D0650530

Serenity can be found in the most unlikely of places.

Best wishes for a
blessed and beautiful
Christmas 2015!

Denay Hartford

533,133

The Christmas Room

Denny Hartford

Copyright © 2015 Denny Hartford

All rights reserved.

ISBN-13: 978-1517588243

For information contact
Denny Hartford
c/o P O Box 34278
Omaha, NE 68134
dennyhartford@gmail.com

Cover design by Patrick Osborne

A Few Words of Thanks

Several friends graciously served to proofread and express comments on the manuscript and their help was truly invaluable. I am deeply appreciative to all of you. Special thanks to editorial specialists Kathy Norquist in Oregon and Craig and Cindy Young in Colorado for their careful, kindly, and wise suggestions. The novel is certainly better because of your insightful help. I also sought out several friends in the caregiving professions who could evaluate how well my characters, setting, and plot measured up with real life. Their comments were deeply gratifying and helpful as well. Thank you then to Sara DeLahoyde, Ann Marie Goettl, Ann Slabaugh, Linda Osborne, and Janine Lehman. Others who conscientiously read the manuscript and offered their advice were John and Ruth Heyer in Iowa; Jeanne Lawson in Colorado; Bryan and Janet Lilius in Texas; David and Janice Mirro in Washington; Leonard and Diane Johnson in Iowa; and Kurt Oyer, Linda Aldrich, and Allen and Cindy Nelson in Nebraska. Thank you so much.

I reserve my greatest thanks, however, for my wife Claire. She patiently listened to me read each chapter as I finished it, offering valuable counsel and encouragement. She then took the yellow notebook pages with my confusing scrawl and typed them into shape on her computer. She also did the investigation into the publishing process; did several proofreads of the manuscript; and handled the innumerable details required to bring the novel to print. Thank you for all of these things, Claire. But even more important help came in all the years of your partnership with me in nursing home ministry and in your exemplary works of love in helping care for your mother and mine in their last years. You are a wonderful model of compassion, strength, perseverance, and kindness in action. And you have my undying admiration, gratitude, and love

Finally, *The Christmas Room* is dedicated to the memory of the two women in our lives who most inspired the novel's protagonist Grace Trinisi. They are our moms, Ionia Ellsworth Hartford and Evelyn Aylward Newman.

Chapter 1
"I Want Her Moved"

"Ms. Kovacs, something has to be done to move my mother to another room. In fact, I can't understand why she was put there in the first place. To be quite honest, I can't understand why you've even allowed the room to be set up that way. It must be confusing, even frustrating for these old people."

Carolyn Kovacs, the Administrator of Villa Vista Care Community, calmly waited to see if there would be any more complaints from the man sitting across the desk from her. She remained patient and undisturbed. One doesn't serve in nursing home management for fourteen years by losing one's cool, making snap judgments, or playing defense to every gripe that comes along.

"Could you be more specific, Mr. Gritzner? The room your mother is in is one of the most spacious we have and it's only two doors down from the nurses station and just a short distance from the cafeteria. Rose, our admissions director, explained to me that you weren't here when your mother was admitted, but your wife and daughters were and they thought the room was wonderful. Most important, your mother loved it. Plus, there's a bonus in having Mrs. Trinisi as a roommate. She's one of the most pleasant residents we have – very sweet and helpful. Your mother has already hit it off very well with her. Please help me understand exactly what is bothering you."

Clark Gritzner was perturbed. He didn't want to be reminded that he was at odds with his family on this matter and he didn't want to be forced to voice his specific complaint. Yet this lady seemed to insist he do so. He hated this whole business of his mother being in a nursing home, especially since this was the fourth one in eleven months he had tried. Was there no place in town that would look after his mother with the care and dignity she deserved? And at a reasonable price?

Carolyn waited for his answer.

"Well, Ms. Kovacs," he drawled out the title, making it almost obvious that he was mocking her. "Do I really have to explain it? I would assume any normal person would know immediately what I'm talking about." Gritzner realized he was being rude but he was too proud, too committed to apologize. Or even to let up.

Carolyn looked down at her desk for a moment. She felt the tension rising, for this was certainly a problem she didn't need this morning. She had to make the final decision on the Montgomery hiring and there was the inspection coming up on Monday. But that didn't mean she was going to let Mr. Gritzner's bullying win the round. She sincerely wanted to please both the residents and the family members. That was her job. But it was also important to have some lines carefully drawn. Mutual respect, understanding, realistic expectations – these things needed to be accepted by everyone involved. And, in this case, she believed that Mathilda Gritzner's long-term care (if she ended up staying there) would be best served by her son learning that clear communication was a must.

She said as much. "Mr. Gritzner, you must surely understand that my care for the residents here cannot be based on guesses and hunches. Open, honest communication is difficult enough in any business but perhaps no more important than in ours. Please, just tell me what's on your mind."

"Okay, Ms. Kovacs, if you're going to make me spell it out for you. Maybe you think it makes me out to be a grinch or something, who knows? But the *honest* problem is that my mother isn't going to be forced into celebrating Christmas when it's April!"

Carolyn tried to hide her smile. Despite what she had said, she had guessed Mr. Gritzner's complaint. "Oh, yes; Mrs. Trinisi's Christmas decorations. Is that the only problem, Mr. Gritzner?"

A red-faced Clark Gritzner was barely containing his anger. "I would think that's problem enough, Ms. Kovacs. Christmas is fine in its place but it's downright silly to have a Christmas tree in April. And those wreaths and the window decorations. I understand that crazy woman even plays Christmas carols all day long!"

Carolyn remained calm but she wasn't about to let that slander pass. "Mr. Gritzner, I suggest that it is untrue, as well as unkind, to call Mrs. Trinisi a 'crazy woman.' She is not. As I've already told you, and I believe your family will agree, Grace Trinisi is a warm, engaging woman who has already become a good friend and companion to your mother. Furthermore, how she and her family decorate her half of the room and the west window next to her bed is completely up to them. And about the Christmas music? Mrs. Trinisi only plays it twice a day, from 10 until 11:30 in the morning and from 6 until 7 in the evening. And it is never played very loud. Her doing so is well within our policies regarding resident privacy and cooperation."

Gritzner realized he'd been outplayed. He knew that he appeared petty and unfair. He had stooped to mean-spirited exaggeration and was caught at it. Perhaps Mrs. Trinisi wasn't crazy. And she did seem to be the nice person everyone was saying she was. So he decided to back off...but only a little. "I apologize for my poor choice of language, Ms. Kovacs. That may have seemed rude." He paused for a moment and drew a deep breath. "I may have spoke out of frustration and I'm sorry if I offended you. However, I must insist that you respect my wishes on this matter. Would you please move my mother to another room?" Gritzner knew he was coming off as overbearing. And he knew there would be a price to pay with Joanna and the girls. Still, this was a battle he wasn't going to lose.

Carolyn nodded. "As you wish, Mr. Gritzner. I hope you'll understand, however, with the reconstruction going on in the south wing and the residents in the annex under quarantine for another three days, it may take a little while to change roommates around. Can you give us a couple of days?"

Gritzner set his jaw and frowned. "No, Ms. Kovacs, I can't. Like I've already stated, I believe it was irresponsible for you to let that lady decorate the place in the crazy way she did." He caught himself. "Note please that I referred to the *decorations* as crazy, not the lady. But no, I want my mother out of there right now."

Carolyn didn't let her frustration show nor her growing dislike of the man sitting across from her. She spoke slowly. "Mr. Gritzner, let me make clear what you're asking. As I mentioned, I know you were out of town when your wife admitted your mother into our facility. That was nine days ago. When she came, she was disoriented and depressed. She was also dealing with some paranoia. I believe the constant upheaval from being moved in and out of different facilities had worn her down. But now she's settled in and quite well at that. She's comfortable and at peace. She has made a good friend in Mrs. Trinisi and, from what your wife has told us, the Christmas atmosphere has really helped in changing her mood. And yet…"

"And yet," Gritzner interrupted, "I want her moved as soon as possible."

"As soon as possible?" asked Carolyn.

"No, Ms. Kovacs, I shouldn't have said that. I should have simply repeated what I said earlier. I want her moved right now!"

Chapter 2
A New Career Path

Brenda took another forkful of the fast food salad and realized the only thing she tasted was the dressing. "That can't be right," she thought. She began to wonder how old the lettuce might be and what kinds of chemicals they had dunked it in to keep it green. Oh, my; better not think about that. Just concentrate on the 180 calories and thank the Lord you had the discipline to refuse the cheeseburger and fries.

These thoughts had distracted her and she forced herself to start reading again from the top of the page of her textbook. Nursing school was a lot more work than she had imagined – a lot tougher than anything she had endured in getting her bachelor's degree in secondary education. That had been a lot of fluff – courses full of obtuse theories, pop psychology, political correctness, and self-help dogma. Brenda had concluded there wasn't much in her previous education of practical value. Four wasted years. No, make it five. That one year of teaching English at Southwest High had to be counted too. Well, not all of it was wasted, she hoped. Many of her students stayed in her memory and affections. She sincerely hoped she had helped them, at least a little bit. And, of course, Brenda had picked up *some* real world experience in that year of teaching – things about youth culture, the largely counter-productive effects of the education system, the coercive power of unions, and a few other things.

It was during that year of teaching that Brenda's grandmother had experienced her first stroke. Helping her Grandma Mattie when she was at the hospital, then the rehab center, and then the first of what had become several nursing homes had awakened Brenda to a new career path. She had started nursing training four days after she taught her last high school class. And whenever her current studies threatened to overwhelm her, Brenda would think back to her third hour class at Southwest (or, for that matter, her fifth and seventh hour classes) and say a prayer of thanks for her new course of study.

Brenda finished the chapter (but not her salad). She then dug out her phone from the purple thrift store purse she loved. It was almost noon. If she was quick, she would have time to get back to school, even if she dropped by the drug store to pick up her prescription. The afternoon promised to be fairly light and, because of everything she had planned for the evening, that was great. After class she would stop by and visit Grandma and Mrs. Trinisi, then head home to have dinner with the family. She was anxious to fill her dad in on how things were going. Dad wasn't the best at keeping in touch with his daughters when he was traveling. In fact, Brenda thought of a couple things her mom had let slip and realized he wasn't doing too well in communicating with his wife either. Something was definitely going on. But even if there was, Brenda didn't expect to be let in on it. She was looking forward to having dinner with him nevertheless. She loved both her parents very much.

Then there was the rest of Friday evening to consider. Brenda had performed in *Fiddler on the Roof* when she was in high school (her sister Reggie had too) and was excited about seeing a professional performance of the play at the Alhambra. They were double dating – Todd taking Reggie and, as Brenda's escort, a friend of his named Floyd they had met a couple of times at Bernie's Beanery. It was going to be an eventful Friday and, if she scored high on the quiz this afternoon, she'd really be motivated to celebrate.

As Brenda walked back to the Landers Building for her next class, she considered that Reggie might not be in the same pleasant mood that she was. Reggie's job had unusual pressures. Selling high-end clothes on commission at a store trapped in a dying shopping mall was a very tough deal. There was also the hectic pace normal for any college sophomore. But there were other issues nowadays. Brenda knew, for instance, that Reggie was more bothered about their dad than she was. He'd been miffed over Brenda's career change but was even harder on Reggie. He always had been. In his mind, Reggie couldn't do anything right.

And then there was the Todd factor. The prospect of a life together for Reggie and Todd no longer produced the thrill it once had. For either of them. In fact, Brenda expected the relationship to fall completely apart any day now. That was fine with Brenda. Todd may be okay – but who wants to tolerate "okay" when what you're really looking for is love and character, comfort and emotional security, and a bit of wow thrown in too?

Brenda's reflections about all these things came to an end when she entered the classroom. She still had a few minutes to go over her notes to be ready for Dr. Layton's quiz on immunology that would follow today's lecture. And, for the next couple of hours, her mind was trained simply on the quiz, with good effect too. She did better than she had expected.

With a light heart then, Brenda drove over to the Villa Vista Care Community a little after five. She parked her car in the almost empty front lot. The staff all parked behind the building. Brenda was eager to see her grandmother. And Mrs. Trinisi too. In fact, she had brought from home a pretty red ornament for Mrs. Trinisi's Christmas tree. What a sweet thing she is, Brenda thought, and what a perfect pal she's proven to be for Grandma.

Then there was the sheer beauty of the Christmas Room itself. When Brenda had visited the ladies after dinner the previous Wednesday, she had seen the Christmas Room for the first time at night. That was a real treat. With the neon candle hanging in the window and the lights on the tree, the whole room invited you to warm your heart. Pretty. Hospitable. Brenda smiled at the memory and found herself singing "It's the Most Wonderful Time of the Year" under her breath as she entered the building.

But even as she walked through the door, Brenda sensed something was amiss. Louise was at the front desk but, instead of her usual bright smile, there was a worried look. And, at the first sight of Brenda, Louise reached for the phone. Brenda heard her say, "One of the granddaughters is here." Brenda stopped and stood in the foyer for a moment, Louise's saddened look now confirming her fear that something was indeed very wrong.

Carolyn Kovacs approached Brenda from her office. "Hello, Brenda. Let me say right away that we believe your grandmother is going to be fine. Just fine. But we did have to send her to the hospital a little while ago."

Chapter 3
A Forced Move

"That's okay, Mrs. Gonzalez. You just go at whatever speed is comfortable for you." The lady looked puzzled and Zachary started thinking through his inadequate vocabulary. "Ah, yes. Cómodo. Fácil. Está bien?"

Mrs. Gonzalez smiled, nodded cheerfully, and eased into a more regular pedaling pace on the stationary bike. She knew she was doing better these last few days and was almost as pleased about delighting Zachary O'Rourke, the handsome young physical therapist, as she was about her hip feeling stronger. The fellow was so friendly and capable. He even tried to speak Spanish so that she would know better what he wanted her to do. What a nice young man. He wasn't Chicano but still, why couldn't her Marta find such a boy to settle down with?

Zachary made sure Mrs. Gonzalez was comfortable with her pace before turning his attention toward Mr. Linkletter. "Link, are you doing okay over there? You've only got another four or five minutes." Mr. Linkletter was at the workbench, hustling his way through a dexterity exercise that involved nuts and bolts. He was way ahead of schedule and Zachary was sure he'd be heading home in a day or two. That was great. It wasn't too long ago that Zachary despaired about Link ever going home. But the old man had strong desire, an exemplary work ethic, and an abiding faith in God. And here he was – about to be booted back home. Zachary would miss the fellow. But he had promised to visit Mr. Linkletter at his home in order to see his elaborate model railroad setup. It had even been featured in the local paper. Zachary had promised him that he was looking forward to seeing it in action. And he was.

This was the part of his job that Zachary most loved. Sure, he missed the regular sessions he had with rehab patients when they were discharged. But they were going home! They had completed their rehab treatments and, through patience and hope and hard work, they were going back to the place and the people they most loved. That was their goal…and his. It was the goal of the whole Villa Vista rehab team.

In fact, when a rehab patient was discharged from the facility, there was a celebratory farewell held in the lobby. Those staff members who could take a short break (no matter what their specific jobs) would form a line at the front door. Then, helped by Kool & the Gang playing "Celebration" over the intercom, the staff sang and clapped along. Some would do a bit of dancing too. Farewell cards and balloons were given to the liberated patient. So too were hugs and kisses. It was a grand event, one that meant an awful lot to staff and patients alike. It was a fun spectacle that brought joy even to the long-term residents of Villa Vista because it emphasized to them that the staff members really were on the residents' side, that their work was more than a job. Zachary had joined a terrific team and he was proud to be a part of it.

An hour later, Zachary had finished his sessions for the day and was now busy with the never-ending paperwork: state and county forms, federal government forms, insurance forms, and plenty of in-house forms too. The bureaucracy grew exponentially and so did the paperwork. It was too bad that the quality of medical care in the country seemed to be heading in the other direction. But at least here at Villa Vista, they were fighting to keep care standards as high as possible. That certainly wasn't the case everywhere. He remembered with great frustration the place where he first worked. That place had gone so far that...

Zachary's thoughts were interrupted by a voice over the intercom. "All available nursing staff, please come to the south station. All available nursing staff, please come to the south station." Since his patients were done for the day, Zachary answered the call as well. Had it been a code alert, he would have only been in the way, but the wording of the announcement suggested a fall, a seizure, a fight – Lord knows what. And, in those cases, he might be of some help. He turned off the lights, locked up, and headed down the hall.

When he got there, things were already under control. Whatever happened had upset a number of the residents in the wing but order was being restored. Nurses were consoling residents as were Carolyn Kovacs and Lois Vendee, Villa Vista's Director of Nursing. Janet Gresham, one of his PT colleagues, was dealing with Miss Dorothy who, at 102, was one of the oldest residents in the place. Miss Dorothy wasn't easily agitated. But she was now. And in the center of the unhappy tableau was a disheveled Mattie Gritzner in a wheelchair. She had obviously been crying – she was crying a bit still – and her eyes retained a look of fright and confusion. Beside her were a couple of south ward nurses and even Greg Kwan, the physician's assistant. That was a break, Zachary thought. He's usually only in the building for a couple of hours.

Lois saw Zachary and came over. "Thanks for coming down. I think it's all over. Well, at least the public uproar. I only pray Mrs. Gritzner will be okay. Her blood pressure went through the roof and we're still having trouble getting it down. Her heart rate is also very troubling. We've called the ambulance and she'll be heading over to the ER."

Zachary looked at Mattie and felt terrible. She was a very nice woman and, though she was new to the facility and wasn't one of his individual patients, she'd been placed in a balance and mobility group he conducted. He liked her a lot. He remembered meeting her family members as well, especially the two pretty granddaughters he met the day she was admitted. Yes, he decided. He liked Mattie's family too.

Janet Gresham waited for Zachary to ask what had happened. He didn't. Zachary was acutely aware of both the spirit and the letter of the HIPAA regulations and, though he thought many of them were silly and even counter-productive, he had made it a habit to know only what he needed to know. Still, he couldn't help but overhear the conversation of some of the staff that had been in the thick of it. He thus learned that Mattie had experienced a panic attack, a big one, after her son insisted she be transferred out of the Christmas Room. Carolyn had apparently warned Mr. Gritzner but he was insistent…and a little bit out of control himself.

Over his shoulder, Zachary heard Carolyn talking to Janet from behind the counter of the nurses station. Carolyn asked, "What exactly went down?"

Janet shook her head sadly and sighed, "Lois asked him to wait for you; she tried to explain that you could kind of ease Mattie into the idea of changing rooms. But he just wouldn't wait. He went in on his own, told his mom he was getting her another room, and started packing up her things right then. He was pretty agitated himself and I think that's what first set Mattie off. She began to cry and then started begging him to stop. And, when he didn't, she tried to get out of bed to stop him. She started crying out for help too. When Gretchen and Bryan got down there, she decided they were in on it and she flew at them too. It was a mess. But, don't you know, Carolyn, it was Grace Trinisi who came to the rescue. She had been in the bathroom but when she heard the commotion, she hustled out and tried to calm Mattie down. Sweet thing, Grace was in such a hurry to help she left her walker by the toilet. Thank God she didn't fall."

Bryan Taliwood came from the Christmas Room where he

had been helping calm Grace Trinisi and he joined the conversation. "That's right, Carolyn. The heroine in our little drama here is Mrs. Trinisi. She got Mattie back into her wheelchair and scolded Mr. Gritzner strongly enough that he left the room. He was sorta flipped out anyhow by his mom trying to hit him with her hairbrush. No kidding. Anyhow, by the time Greg came back with a sedative, Mrs. Trinisi had pushed the button on her CD player and had Bing Crosby singing Christmas songs. It probably worked better than the drug would have. She had sat down with Mattie and, like I said, she was fairly settled down by the time Greg got in there."

"But her blood pressure?" asked Carolyn.

"Oh, well, that's not good," answered Janet. "Not good at all. Greg said her heart is also racing and way out of rhythm. Though the outward panic may be over for now, she's still scared and confused. And she's a pretty sick lady. I'm afraid she does need to get over to the hospital to make sure everything's okay."

Zachary's eyes scanned both hallways and his stern visage must have communicated his thoughts. Janet spoke, "If you're looking for Mr. Gritzner in order to slap him, don't bother. As soon as he saw Greg preparing the sedative, he said, 'It's about time,' and took off."

"Took off?" asked Zachary. "Where on earth to?"

"To parts unknown, I guess. Gretchen looked out and said the guy's car isn't even in the parking lot anymore!"

Chapter 4
"Takk for Sist"

Grace Trinisi sat in her blue stuffed chair sipping occasionally from one of the small bottles of Diet Coke which her son kept plenty of in her closet. Carolyn Kovacs was just a few feet away, seated comfortably on the fold-down seat of Mrs. Tranisi's maroon walker. Carolyn had a coffee from the nurses station. All signs of the disturbance from an hour ago were gone. The whole wing was quiet. But here in the Christmas Room, there was a special serenity. Bittersweet, perhaps, but genuinely, thankfully peaceful.

Dusk had fallen and Grace had turned the lights on her Christmas tree. The little switch by her chair posed no problems for her. But Carolyn was needed to push the button on the safety relay which lit up the candle in the window. It was a simple enough task but it was one of the many things that were beyond Mrs. Trinisi's understanding nowadays. The frontal lobe dementia that increasingly affected her balance, her memory, her judgment, and even some of her basic motor skills had simply put some tasks out of her ability.

There were other medical issues that she had to contend with as well. Diabetes, arthritis, a hiatal hernia, a weak heart, and occasional bouts of depression and obsessive behavior. It was remarkable that she was as contented as she was. Kind-hearted too. And grateful, patient, and funny. Carolyn knew a bit of her history and understood that these character traits didn't just happen. They came from Grace's religious faith, a long and happy marriage, a sweet family life, and an ever-present wonder and appreciation of the world around her.

Carolyn took in the scene as she stirred her coffee. "This room is so beautiful, Grace. I love coming in here." And she did. In fact, Carolyn had taken to coming down throughout the week and spending a few minutes in the Christmas Room before she left for home. Other staff members did the same thing – as did many of the residents who were able to get around. Other than the dining hall and recreation room, it was the most popular spot in the whole nursing home. The staff did their best to make all of Villa Vista an inviting, pretty place but there were always limits. Freedom of access. Function. And, of course, finances. But Grace Trinisi's family had created a very special atmosphere in this room. And the engaging warmth of Grace herself completed the charm.

Carolyn looked at Grace over her coffee and wondered exactly how she could bring up the subject of…well, of the explosive scene that had been enacted earlier in the evening. There was nothing she could do right now for Mrs. Gritzner. The word had come from the hospital that she was comfortable and doing pretty well. Since Grace had been right in the middle of the turmoil too, Carolyn wanted to make sure she was okay. This was just the kind of thing that could threaten the fragile balance in which Grace lived.

But before Carolyn could broach the subject, Mrs. Trinisi did. "Mattie was sure upset tonight, wasn't she? Did you know she was trying to hit that man with her brush? I don't think she connected but she sure took a couple of good swipes at him. What on earth did he do to get her so mad?"

"Well, I'm not sure, Grace. You do know, don't you, that the man is her son?" Carolyn didn't want to let Mrs. Trinisi think that men simply strayed in from the streets to frighten the residents. "He's been out of town and this was his first visit. I guess that…"

Grace interrupted her. "Oh, that was her *son*." She pondered that revelation for a moment. "Okay, that makes sense. He did kinda look like her." Then she smiled and arched her eyebrows. "I guess maybe they're never too old for their mom to take a swat at 'em, huh?"

Carolyn laughed. "Maybe, you're right. Although, knock on wood, I never had to get physical with my brood. They behaved themselves pretty well."

"Yes, but you had all daughters, didn't you?"

"Yes, four girls. Was it different with you? You had boys *and* girls, right? Did any of them need to be reined in?"

"Oh my, honey. They all did. Although to be honest, I guess the girls didn't need much. You could take away some privileges or make them stay home – that was plenty to keep them behaved. But the boys were a different story altogether. Frank and I loved them and they loved us but they sure broke our hearts a lot of times along the way." She sighed and sat quietly for a few moments. Then she brightened up again as she whispered, "Maybe I should have had Mattie living next door. I could have let her loose with her brush on 'em and maybe we wouldn't have had all that trouble!" She laughed and waved her hand as if she was doing the chasing herself. "I do hope she comes back though. I really liked her. But, of course, I still miss Rosie. I think she was my best friend since I lived here." There was a silence as Grace's mind sought to capture a few memories of her good friend. She then asked quietly, "Did she die?"

Carolyn was familiar with this question. Mrs. Trinisi asked it every once in a while. "Yes, Grace. Rosie passed away a few months ago. Do you remember your son taking you to her funeral? It was raining and he fixed up a wheelchair with an umbrella?"

Grace smiled. "Oh, yes. That was funny. But it worked, didn't it! You know, there was a long time that Tony wasn't so good with fixing things. His dad tried to teach him things but all Tony wanted to do was play ball. And then, later…well, later he wanted to play with other things. But I won't think about that now. And anyhow, that umbrella sure did work. Bless his heart."

"He's a very good son, Grace. He sure loves you and we all think the world of both him and Marsha. You did a great job with him anyhow – hairbrush or no hairbrush!"

"Yes. He *is* a good son. And his wife surely is a treasure. I love her as much as I do my own kids. And, you know, Carolyn, all my kids turned out great. It took a while for my boys but God finally straightened them out. And so I can say God is watching over all of them now. That's a comfort."

God is watching over all of them. Carolyn thought of her girls and found consolation in Grace's observation. "Amen to that. And now I better get home. You know, Grace, two of my girls are still at home and they'll be wondering where I am. Plus it's almost 6:30 and that means Tony and Marsha will be by to take you to dinner, right?"

"Oh yes, is it Monday already?"

"No, Grace, it's Tuesday. It's Tuesday and Friday that you guys usually go out to eat."

Grace grinned. "Whatever you say, honey. I hardly ever know what day it is anymore. Ever since they took my car away, I only sit here until someone comes and tells me to go there, do this, come here, and so on. But that's okay. Everyone takes care of me just fine."

"Okay, Grace. I'll see you tomorrow. And thanks again for letting me share the Christmas Room for a bit. Please tell Tony and Marsha hello for me. And thank them again for helping with the St. Patrick's Day party."

"I will, Carolyn. And thank you for the visit. *Takk for sist.*"

Grace Trinisi almost always finished conversations this way. It was a Norwegian phrase, something she had grown up with in the days before she married into a large, generous Italian family. She had explained to Carolyn that the phrase meant "thanks for your time" or something like that. It was a perfect phrase for Grace for she was genuinely grateful for people spending even just a few moments with her. But tonight was a bit different as Grace had another closing line. As Carolyn started to walk out the doorway, Grace stopped her. "Oh, Carolyn? One more thing, please?"

"Yes, Grace. Of course. Anything I can possibly do."

"Would you please say a prayer that Mattie gets better and that she can come back and be my roommate? Because Rosie can't be my roommate anymore. You know, Rosie died."

Carolyn had to force down the lump in her throat. "Yes, Grace. I will pray that Mattie gets better and that she comes back to be your roommate."

As Carolyn walked out to her car, she did pray that prayer. But she added, "Lord, to make that happen, You're going to have Your hands full with Clark Gritzner. And I'm afraid he's going to require something bigger than his mom's hairbrush too. But, enough of my ideas. I'll leave him to You. I've got a few prayers now about my girls." And that's what occupied her mind during the drive home.

Chapter 5
"We Know All About It"

There was an ominous silence in the hospital room where Mathilda Gritzner lay. She was sleeping peacefully now, the forced sedation giving way to a natural and well-needed rest. Her granddaughters had gone home to bed, Joanna Gritzner finally convincing them that Grandma was going to be okay and that she and their father would watch over her a while longer. Joanna now sat alongside her mother-in-law holding her hand. That hand was so thin with wrinkles and protruding blue veins, yet it remained graceful and lovely. The nails were a bright red, Mattie's favorite color, and Joanna could tell that someone had recently painted them. And there was the simple gold ring on her finger, a ring that had been there 63 years.

Clark sat across the room looking out the sixth-floor window. Normal visiting hours had ended quite a while ago. The parking lots below were nearly empty and there was no movement at all.

Clark stared out the window in order not to look at his mother...or his wife. Yet the view, as pretty as it was, gave him no peace because the twinkling of the downtown lights through the misty night painfully reminded him of the

Christmas Room back at the nursing home. Beyond those lights, his pride and joy, the *Blue Wave*, rode at anchor in the bay. How he wished he was aboard her right now…away from here and out of this desperate situation.

He knew he had acted irrationally and was deeply embarrassed about what had happened. Nevertheless, he was still angry too – and anxious to find someone else to share the blame. "The people over there certainly need some instruction about how to properly run a nursing home. No doubt about that. Very unprofessional." Clark continued to look through the window as he spoke. But there was no answer from Joanna. He waited for another minute but she remained silent. "Knowing how fragile Mom is, they should have been more considerate, more supportive. And they should have been in there with a sedative to quiet her down a lot quicker than they were. Completely unacceptable."

Still not a sound from his wife.

Clark tried again. "And then there's that roommate. I think she may be insane – a bit anyhow. She has no business being there, not with that violent temper of hers. You know, she could really be dangerous to someone."

At that, Joanna finally spoke. "Did she hurt you, dear?" She asked the question slowly, letting the barbed irony have its full effect. "I know that Mrs. Trinisi was upset with you. It's my understanding that she rebuked you and asked you to get out of the room. But the violence, as I understand, came from your own mother, dear. *She* was the one who got physical with you. With her hairbrush, wasn't it? The one Reggie gave her for her birthday?"

"What on earth are you talking about?" Clark felt his face flush and he wondered if he looked as guilty as he felt. Joanna's gaze on him was steady and challenging. Yet she waited several moments before she asked her husband, "Didn't she, Clark?"

It was now Clark who was silent. Though he was well aware that his silence tended to confirm his guilt, he didn't know what to say. Did Joanna *know* all that had happened back at the nursing home? Could the nursing home director be so unprofessional, so vindictive as to go tattling to his family?

Joanna interrupted his thoughts as if she'd been reading them. "No, Clark. The staff didn't tell us much about the why of Mom's meltdown. Not about *your* part in the mess anyhow. But other people were there. You wouldn't know this, not having been around the place much, but there are some residents of Villa Vista who spend most of their time either at the nurses stations or in the foyer next to the front door. And they know just about everything that goes on there. They knew about your graceless demands to Mrs. Kovacs to move Mom out of her room, your insistence on packing her things yourself, your cold-hearted indifference when she was begging you to stop. And, yes, about Mom getting so scared and angry that she tried to hit you with her hairbrush. We know all about it, Clark." Joanna's eyes then turned away coldly and he felt the sting of her disgust. "We even know about your running away from the place before determining your mom's condition. None of it is too ennobling, Clark."

Clark was stunned. He'd been ashamed of his actions earlier but that was a personal thing. He could deal with that. Hadn't he already been dealing with a load of personal shame these past several months? But the fact that Joanna knew exactly what happened at the nursing home bothered him terribly. Should he try an outright denial? No, her look showed him that she was quite sure of her information.

Then one terrible word emerged from his confusion. We! "We? What do you mean, Joanna, that *we* know all about it?" Clark felt like a child caught in a terrible act.

Joanna refused to turn toward her husband. Instead, her gaze stayed on Mattie sleeping comfortably beside her. "Don't you remember, dear? Brenda arrived at Villa Vista shortly after the ambulance had left. And those residents I was telling you about? Well, they and the girls have become pretty good friends these last few weeks." She let that sentence hang before she added, "And friends talk."

Clark understood now. The nursing home residents weren't constrained by privacy regulations. They had told Brenda what they knew. And Brenda had told Joanna and Reggie. No wonder the girls had been so distant and cold toward him earlier. It was all known and it all put him in a very bad light. His anger, impatience, selfishness – his family was learning what he was made of.

Clark tried to find some solace in the fact that his family didn't know about everything else going on in his life. Not yet anyhow. He gazed back at the lights downtown, enduring the hard silence there in the hospital room. He wanted to say the only thing he could that might alleviate Joanna's anger and disappointment. He wanted to say he was wrong, that he was sorry, that he did still love them all. But he couldn't face saying these things. Not until he was able to prove the truth of his words. Not until he somehow fixed the other things he had broken.

***

As the lights of the city twinkled beautifully in the darkness of the early morning hours, the lights in the Christmas Room twinkled too. Normally, they would have been turned off long before this. But because Grace Trinisi had the room all to herself tonight, the staff had granted her wish that they be left on. Earlier she had used those lights to read a bit from her large-print Bible. Grace had to read very slowly nowadays and she often paused to go over in her mind what she had just read. It took more work but she wanted to keep up the habit. She believed God understood and was pleased with her efforts.

Having set aside the Bible for the evening, she was now spending these quiet hours praying and thinking. And remembering. She was often occupied by these things after everyone had gone to sleep. In fact, she herself seemed most awake at this time. But tonight there were more reasons to talk to God than ever. There were so many things going on with her kids and her sisters in Missouri who were in bad health. And Grace wanted to talk to God about the family she saw on the news earlier, the family whose house had burned down. There were also prayers for what the president was doing, for Reggie's boyfriend who Grace didn't think was the right fellow for her, and for her new friend Mattie who had gone to the hospital.

And she had a prayer too for Mattie's son who seemed to have such sadness and anger inside him. "Lord Jesus, that man has things wrong in his heart. That's plain to see. He has gone astray somehow…maybe, pretty far astray. So, please fix him and make things right, okay? You did this for my boy when he had run far away from You and so I pray that You would fix things for my friend Mattie's boy too. Amen."

Chapter 6
Nixon's Mustache

Lois Vendee had just given her boss, Carolyn Kovacs, an update on Villa Vista's quarantine situation when she noticed Tony Trinisi pull up in the parking lot in his lime green Mustang convertible. Lois' grandpa would call it a "cool as cucumbers" kind of ride. And she would agree. But to the staff and residents of the Villa Vista Care Community, Tony and his family were "cool as cucumbers" too, real favorites of everyone. Tony and Marsha had become involved in all kinds of activities at Villa Vista. So had their kids and even Tony's construction company. Lois thought of the phrase that Carolyn frequently used of the Trinisi family – they were "efficiently kind." She knew exactly what Carolyn meant. Without being maudlin or paternalistic toward the residents, the Trinisis were caring and interesting and downright fun. And, without interfering or second-guessing, they were the same with staff members.

Carolyn wondered why Lois had stopped talking. "What's up?"

Lois motioned to the window behind Carolyn. "Tony Trinisi just drove up in that slick Mustang of his and he's got the top down today."

Carolyn turned around in time to see Tony pull out a large bag of bird seed from the backseat. She laughed. "More bird seed, already? Those little guys sure go through that stuff. Didn't he just fill those up last weekend?"

"He might have," Lois said. "I didn't work last weekend. But I know he does it an awful lot."

The Trinisi family had put in a large birdfeeder as soon as Tony's mom had come to Villa Vista. They had cleared the idea with maintenance and promised to keep it clean and filled. And they did. But by the time the doctors suggested Grace remain at Villa Vista as a permanent resident, Tony and Marsha had already put in another half dozen birdfeeders outside the windows of various residents they had befriended. Those feeders proved to be a great source of comfort and entertainment for the residents, drawing not only plenty of birds year round but also tree squirrels, ground squirrels, rabbits, and a couple of times, even deer. Carolyn knew it must be a rather expensive venture but Marsha had once explained that a couple of their friends from church routinely brought over large bags of bird seed they picked up at a discount farm store. That was really nice, thought Carolyn. There are so many ways to show friendship and support. And it pleased her to know the Trinisis had quality friends.

Carolyn buzzed Louise up at the front desk. "Hey, Louise, Tony Trinisi is out there filling his birdfeeders. When he comes through, could you tell him to stop in my office for a few moments? Thank you."

It was about 15 minutes before Tony appeared in the doorway. Lois had scooted off and Carolyn was alone at her desk. "Afternoon, Carolyn. Louise said you wanted to see me. What's up?"

Carolyn took a deep breath. It was a purposeful action, designed to let Tony know the topic was something of importance. "Well, I wanted to talk to you about what happened last night in your mom's room. You've probably heard about it already but I wanted to make sure you knew the details."

"You mean about Mattie going to the hospital?"

"Yes. Well, yes and what went on *before* that as well. I did spend some time with your mom afterward and she seemed fine. But I wanted to check in with you. Did you guys see her last night?"

"Oh yeah. We took her down to Summer Kitchen for the usual."

Carolyn smiled. She knew there were certain patterns the Trinisi family followed faithfully. They were a means to help Grace cope with everything happening to her. Carolyn said, "Okay, you've got my curiosity up. Just what is the usual?"

Tony chuckled. "Oh, the usual at Summer Kitchen means Mom looking over the menu for a long time and having me explain everything in detail. Then Mom changes her mind several times before she finally tells me to go ahead and order whatever she had the last time."

Carolyn held out her hands in appeal. "Which is?"

Tony grinned. "Which is mashed potatoes and white gravy, a dinner roll, and three slices of bacon that are extra, and I mean, extra crisp. She never wants dessert. In fact, she always insists that she just had the best meal ever and she couldn't eat another bite. But that only lasts till we roll her by the checkout counter where they display all those gorgeous bakery treats. Then Mom decides that she'll take some dessert home with her after all. In fact, she ends up taking two desserts, one for her and one to share with whoever is her roommate."

Carolyn could easily imagine. Grace Trinisi was always giving someone something. "Your mother is such a sweetheart. And in so many ways too. But getting back to last night's adventure, did she tell you what happened?"

Tony shrugged. "Not much, really. By the time we got here, I suppose an hour or more had passed since the incident. You know how it is. Mom had forgotten most of it and even what she remembered kinda got mixed in with other stuff." Tony chuckled again. "I'll give you an example. She was telling us that Mattie's son had a little dog and he made it pull a lawn mower. I suggested to her that didn't make much sense. A dog pulling a lawn mower? Well, she thought a few seconds and then said that maybe Mattie had told her that story. Then Mom laughed and reminded us that we had to be patient because she gets confused quite a bit. I said, 'Who gets confused, Mom? You or Mrs. Gritzner?' Mom said, 'Well, I don't even know any Mrs. Gritzner. I'm talking about Mattie who lives in my room here. And you know it's both me *and* her that get confused a lot. Goodness, son, you oughta' know that by now!' Then she laughed some more."

"So she didn't seem upset about things?"

"No, I don't think so. The only thing that seemed to stick in her mind was the plight of that poor pooch. Midway through our meal, she turned to Marsha and, just as serious as can be, said, 'You wouldn't think even a little dog would put up with that kind of behavior would you? For heaven's sake, pulling a lawn mower! You know, when Richard Nixon picked *his* dog up by the ears, he turned and bit his vice president something awful.'"

That provoked laughter from them both. Carolyn grinned. "Wasn't that Lyndon Johnson that picked up his dog by the ears?"

"Yeah, Tony answered. "It was one of his beagles and there was a storm of protest over it. But Mom has somehow connected the incident with Nixon. And, of course, there was no biting and no vice president. But it was her story and I didn't bother to mess around with it. But then it got even better."

"How so?" Carolyn asked.

"Well, Mom explained that the vice president wouldn't show his face for a month because of that dog bite. And when he finally came out of hiding, he had grown a mustache to hide the scar. She then argued that the mustache was a terrible one, so bristly and unkempt, that it was the end of his ever becoming president. And so that's why politicians don't wear mustaches anymore."

Carolyn had heard other funny stories from Grace but this was one of the best. She wondered though if Grace wasn't more purposeful than what people might think. "Tony, do you suppose that your mother knows full well that she's teasing us when she tells those stories?"

Tony gave her a big smile. "Oh, there's no doubt she does. Some of the time, anyhow. You know, my father was a great storyteller and I figure she must have picked up a few pointers from him along the way. But there are other times when I know it's the dementia and confusion. But that part isn't a problem. As you know, Carolyn, our real heartbreak is how the dementia has affected her judgment and balance." He paused for a moment as he thought of something else sad. "And, of course, there's the paranoia and the panic attacks."

"Yes, I know," said Carolyn with true sympathy. "But it's been quite a while since we've had any signs of them, hasn't it? Thank the Lord, right?"

"Thank the Lord, indeed. I pray every day we will never have to go through one of those nights again." Tony shook his head at the memory of one particular event, a manic episode far worse and far longer than what Mrs. Gritzner had experienced the night before. He then came back to the moment. "But to return to your question, Carolyn. No, Mom didn't seem to be adversely stimulated by what happened last night. She was in fine form. Cheery and conversant."

Carolyn nodded her head. "That's good to hear."

"However," Tony added, "she did tell us that we should be sure to say a prayer for Boris."

"Boris?"

"Yes. Isn't that the fellow's name?"

"Mattie's son? No. His name is Clark."

Tony looked puzzled and then broke out with a bit more laughter. "Well, either Mom *thinks* the guy's name is Boris or she thinks Boris is the name of that poor, overworked dog!"

Tony started to turn for the door but then hesitated. "Hey, I want to visit Mom a few minutes before I head back to work. But Carolyn, thanks a bunch for checking in with me about last night. I really appreciate it. And thanks for looking in on her after it all went down. Oh, one more thing. I don't want you to think we learned the details from any of your staff. Mattie's granddaughter Reggie called us last night after we got home."

"Reggie Gritzner? How did she know?"

Tony motioned over his shoulder. "Apparently, some of the gals out front here shared the straight skinny with Reggie's older sister. And Reggie then called us later from the hospital."

Carolyn was puzzled and her face must have shown it. So Tony explained, "Don't be too perplexed. Reggie is about 20 and in the last stages of a failed romance."

"What's that got to do with anything?"

"You forget I've got a very handsome, very engaging 23-year-old son at home. And Albert was the sympathetic person to whom Reggie told the whole story."

Carolyn smiled. "Say no more."

Tony waved as he left the office. "I won't!"

Chapter 7
A Sister's Revelations

It hadn't been her most productive day and, though she was relieved it was finally over, Brenda sure wasn't looking forward to going home. Both she and Reggie had been grieved to learn the ugly part their father had played in last night's disaster. But Reggie seemed particularly bitter. Brenda had been gravely disappointed in her dad but Reggie acted almost like she'd been expecting something like this. Nothing substantial had been shared on the drive home but, after they had prepared for bed and Brenda was just about to turn off her light, Reggie came in. In tears, she announced that she simply had to talk to Brenda or, as she put it, she was going to bust wide open.

Reggie's revelations turned out to be deeply troubling for Brenda too. Reggie spoke of their dad's increased drinking, inexplicable absences from home blamed on work and, this was the most devastating news of all, Reggie's conviction that there was another woman in their dad's life.

On the last point, Reggie admitted the evidence wasn't conclusive. But it was the explanation she thought made the most sense of everything else. And the drinking? Well, that was more than clear. Reggie had found three quarts of bourbon behind lawn sacks in the garage. Even worse was a nearly empty pint bottle she discovered under the front seat in the Chevrolet.

Reggie was livid with her father. Did he need a drink to fortify himself for the trial of coming home to his family? And booze in the car? What about her dad's beloved Uncle Lou, killed at 47 by a drunk driver? Had their father become so callous and self-centered that he would endanger the lives, limbs, and livelihoods of other people by driving under the influence? She told Brenda she hadn't checked but she figured that the *Blue Wave* was probably full of liquor as well. "God only knows how much he's got stashed there. After all, he spends more time aboard her than at home nowadays. And, let's face it, Brenda, a drunk at the helm is almost as dangerous as a drunk behind the wheel."

Reggie's disgust was almost violent. Brenda could see it had overcome whatever love and loyalty Reggie had once felt for their dad. Then Reggie explained her plans for the future – plans that included an immediate and complete exit from the family home. She told her older sister that she had been thinking of it for quite a while. She even admitted that was one of the reasons she had held on to the relationship with Todd. But she'd come to her senses a few weeks ago. She didn't love Todd. She didn't even really like him much anymore. So, as much as she wanted to split town immediately, she had decided to keep her head. That meant finishing the school year and transferring to another college somewhere far away next fall. But she would need to find another place to live in the meantime. "Brenda, I'm not going to stay here. I figure I've got to find a place by the weekend or go nuts."

Brenda nodded and held her sister's hand. As much as she was hurting over their father's failures, the news about Reggie breaking it off with Todd provided at least one ray of light. Todd had been just another in a long list of losers that Reggie had unluckily picked. "What are your possibilities, Sis? You don't have much money, do you? And I'm tapped out too."

"Not to worry. Like I said, I'm not going to do anything crazy. I toyed around a little with heading out to the coast and staying with Laurie for a while. Or maybe Aunt Geri's in the mountains. But I decided to finish school, probably moving in with Chita and Beth who live near the college. Then I can transfer my credits somewhere else next year."

This was hard news for Brenda to take in. Very bad news about their father. And bad news too about her sister. She loved them both and hated the notion of being separated from either one. And their mom's heart would be breaking too over the whole mess. Doggone it, Dad! Why are you putting all of us through this?

But the bad news wasn't over yet. Reggie had still more revelations of their dad's misbehavior, things that led her to the conclusions about another woman. Suspicious that their father had been lying about those long absences from the house, Reggie had started playing detective. With help from her old cheerleader buddy, they had called her dad's office. Chita pretended she was a client who needed to get hold of Clark Gritzner as soon as possible. On two of the occasions they had pulled this stunt, they found out that he wasn't traveling for work like he had told his wife. One time the office secretary said he was on personal leave; the other time the switchboard simply connected Chita to his office where he himself answered the phone!

Brenda asked, "Do you think he's just been escaping out to the boat? You know, hiding out from whatever troubles he feels are chasing him?"

"I thought of that. And it could be. We know how much that thing means to him…more than any of us, it sometimes seems. But I still don't see how that would track with the drinking, the lies to Mom and us about travel, the rather poisonous irritability he's developed, and the distance he's created between himself and his family. Except once in a blue moon, he won't even go see his own mother! And then look what he pulled last night! What else could explain all of this, Sis? I agree with you that Dad certainly doesn't fit my idea of a philandering husband. But who knows what booze does to you? How do we know just what kind of man our dad has become?"

Brenda was quiet. It was a lot to take in. And, of course, even Reggie's wrath had left out a few items like their father's coarseness toward Carolyn Kovacs and acting like Christmas lights were some kind of voodoo magic. Their dad used to love Christmas as much as anyone. Reggie was right to ask the question. Just what kind of man had their dad become? And why? And what, if anything, could his daughters do about it?

Brenda suddenly looked up and wiped away her tears. "What about Uncle Durward? Do you think we might get him involved in figuring out this mess?"

Reggie frowned and shook her head. "I thought of that already. We both know he's had experience with some of these things and, for all appearances, it looks like he's put them behind him. That's a point in his favor. But, on the other hand, think about how much Dad hates him. No, I'm afraid getting Uncle Durward involved would be like throwing gasoline on a fire."

"Yes, all that's true, Reggie. But, like you said, Uncle Durward managed to overcome quite a bit in his life and he got his act together. He's no stranger to trouble but he's also known personal victory…even over liquor. He could give us some good advice. Don't you think?"

Reggie thought it over a while. "No, at least not yet. Let's wait a bit. I'm really afraid of how Dad could go off the deep end if we brought Uncle Durward in. You know how deeply he's set against him, Sis. If Dad doesn't care enough right now for the good opinion of his wife and daughters, I can't imagine him paying attention to his long-estranged brother who's done time in prison."

Brenda acquiesced. Reggie's conclusion was sound. If this thing was going to get cleaned up, it was going to have to be done by their father. But would he even want to try? Was it too late? And what was behind the drinking, the lies, and the meanness?

Reggie's emotions had exhausted her and she now lay asleep at the foot of the bed. Brenda tucked a blanket around her sister and did a bit more crying herself before finally drifting off too.

Chapter 8
In the Glow of the Christmas Room

The job of a physical therapist was certainly rewarding. But it wasn't always enjoyable. Nor was it easy. And a physical therapist working in a nursing home faced special challenges. Unlike many of his friends in the physical therapy field, Zachary O'Rourke never sent anyone back to their football team or jogging routine or work. His successes, when they did occur, meant that people (usually, but not always, elderly) became a bit more ambulatory, recovered some of their limbs to more effectively eat dinner or play cards, established more balance to keep from falling, maybe even live longer and more comfortably because their circulation or breathing or pain management had improved.

Still, though Zachary sometimes pondered the differences between his career and those of most of his peers, he was never so discouraged that he was tempted to move in a new direction. The successes he did have were of extreme importance. After all, the reason he chose physical therapy was to help the people who most desperately needed his skills. And places such as Villa Vista allowed him plenty of opportunities to pursue that calling. Today had been one of those days that made him embrace it with fresh gratitude and resolve.

Zach finished up his paperwork (computer work actually, though everyone still used the old word) and he was half-expecting Ralph to come by. Ralph Yarborough was Villa Vista's head custodian. That was his title anyway. But the position, as Ralph envisioned it, was something more fluid and expansive. He had a couple of assistants on staff to help clean up and there was another who helped him manage the physical structure. Ralph did more than his share of these duties yet he also did lawn work in the summer and shoveled walks in the winter. He was an in-house transport aide also, helping get residents to and from meals, appointments, and social activities. He ran errands, washed windows, and fought a perennial war with the moles in the Villa Vista grounds. He was the busiest person in the place and easily one of the most important in keeping the Villa Vista ship sailing on course. It was all a little ironic too, because at 84, Ralph Yarborough was himself as old as many of the residents in the place. He was quite a guy and Zachary really appreciated being his friend.

The clock had moved past six, however, and Ralph hadn't shown up. He must be busy somewhere else. So Zachary put his stuff away and decided it had been the kind of day that had earned him a visit to the Christmas Room. Zachary knew the residents of the south wing would be eating dinner and Grace Trinisi would probably not even be in her room now. But that was okay. He would stop by for a few minutes anyway.

Zachary was one of several residents and staff members who had discovered that the charms of the Christmas Room often provided just what a person needed in stressful times. Need a little comfort or cheering up? Perhaps a dose of inspiration and spiritual perspective? Maybe it was just a splash of beauty in an otherwise drab day. Whatever it was, the Christmas Room was the place. Mrs. Trinisi, even when unmoored from certain temporal realities, was never without a heart full of tenderness, humor, and social graces. She was the kind of welcoming, nurturing soul that everyone loved to be around. And part of her magic remained in the Christmas Room even in her absence. The tree, the decorations, the candle in the window – all of this called to Zachary this evening, inviting him to come and relax a few minutes before facing the drive across the city. Come on in, the room suggested. Sit a while and take a little Christmas home with you.

But when Zachary entered the room, he found another gift awaiting him, unexpected but certainly not unwelcome. Brenda Gritzner was sitting in Grace's easy chair looking out into the dusky sky. Zach couldn't help but think, "What a lovely woman she is."

Brenda turned when she heard Zachary's step and gave him a big smile. She cautiously reached up to her cheek to make sure there wasn't a teardrop lingering there. For she too had been experiencing the depth of stress and trouble that made a visit to the Christmas Room desirable.

"Good evening, Mr. O'Rourke. Grace is still down at dinner."

"Yes. I figured she would be. To be honest, I only dropped in to soak up a bit of Christmas in order to make the drive home a bit more cheerful."

Brenda looked around at the decorations before letting her eyes move back to the handsome young therapist. "It is an excellent room for that, isn't it? That's why I'm here too, I guess. I wanted to spend a little time with Grace this evening but it's also nice just to do a little thinking in this lovely room." She paused and Zachary noticed she was holding one of the sheep from the nativity set that Grace kept on the windowsill. The motion of her hand suggested a gentle petting but when she caught Zachary's gaze capturing the movement, she was suddenly embarrassed. She returned the sheep to its place alongside the figures of the Holy Family.

Zachary softened her self-consciousness by agreeing with her statement. "I know exactly what you mean. That's why I like coming in here too. And, maybe you know this already, but I'm sure not the only one. This is a very popular spot here at Villa Vista." He tossed his bag onto the floor next to Grace's bed. "Hey, I know it's not very dark but let's turn on the lights anyway. What d'ya say?"

"Good idea, Mr. O'Rourke. A very good idea." She reached up and flipped the switch while Zachary moved to the corner and plugged in the Christmas tree. The beautiful white candle with yellow flame and green garland lit up the window and the tree glowed gloriously in response with its own blaze of light and color.

Brenda's eyes reflected the pretty glow of the Christmas lights around her. They were gorgeous, thought Zachary. The lights *and* Brenda's eyes. And, before he planned on saying such a thing, he heard himself asking, "Brenda, do you have plans for dinner tonight?"

Once said out loud, Zachary knew he had wanted to make an invitation of that sort almost from the moment he had met Brenda. But he suddenly felt awkward. "Of course, I suppose your family is waiting for you at home or maybe you already have another dinner date but, you know, I was just thinking." Zachary stopped, unsure of how to proceed. He hadn't asked a girl out for a date since his fiancée Roxanne had jilted him last summer. And, if you didn't count those eighteen months with her, his last date had been back in his undergraduate days.

Brenda came to his aid. "Mr. O'Rourke, if you're suggesting we go to dinner together, I think I might enjoy that very much. Is that what you were asking?"

Brenda smiled broadly, giving Zachary the confidence to reply. "That's exactly what I was asking. As a matter of fact, I've been wanting to ask you that ever since I met you guys when you were taking the tour a couple of weeks ago. Do you even remember meeting me down in rehab?"

"Of course, I do, Mr. O'Rourke. But if I may be so bold to say it, my impression then was that you were more interested in my sister, Regina." Brenda tilted her head and gave him an impish smile.

"Oh really?" Zachary grinned back at her. "Your sister, Ms. Gritzner, is a very personable young lady. And I'm sure part of that is from your own influence. But, now if I may be so bold to say it, it is *your* charming presence that lights up a room when you enter it. Maybe as much as Grace's Christmas tree here."

Brenda blushed at the extravagant compliment but it also made her laugh. "I'm afraid the festive atmosphere of the Christmas Room may be affecting you, Mr. O'Rourke. But I'll allow for that. Plus, I generally accept all superlatives. Where do you have in mind?"

"Do you know Nick's over on Piedmont? Or do you even like Italian?"

Brenda laughed. "Well, if I didn't, I would never admit to it sitting here in Mrs. Trinisi's chair! It so happens though that I love it. Chicken Parmesan. Spaghetti. An Italian sausage sandwich with peppers and black olives. Pizza. I love'em all. Oh, no; I tell a lie. No shellfish – Italian style or any other way. I'm allergic."

"Okay. It's a deal. Would you like me to follow you home and then go together? Or would it be better for each of us to take our own cars?"

"Let's go for the latter, if that's okay, Mr. O'Rourke. I have reasons that I'd rather not stop at home for a while. But listen; why don't we stop down at the cafeteria and say hello to Grace before we go?"

Zachary agreed. "Good idea. I'd like to speak briefly to Mr. Stein also and to Ralph Yarborough if I see him. And, one other thing, Ms. Gritzner."

"Yes, Mr. O'Rourke?"

"Let's try and work our way round to first names before Nick serves the spumoni."

Zachary and Brenda ended up having a nice visit with Mrs. Trinisi. And Zachary was able to talk to Mr. Stein, Mr. Jenkins and even to Ralph too who was there way after his shift had ended. In fact, it was almost 7:30 before they finally left the cafeteria. And though both of the young people were now familiar figures at Villa Vista, there were several perceptive diners who noticed they looked especially nice as a pair.

Chapter 9
"A Little Slip of a Thing"

Rita Costello, a young CNA who had become a favorite of the residents in the south wing, helped Mrs. Innes get situated back in bed after returning from the bathroom. Rita was feeling very grateful because things had gone well which wasn't always the case with Mrs. Innes, poor thing. Tucking her in now, Rita thought Mrs. Innes would probably sleep through the night. But, on the other side of the curtain, she knew Mrs. Ridgeway was anxiously awaiting her attention. Lucretia Ridgeway would need to use the bathroom also but she would then need her heel to be re-wrapped. She would then probably want someone to sit with her for a bit. Normally Rita wouldn't have time and would have difficulty breaking away. But with Mr. Tyree moved to the north wing and Mrs. Gritzner not yet back from the hospital, Rita would have a few extra minutes tonight. She might even grab a cup of coffee and take her break while listening to Mrs. Ridgeway talk about her late husband. Surprisingly though, Mrs. Ridgeway fell asleep quite quickly so Rita decided to take her break down in the cafeteria. Maybe Betsy or T.J. would be down there too.

But as she approached Number 14, the Christmas Room,

she had another idea. She peeked in and saw Mrs. Trinisi sitting in her blue chair looking through her window out into the night. That was par for the course. Grace Trinisi was almost always the last to be put to bed and the first to be helped up in the morning. She sometimes would drift into a nap or two during the day but how she retained so much energy and good humor while getting so little deep sleep amazed the entire staff. But working with the elderly had given Rita many moments of amazement. The powers of memory and emotion (and the quirky nature of both). The complex integration of the body's systems. The capacity for endurance. The effects of drugs on both body and mind. The retention, even in the most difficult of trials, of gratitude, good humor and other social graces. Yes, working here at Villa Vista had given Rita constant grounds for wonder. And constant grounds too for the observation of human beings to show remarkable levels of warmth as well as coldness, emotional endurance as well as weakness, love as well as selfishness.

But more than merely learning about other people, working here had taught Rita much about herself. She had learned responsibility and patience. She had developed new perspectives on life and found reservoirs of strength and other-directedness that had really surprised her. She smiled and thought to herself, "I bet it would surprise my parole officer too!"

Mrs. Trinisi must have noticed movement for Rita heard an invitation for her to come in and say hello. She did just that. "Good evening, Mrs. Trinisi. You sure look good tonight. How are you feeling?"

"Oh, I'm fine." She was looking hard at Rita, trying to remember her name. She finally gave it up. "I'm just fine, honey."

Rita smiled. The old folks used these terms of endearment all the time and they used them without being patronizing or cute. They truly felt warm-hearted toward the people around them. Well, okay. Not all of them, Rita admitted. She had a quick vision of Mrs. Claxon, for instance, and that reminded her there were plenty of other problem folks. But for most of Villa Vista's residents, words such as honey, dear, darling, pet, sweetie, sugar, and a lot more were on their lips all the time. Rita loved it and thought it a nice reminder of what must have been a kinder, more sociable era.

What a sad thing that the politically correct standards of today were so set against this pleasant practice. Rita knew that in many institutions (including the immense senior center across town where her mother worked), staff were strictly prohibited from using any terms of endearment at all. The bosses insisted that it was paternalistic and unprofessional. Good grief, what foolishness, Rita mused. As if respect and appreciation were somehow incompatible with kindness and affection...and common sense. Rita had told her mom her opinion over coffee just yesterday: "Some of these paper pushers won't be satisfied until health care is passed on to robots or, worse still, to cold-fish bureaucrats like themselves!"

Grace Trinisi was sitting with her hands in her lap, a lovely brown afghan spread out to cover her. "Would you like to sit down, dear? There are a couple of chairs folded up by the Christmas tree there or you could take the seat on my walker. If it holds me up, it will be strong enough for a little slip of a thing like you."

Rita chose the walker. T.J. had told her that Mrs. Trinisi had once been a heavy woman and she knew Grace still tended to think of herself in that way. The truth was, she wasn't much more than "a little slip" herself nowadays. Poor thing. Rita patted her hand. "It's good to see you, Mrs. Trinisi. And it's always nice to come and sit a while in this beautiful room."

"Thank you, dear. I'm pleased to hear that. You know, my son and his wife do all of it. Well, and their kids too. But I got rid of most everything I had in my apartment. These Christmas things might be the only stuff I still have." She said this quite matter of factly, something Rita had noticed was very common among the people she served here. The anxious race to acquire stuff that marked the earlier decades of their lives had slowed down or even stopped altogether. Now they thought more of the simplest, most basic things. Being clean and warm. Enjoying a cup of tea or Gloria's macaroni and cheese down in the cafeteria. Having someone to talk to. Maybe this was the most important lesson that Rita needed to learn from working here. Get the right perspective on stuff. On people. On life and death.

Rita noticed that the music she'd heard from down the hall earlier in the evening was gone. "Weren't you listening to Christmas music earlier, Mrs. Trinisi?"

"Yes, I think I was." She seemed perplexed for a few seconds and Rita remembered how, in addition to many other health issues, Mrs. Trinisi had to deal with confusion and forgetfulness. Rita then recalled the protocol for Grace's music. Because his mother was no longer able to work the CD player, Tony Trinisi had created a simple arrangement for the staff. The red box beside the player had CDs with Christmas music, labeled for the successive days of the week and exactly timed to fit the limits suggested by the Villa Vista staff. But because putting the disc in or even turning on the machine was usually beyond Grace, the staff had been asked to put in the proper CD and turn on the player. And when that particular disc had played through, the machine shut itself off.

Recognizing that Mrs. Trinisi wasn't yet ready to go to bed, Rita suggested she turn the music back on for a little while. "Because a lot of people have already turned in for the night, I'll lower the volume a little. But since you've got the room to yourself again tonight, it won't hurt to play it some more. What do you think?"

Mrs. Trinisi thought that was a wonderful idea. Even better was that Rita agreed to take one of the Diet Cokes that Tony Trinisi kept piled up in the room. It was only another ten minutes they had together but they enjoyed them, Grace talking about Christmas in the old days and young Rita listening, learning, and admiring. It put both of them in a great mood the rest of the night.

***

While Rita and Mrs. Trinisi were having their pleasant chat in the Christmas Room, there were other conversations going on too. Reggie Gritzner and her girlfriends were discussing the details for her moving in with them permanently at their two-bedroom apartment in the city. Brenda Gritzner and Zachary O'Rourke were at Nick's Ristorante getting better acquainted. Tony Trinisi was on the telephone conducting a conference call with his siblings scattered all over the country, informing them of the latest news about their mom. Carolyn Kovacs was enjoying a late-night snack with two of her daughters and talking about the old Anna Neagle movie they had just watched together. Clark Gritzner was having a rambling on-again, off-again conversation with a bartender who couldn't have cared less.

And Joanna Gritzner? Well, she was having a conversation at this moment also. Joanna was, for the first time since she was a little girl, having a talk with God.

Chapter 10
An Unexpected Request

The inspectors had finished their two-day visit at Villa Vista and though they couldn't officially discuss their conclusions with Carolyn Kovacs, the lead official had indicated they had found things exceptional. Carolyn had been pretty confident that the facility would do well but then you can never tell with bureaucrats. She had breathed a big sigh of relief and called in the leadership staff to commend them. In fact, she had written a memo that would go to all the employees to thank them for jobs well done. That hurdle cleared, Carolyn concentrated on the next task at hand.

On her desk were the night reports and as she went through them, Carolyn was very surprised to see a re-admittance form for Mathilda Gritzner. Carolyn had checked in with the hospital every day since Mrs. Gritzner had been taken to the emergency room. She had been pleased to hear that Mattie had not only recovered substantially from her manic episode but that Dr. Wittman, a young and gifted physician about whom she had been hearing good things, had changed Mattie's blood pressure medicine and adjusted her Coumadin prescription. The result seemed to have brought Mrs. Gritzner back much better than before. That had been great news to Carolyn but she never imagined she would see Mrs. Gritzner again...not after the fit her son had thrown in the Christmas Room.

There was, however, a greater surprise in a note attached to the hospital report. It read, "The family wishes to sincerely apologize for their unwarranted interference in Mattie's care and they would consider it a great blessing if she would be allowed to come back to Villa Vista. Furthermore, after talking to Mattie herself and all other members of the family, we would deeply appreciate her being allowed to return to her previous room with Mrs. Trinisi. Mattie misses her friend and the staff down in the south section who have shown such kindness and professionalism. Mattie longs for the beauty and serenity of the Christmas Room. So, if it's at all possible, could she please come back to it?"

The note was signed by Joanna Gritzner but she had added a postscript. "P.S. My husband is out of town as I write this and he won't be back for another few days. However, please know that he concurs completely with this request. So, may I close with a heartfelt repeat of our appeal? Please let Mattie come home."

Carolyn put the letter down and was lost in thought for quite a long time. Readmission in such cases was a matter of routine but she hadn't entertained any expectations at all that Mrs. Gritzner would be coming back to live at Villa Vista. Not that Carolyn thought she would do better anywhere else. No indeed. The best place for Mattie Gritzner, Carolyn was absolutely convinced, was the Christmas Room at Villa Vista. But now that the request had been made, Carolyn felt cautious, even skeptical, about giving her okay. She had established affectionate attachments for Mattie and Joanna and the daughters, but could she jeopardize the balance and efficiency of her facility by giving Clark Gritzner new opportunities for interference?

She picked up the form and reread the medical report from Dr. Wittman. Then she reread, slowly and pensively, the attached note from Joanna. But before she got to the postscript again, Grant Katulka knocked on her door and stepped in.

"A fax just came in that is addressed to you personally. I thought you might want to see it right away."

"Sure, Grant. Thank you. Is it from the health association?"

Villa Vista's business manager shook his head. Grant, an older gentleman, retired from the railroad and working now on his second career, was always a subdued person but this morning he seemed almost grim. "No, Carolyn. I'm afraid it's from Mr. Clark Gritzner."

Oh, bother. Carolyn took the fax from Grant and began reading aloud. "Attention Carolyn Kovacs, Director, Villa Vista Care Community. Dear Mrs. Kovacs" (Carolyn noticed – and appreciated – the thoughtful change in title.) "I write first of all to beg your forgiveness for my rude and thoughtless behavior of April 16. There is no excuse for my conversation or behavior. And I am all too aware of what my arrogant actions created. My mother has received excellent attention and the most professional care at Villa Vista. I realize that now. And again, I humbly apologize for suggesting that wasn't the case. Furthermore, I now understand the beneficial effects my mother has received from sharing the room with Mrs. Trinisi. I do not deserve your consideration, Mrs. Kovacs, but I dare to ask on behalf of my mother and the members of my family, could you possibly allow my mother to return to Villa Vista? I firmly promise not to repeat my earlier offenses. Thank you for considering my request. And again, Mrs. Kovacs, I truly am sorry. Signed, Clark Gritzner."

Carolyn closed her eyes momentarily and Grant noticed a slight shake of her head. When she looked up at him standing in front of the desk, he thought she looked a little dazed. "Okay, Carolyn," he spoke softly. "What's it all mean?"

Carolyn swallowed and took a deep breath before answering, "I think it means the age of miracles has not yet passed." She paused and noticed Grant was waiting for a clearer answer. "It means Grant, that later this afternoon, Mattie Gritzner will be coming home!"

Chapter 11
"They Make a Cute Couple"

It had been a wet, windy, and warm spring but as April gave way to May and May, in its turn, gave way to the deeper heat of June, the atmosphere was particularly muggy. The air conditioning at Villa Vista Care Community had been turned on early and it stayed on. Fans were working overtime too. And so, though the electric bill went through the roof, the residents remained comfortable. The conditions had been great for Villa Vista's grounds, however, and that was a welcome delight for those who enjoyed the flowers, bushes, and lawn. The patio area on the southeast side of the building and the long shaded portico at the entrance were very popular spots now. And Grace Trinisi was one of those who enjoyed these outdoor locations the most.

It was a Saturday morning and Grace was sitting in a wheelchair under the portico. Her daughter-in-law Marsha sat on a bench next to her. Across from them were Thelma Keith and Horace Jones. They were catching up with each other's lives because it had been several weeks since they last talked.

Things had been up and down for Grace during that spring. She had suffered a couple more falls, one that gave her a deep laceration on her hip that hadn't wanted to heal quickly. There had also been another urinary tract infection that brought with it fever, pain and increased agitation and confusion. The Trinisi family and staff were very grateful, however, that the UTI hadn't triggered a panic attack or any other health setback like before. Grace had spent two nights at the hospital but, toward the end of May, she had begun to recover. The family realized, of course, that with every such event, Grace didn't quite bounce back to the same level. In health, in memory, in understanding, and in strength, Grace continued to decline. But her moods were stable now and positive.

As for Thelma and Horace, things had all been up. They were both "graduates" of Villa Vista, testimonies to Zachary O'Rourke and the rest of the rehab team who had helped them both recover from joint replacement surgeries and successfully prepared them to return home. But in the days they had spent at Villa Vista, very significant things had happened to Thelma and Horace. They had, for instance, rediscovered the gift of intimate friendship. Both had lost their spouses years earlier and neither had children living nearby. Retired from their jobs, they had lost the companionship of co-workers too. And, though both had been active in their churches in years past, they now felt set aside and lonely there. Horace, once talking to Ralph Yarborough about this, had bemoaned his pastor's attitude toward his older church members. "It's like the preacher tells us senior citizens to keep writing your tithe checks. And to remember the importance of estate planning to keep the church going. And now, if you will, please go back to stuffing the church newsletter in the envelopes and don't bother us younger folks because we'll do all the important stuff."

But at Villa Vista, Thelma and Horace had once again made good friends. Stripped of ego and its trappings by sharing a room with someone, eating in a cafeteria, needing help to use the bathroom, and all the rest, you could better see what was most important in life. Social status, bank account, clothes, and cars – none of these things mattered so much in a nursing home. But humility and compassion, respect and gratitude, kindness and good cheer? These things loomed large indeed.

Villa Vista had also opened new possibilities for significant service for Thelma and Horace. Living at Villa Vista, even for the short time they were there, had shown them how useful they could be to others. They didn't know nursing skills or physical therapy techniques, but they could do for others what had been done for them. They could be kind. They could comfort. They could talk with people, listen to them, sometimes pray with them. They could help alleviate the loneliness, fear, boredom and sense of being cast aside. They could be there.

Thelma and Horace learned that they weren't above stuffing envelopes. Certainly not. But they were worth more than that too.

Thelma and Horace found one other very wonderful thing. They found love. And as Marsha Trinisi heard them talk about their new involvement as volunteers here at Villa Vista and as she saw them holding hands and savoring each other's company, she realized anew how sweet and curative and beautifying was romantic love.

Even Grace couldn't help but notice. She had drifted off into one of her quick naps so Thelma and Horace had lowered their voices, thanked Marsha for spending time with them, and made a quiet exit. But as they walked away, Marsha heard Grace chuckle. She turned and caught Grace's wink. "They make a cute couple, don't they? Very much in love, I think."

"Yes, I think so, Mom. Very much."

"You know, they met right here. They used to come down to my room when I played music. The man…I forget his name."

"Horace," Marsha said.

"Yes, that's it. Horace. Like the poet. Anyway, he used to talk to me about his travels and I talked to him about growing up on the farm."

"I remember that, Mom. Do you remember that he was the man who gave you the calendar with the pictures from Ireland?"

"Oh, is he the fellow? That was nice of him. He put one of the pictures on my wall. By the mirror, isn't it?"

"Well, kind of. Tony cut it out because it looked so Christmassy. He put it in the picture frame that sits on your table. Right under the mirror."

Grace wrinkled her face as she tried to picture her room. "Oh yes. That's right. The picture in the frame." She paused a moment before leaning toward Marsha. She whispered, "I think I might give that picture to my roommate. She likes Christmas too. What do you think, honey? Do you think Tony would mind if I gave it away? Or that other man, the world traveler? Do you think that would bother them? I wouldn't want them to think I was ungrateful for such a pretty present."

Marsha felt tears well up in her eyes as she softly wrapped her mother-in-law's hands in her own. "Mom, I think they would love the idea. They would be proud of you for passing it along to a friend. And I'm sure Mattie would think it a splendid gift."

Grace smiled. "Yes. Yes. Her name is Mattie now, not Rosie. Rosie is gone. But Mattie is very nice too, isn't she?" Grace considered that a moment and then let her eyes close again. Marsha was silent but still held her hands. And after a minute or two had passed, Marsha saw Grace's lips turn up into a smile. She kept her eyes closed but started to hum and sway her hands as if she were dancing. Marsha listened closely and tried to figure out what song it was. One of her Christmas favorites? Maybe a love song inspired by Thelma and Horace? Then suddenly, Marsha had it. Grace was thinking of that Irish scene she was going to give Mattie and humming an appropriate air, "Too-Ra-Loo-Ra-Loo-Ral."

Chapter 12
Awkward Moments

It was one of Clark Gritzner's rare visits to his mother and, though he hadn't seen her for almost a month, he was already working on the excuses he would give for his absence in the next couple of weeks. He didn't have much time to spend with her now either. He had stopped at a drugstore and bought a big box of chocolates, the kind his dad used to give her at Christmas. But he was blocks away before he remembered that she wasn't supposed to have candy anymore. He had turned around and driven back to the store, created a bit of a scene in demanding they exchange the chocolates for a pot of little flowers, and now he had to park in the blazing sun. It wasn't a good start.

It got worse.

Clark's mother wasn't in her room. She wasn't in the nursing home at all. Joanna had taken her to a doctor's appointment. It was his own fault, he knew. Had he simply called his wife after getting off the plane, he wouldn't have had this infuriating hassle. Even if he had stopped at home instead of going to the marina to check on the *Blue Wave*, he wouldn't have wasted his time here. Clark started to ask at the nurses station how long his mother was expected to be gone but, realizing he wouldn't stick around regardless, he decided against it. Instead he motioned to a nurse (some young woman dressed in white anyway) and gave her the plant.

"Could you leave this for Mattie Gritzner in Room 14 and tell her it came from her son. Tell her I came to visit but I couldn't stay, alright?" The young woman (Territa, one of the kitchen crew who had just taken a lunch tray down to Mr. Pylonski) nodded and took the plant.

To avoid Carolyn Kovacs' office, Clark turned down the hall toward the south exit. He hoped it was open because he didn't want to have to ask anyone for an exit code. As he walked quickly down the hallway, he noticed a man in a tall, slanted wheelchair. The man's body seemed to be twisted up but he was unquestionably young, much younger than the other residents of the facility. More surprising to Clark, however, was that the young man looked familiar. Very familiar. And when he heard his name called, Clark knew at once who he was. The voice was raspy and a bit forced, the face lean and bearded, the body sadly misshapen. But he knew it was David Youngville.

The voice sounded again. It came almost in bursts, sounding as if every word came not only by special effort, but perhaps also with pain. "Do you remember me, Clark? I'm David from the 55th Street office."

Clark nodded. Yes, he remembered. But Clark didn't speak for what he knew was an awkward time. He recalled David as a nice fellow and a talented draftsman, one of the young hotshots that Blake had hired away from Kensington Grove. David had nearly been killed outright in a traffic accident but Clark hadn't followed David's story. He had forgotten him and never knew the young man's fate.

Now he did.

David sought to relieve the tension by speaking himself. "I know it can be a difficult moment, you know, to take in the change…to try and keep the shock from showing. But, really, it's alright. It's completely normal and I'm pretty used to it by now. Don't worry."

The young man was smiling and Clark instinctively believed he was being sincere. And, remarkably, it did help put Clark at ease. Enough to where he finally found his own voice. "I'm sorry, David. And thank you for helping me get a grip here. You're right, of course. I was shocked and I've always been terrible knowing how to handle tense situations like this."

Clark winced at his own words and the lack of sensitivity they revealed. He thought, "Here's a young man unfairly crippled up and in a wheelchair and yet I'm the one complaining about feeling awkward."

David expressed his surprise. "You're kidding. The company's top salesman? You always seemed so completely in control. So relaxed and confident."

Clark found himself strangely disarmed by the calm demeanor of the young man in the wheelchair. And his response was perhaps the most candid and trusting thing he had said for months. "David, I'm afraid I'm nothing like what you think. I never was really. But I'm certainly not nowadays. First of all, I haven't been the top salesman for quite a while. In fact, to be completely fair, I'm not very far away from being fired."

"Oh man; I'm sorry, Clark. Maybe you're just going through a bad patch right now."

Clark shook his head. "I'm going through a bad patch, that's for sure. But it's not just work. In fact, work may be the very least of my troubles."

From his wheelchair, David's sigh was loud. And it made the sincerity of his next statement seem particularly sincere...and significant. "I'm really sorry to hear that, Clark. Life can be awfully hard sometimes. Unfair. Ugly. Even when you're trying your best."

Clark was moved. Here was a man who had great promise – a talented, good-looking, personable young man who was quickly moving up the ladder. And now here he was in a motorized wheelchair, broken and helpless. Yet Clark saw that he wasn't consumed with his own problems. He was genuinely hurting for someone else – someone he hardly knew, someone who hadn't even been particularly nice to him. Clark felt ashamed and convicted of his own shallowness. He felt it at a considerably stronger level than he had for a long time. Yet, Clark also found a sense of safety with his former colleague.

David again broke the silence. "Look Clark, I don't know what kind of time you've got but if you'd like to talk a bit we could go down to the lounge or cafeteria. You could get a cup of coffee or a Coke."

Clark looked down and felt the warmth in both David's invitation and his smile. And he almost accepted. In fact, he was so close to saying yes that he felt pained when he said no and made up a lie for an excuse. "Thanks, but my wife is waiting for me to pick her up. I'd sure like to do that sometime though. My mother lives here now and so I guess we'll have other chances. What's your room number?"

"27."

"Great. I'll look forward to it. Is there any particular time that's best?"

David laughed. "You come anytime, Clark. You'd be surprised just how much time a partially paralyzed guy confined to a wheelchair and living in a nursing home has on his hands!"

Clark gave a sheepish grin and made a quick exit. As he hustled down the south hallway, he was aware his cheeks had reddened for he was certain David knew he was lying. But Clark knew the biggest reason he felt flushed and frantic was that he suddenly recalled the cause of David's accident. He'd been hit by a drunk driver.

Clark promised himself, though not with a lot of confidence, that he would have to slow down his own drinking. Like everything else in his life, he had lost control there too. And he would have to get a grip before he left somebody dead. Or in a state like David Youngville.

Chapter 13
Farmers Market

Browsing through the farmers market early on Saturday mornings had now become a matter of course for Brenda Gritzner and Zachary O'Rourke. She favoring the variety and quality of the vegetables that were available, he the strawberries, conversations, and "unplugged" music from street performers.

Their primary interest, however, was in one another.

Brenda hadn't really been interested in a serious relationship. She wanted to concentrate on her studies and get a bold start in her new career. But Zachary had changed all that. She still wanted the other things but she now wanted him too. And, at least so far, that seemed possible. In fact, their relationship enhanced her previous priorities still further. Her grades remained high. Her appreciation for the healing professions had grown. Even her connections for jobs after graduation had increased through contact with Zachary's friends and associates. Yes, he had been good for her in every way she could imagine.

The couple walked hand in hand through the market, combining small talk with big talk, observations with opinions, feeling both the comfort and the charge that love creates.

Not all of the subjects they talked about were easy ones. Brenda had relayed to Zachary the latest news about the disintegration of her family while Zachary had told her about the sudden death from a brain aneurysm of Mr. Atwill. He had been the third resident of Villa Vista to die in as many weeks but the other two had passed away in the hospital. Mr. Atwill was a rather cranky fellow who had given the staff a lot of trouble in the months he'd been there but Zachary attributed a lot of that to fear and grief. He was sure Mr. Atwill was starting to adjust and a new CPAP machine had begun to give him the first restful nights he had experienced in years. Then, right in the middle of bingo, Mr. Atwill had fallen over, probably dead before he hit the floor.

"It was pretty hard on some of the residents to observe," Zachary explained. "And, though it's been almost a week, there are a few who can't seem to get over it, including a few of my rehab patients. I feel like I've had to be a counselor as well as a PT this week. And I certainly don't feel very skilled with the former duty."

"I'm sure you've done fine, Zachary. You're a good friend to those people. You listen. You sympathize. You offer good advice when it's needed. A professional counselor couldn't do any better than that."

"Thanks, Brenda. I don't think I was hinting for affirmation. But I'll certainly accept it. I appreciate it."

Brenda smiled. But it soon disappeared as she brought up a related subject. "Zachary, I worry quite a lot about how I'm going to respond to crises and tragedies like the one you've just described with Mr. Atwill. I see the value of nursing. I do. It's a noble, heroic calling. And I want my life to count, really count by being a nurse. But I often have real doubts that I'll be able to handle patients dying. Even dealing with people enduring suffering seems like it could so easily be overwhelming."

"Sometimes it is," Zachary answered soberly. "It wouldn't be honest to deny it. And asking those questions of yourself is a good thing to do, Brenda. I agree with you about the nobility of the healing professions. However, I don't think everyone is cut out for caregiving, let alone for ministering to people nearing the end of life or people coming into an emergency room or an ICU. It can be very, very hard. There's no doubt about it. I suppose it might be easier with certain personalities and it almost surely becomes less difficult with experience. And good training. And a strong resolve to do what needs to be done. But it will always be a tough job."

"You don't have doubts anymore, do you?" Brenda asked.

"No, I guess not. Depression? Yes. Frustration? Yes. Anger? Yes to that too. But no real doubts to speak of. As I've explained before, my profession suits me. I want to provide care to those who most need it. And working with the elderly fits my personality and my gifts. It's often difficult and sad but I know it's what I was called to do."

"Calling. That's the key for you, isn't it?"

"Yeah, I guess so. I realize it's a very individual thing. God puts together a person's background, their temperament and skills, their sense of need and He then matches those up with available opportunities. I know it's right for me. And yet for others the call is to be an airline pilot or soldier or hod carrier. You've got to be open to what He has in store for you. And if you're willing to let Him set the agenda, then it's cool. Hard job, boring job, fun job. If it's His calling, it will bring you satisfaction. And it will make a difference that's very important too."

Brenda walked quietly for several strides before she stopped and looked up at Zachary. "What do you think about me, Zach? Do you believe I'm called to be a nurse?"

The young man smiled and tenderly squeezed her hand. "I don't know, Brenda. And I don't think you necessarily need to know that right now. I think it's enough to believe you're called at this moment of time to be in nursing school. Whether or not you ever practice, we don't know. Your training may convince you one way or the other. Or, like with teaching, you may have to get out and start before you know there's something else for you."

"You mean I might waste *another* few years before I find out what I want to be when I grow up?"

Zachary smiled and shrugged. "Maybe. But don't get ahead of yourself."

They started walking again, heading toward the fellow playing the saxophone in front of the craft booths. They listened to one of his songs. He wasn't very good but Zachary dropped a couple dollars in his open case anyway.

As they strolled through the farmers market, Brenda asked, "Can I come back to the matter of choosing the right career? How do you make absolutely *sure* you don't miss God's call?"

"Good question. Come on, let's sit down over here and have a Coke or something." They sauntered over to the tables set up outside the Java Jive. The waitress was heavily inked and pierced, and she sported a hairdo that involved a variety of colors. She wore a name tag but the name written there was unpronounceable. She was, however, very friendly and efficient. Within minutes the couple was sipping the brew of the day, a light, frothy mocha called Delicate Dominican Dream.

"Okay," Zachary began. "The most important calling of God in any person's life concerns character. That's where you start. And, for that matter, it's also where you end. As a convert to Christianity, I'm aware that God wants me to be a person of integrity and compassion, virtue and courage. As the Westminster creed puts it, I'm to worship and enjoy God forever. So, if I'm centering on those basic things, what I do for a living or where I live is secondary. Not unimportant…just secondary. They find their relevance in the first principles."

Brenda was listening closely and she was agreeing too. Ever since she had become a Christian back in high school, these truths had been a part of her worldview. But Zachary seemed to have a tighter grasp on them. He had certainly lived them out in more straightforward ways than she had to date. Still, she was delighted and deeply grateful that Zachary shared her faith. But beyond the big issues of life, there were a lot of other things that concerned her...especially now with what was happening in her family. She hoped Zachary might be moving toward talking about some of them too.

He was. "So those are the basic elements of a life well lived, the foundational truths. But with all that said..." He paused and noted the look of anticipation on Brenda's face. "With all that said, I believe God's love for His children is so personal, so deep, so comprehensive that He is going to guide and protect them in the daily decisions of life too. We pray. We seek good advice. We test options. And quite often, we will end up reversing course and trying a different route. But, in the end, if we are truly focusing on the main things, God is going to help us find *exactly* where we're most needed and most fulfilled."

Brenda nodded. "That makes sense. And it means that if I'm being faithful in my relationship with Christ, I'm not wasting my time in nursing school. No matter what happens."

"Exactly." Zachary agreed. "As much as you sometimes suggest that your bachelor's degree and your year of teaching was a failure, I think you know it wasn't. You saw corners of life you never would have seen. And you learned things. You grew as a person. And you touched other lives."

"That's a comforting idea, Zachary. I suppose I should appreciate that a lot more than I have." She sipped more of her coffee and considered what her boyfriend had been saying. "You know, that's true of nursing school too, isn't it? No matter where I nurse or, maybe, if I never even do it as a living, I need to make the most of my experience now."

"Spot on. Even if your nursing training is only used when you volunteer at a crisis pregnancy center or on a mission trip, it will be of great value."

Brenda blushed and looked down at her cup of Delicate Dominican Dream. "Even if I use it someday to take care of my own kids."

Zachary looked longingly at the young woman with whom he had fallen in love. "That's a wise application, Brenda. Very wise." He smiled coyly and slowly stirred his drink. "Yes, a woman with nursing training might go to the head of the list for a lot of men who are considering marriage and family."

Brenda looked up and their eyes met. "Would that help you make up *your* mind, Zachary?"

He reached over and grabbed her hand. "Oh yes, Brenda. Without a doubt. In fact, I guess it already has."

:

Chapter 14
The Origins of the Christmas Room

The Christmas Room at Villa Vista made for continual conversation. Prospective residents and their families who were taking a tour of the facility asked about it a lot. Volunteers from organizations and churches talked about it with great curiosity and amusement. Health officials, ambulance crews, deliverymen – everyone found the Christmas Room of enormous interest. And almost all of that conversation was favorable. Even in the surrounding neighborhood, where people couldn't help but notice the distinctive decorations that lit up the room so colorfully at night, the Christmas Room was embraced as a unique blessing. For even if people found it quirky, they also thought it quaint and pretty. It also helped persuade everyone who knew of the Christmas Room that the staff respected the individuality of the residents, that they were conscientious and kind and accommodating. It had proved its value to the residents and care staff in many ways. Even the business office had great reason to appreciate the Christmas Room.

But there were always a lot of questions and the staff had learned to give answers that were honest but didn't cross the HIPAA laws or surrender the privacy rights of the residents.

So there were only a few who knew the whole story.

Grace Trinisi had experienced her first stroke over a year ago. She was living with Tony and Marsha as she had been for several years. Grace had been widowed quite a while earlier and had struggled with several serious health problems including severe mood swings and manic episodes stemming from depression and the onset of dementia. They had been tough years for the family, but the Trinisis had done a good job in providing care and protection...and love. But the stroke changed things dramatically for Grace. There were almost two weeks in the ICU and another eight days in the hospital before a second stroke and subsequent surgery put her back in the ICU for another eleven days. The doctors had then recommended that the family admit Grace to Villa Vista for a trial period, believing that the rehabilitation programs, the socialization, and a more enveloping "safety net" would all be to Grace's advantage.

It was. Grace responded well and there was rapid improvement in her physical health. But it was in Grace's emotional condition that the family saw the most surprising and welcome changes. Her general depression lifted significantly. She started smiling and laughing again. She loved being around people her own age and she made friends fast. It was terrific.

Previously, even before the stroke, Grace had not been happy. She was profoundly bothered by guilt, believing that her presence in her son's home was a harsh interference. She hated the idea of requiring constant help from them without being able to give anything back. And assurances from the family that her very presence was treasured carried little weight. Like so many of her generation, she had a deep fear of being a burden to those she loved. She knew they meant well and she had been generally grateful and pleasant. But in that last year before the strokes, Grace had become more withdrawn. Her depression and anxiety had increased as well. The doctors surmised that the resultant stress might even have been a factor in hastening the stroke.

At Villa Vista, however, Grace felt free. Whereas she had become sullen and resentful in those last months living with them, she now cherished the attention of her family. She was also enjoying her many new friends (both residents and staff) and even embraced a sense of purpose. As she put it, she had "a ministry with these old people" by encouraging them, having conversations, praying for them, being hospitable by sharing her room and her refreshments. There was no doubt. She was happier and more fulfilled than she had been for years and, even though Tony realized the extent of her limitations and the fragility of her health, he was happy to have his mom back.

But what of the Christmas Room?

Grace had suffered that first stroke in February but, in her restless mind, she believed it was Christmastime. And she wondered, with no small amount of consternation, why Tony hadn't bothered to decorate her room. He tried to explain the situation several times. So too did the nurses and aides attending her but no one seemed to get through to Grace. So, after an evening when Tony saw his mom cry because she feared she would never see a Christmas tree before she died, he drove home, crawled up into the rafters of the garage, and unpacked the tree and decorations he had put there just weeks before. He also grabbed some Andy Williams and Johnny Mathis Christmas tapes and his old boom box and tossed them in the car. Within the hour, Tony, Marsha and the kids were back in the ICU room, listening to music (low volume, of course) and trimming the Christmas tree he had set up in the corner. And Grace? She was wide awake and enjoying every moment, calmer and happier than they had seen her in a long while.

The charge nurse at the hospital, one Ms. Callahan, wasn't at all pleased with what was going on and unloaded all kinds of threats, including putting in a call to security to have all of them and their "Christmas stuff" removed from the hospital. But the family was undeterred, Tony suggesting that she first ask Dr. Worthington or Dr. Mubarik or whoever was serving as the hospitalist to come up and evaluate the situation. Meanwhile, he would call the newspaper and a couple of the local TV stations because he thought it might make a story they would find of great interest.

The Trinisis stayed. And so did the Christmas tree.

Somewhere along the route to Grace's recovery, Tony suspected that his mom recognized it wasn't really Christmastime any more. But it had seemed to have been such an important part of her emotional turnaround that he was reluctant to drop it. The doctors agreed. Dr. Li had once taken him outside the room and, in an exaggerated conspiratorial whisper, said, "Look, Tony. As you already know, a couple of the nurses up here and even one of my colleagues are playing the humbug on this whole Christmas thing. They're afraid that it's giving your mom a false sense of comfort. That's balderdash. These kinds of people are driven by protocol and pharmaceuticals. I ask them what they want – to rely only on drugs to control a patient's moods? To keep them manageable by just keeping them stoned? That's crazy."

Dr. Li continued, "Pills are not the whole of healing. If anyone should realize that, it's doctors and nurses. Not that I'm suggesting, of course, that your mother isn't positively served by various medicines. She is and we'll continue that treatment and change it as necessary. But the fact that your mom finds comfort and happiness in the trappings of Christmas shouldn't be discounted. In fact, why should we be surprised at that? Most of us do. It's just that your mom is blessed enough to want it more than just in December. So as long as it's helpful to her, I'm all for it. So is Dr. Worthington. And, for that matter, so is Carolyn Kovacs over at Villa Vista Care Community which is where we've suggested your mother go, at least for a while when she's discharged. And, who knows, your mother may well be blazing a new trail for us. After all, wouldn't it be super if we could cut down on the angst and paranoia of some of our patients, not so much by drug drips but with a bit more Santa Claus and Bing Crosby?"

Tony couldn't have agreed more.

But the Christmas approach *did* end up presenting a problem...a rather unexpected one with surprising results. And that problem began when Tony and the family removed the tree, the lights, and the music from the hospital to re-establish them in Grace's new home at Villa Vista. As Dr. Mubarik explained it later to Tony when they ran into one another at a baseball game the following summer, "It took our staff until about April to get over the post-Christmas blues that set in after your mom left us. I'm not kidding one bit either. It got to the point that Ms. Callahan herself started bringing in Christmas cookies every Thursday instead of donuts! So you be sure to wish your mother a merry Christmas from the whole bunch over there. And I mean the *whole* bunch!"

Chapter 15
Home Alone

Joanna Gritzner put her phone down on the counter. Brenda had just called and told her she wouldn't be home for dinner. She was going out with Zachary for Chinese. Joanna couldn't help but note how happy and excited her daughter sounded. Joanna was happy for her too, though it tended to emphasize her own sense of sadness and helplessness that she felt in her relationship with Clark. Clark had been her high school sweetheart and only love. As her husband, Clark had given her much joy and satisfaction and safety these past 27 years. But he had now become a stranger to her, a man she didn't care for very much. Sour. Selfish. Short-tempered. Secretive. When she first realized he had started drinking, she thought that explained the changes in him. She now thought differently. She suspected it was more likely that Clark was looking for an escape from a deeper, more exasperating problem. And Joanna couldn't help but conclude the problem must be her.

And yet Clark's attitude toward his daughters had radically changed too. What could the cause of that be? The girls had been the treasures of his life but, in recent months, he had been coldly dismissive even to them. Brenda hadn't felt it as much as Reggie but that wasn't really surprising. Brenda had long established more independent attitudes and beliefs. She was her own person. But in recent weeks, Joanna believed both daughters had come to feel about their father what she as his wife did – shame. And the realization that her girls had lost the love and respect they once had for their dad was the most painful thing of all.

Joanna knew they would all deal with things differently. Brenda was strong. Even a disaster (if it came to that) would not crush her. Brenda had spiritual convictions that the others in the family didn't possess, the result of a religious experience she had at a Christian camp in the spring before her high school graduation. Ever since then she had been different and Joanna appreciated the changes. Brenda didn't preach at the rest of the family. Well, not very much. But she clearly had a moral vision now and inner resources that set her apart. No, Joanna had no doubts about Brenda. She would survive and still be sweet and savvy and joyful.

But Regina was another case altogether. She was strong too but in a more calculated, self-centered way. Her reaction to her father's change had already shown up in bitterness and rejection. Regina wouldn't emerge unscathed from the coming disaster. She would rebel and strike back. Joanna could easily conceive of Regina disregarding everything from their life before and retaining only the hurt her father had caused.

And what about Joanna herself? She would be the one to just shrivel up and die. She was all too aware that she had no religious strength like Brenda had. She had no vantage point from outside herself, no sense of objectivity. Nor did she have the self-assurance and pride that Regina possessed, the confidence that would drive her to be an instrument of justice. No, Joanna had nothing. Without Clark's love and protection as well as the interests they had shared – mostly, the love of their daughters – Joanna felt empty and powerless.

Tonight was particularly hard. Clark had announced

another sudden business trip and had left for the airport hours ago. Regina was spending the weekend with friends and had, in fact, made it plain she was going to make it a permanent arrangement. Joanna couldn't blame her for wanting out of the house. No one really lived here anymore.

No, Joanna thought suddenly. There's Brenda. She's still here. And she's alive in every fiber of her being. She's alive and she's free and she's strong. She carefully considered the question. Was it because she *really* did find God at that summer camp? Joanna sighed and suddenly said out loud, "Tonight of all nights, Brenda, I think we could talk about those things. But you won't be here. You're busy. You may even be in love, and that means it won't be long before you'll move out too. And, honey, I can't begrudge you what happiness you can find. But I sure do wish you were here tonight."

Joanna began to clear the dining room table of the dishes she had set out for her and Brenda. She put the casserole back on the counter and the glasses in the cupboard. Without realizing it at first, she had begun to cry. She sat back down and wept quietly there at the table. Sad. Alone. Helpless to control her emotions and helpless against the mysterious forces that had broken the happiness and security of her life.

Several minutes passed before Joanna realized the sound she heard was the ticking of the wall clock. It wasn't even five o'clock yet. Brenda might not be home until late. Clark and, of course, Regina wouldn't be home at all. How on earth was she going to get through this lonely night? She noted the time again. Her friend Sheila would be headed to the gym pretty soon and some of the other girls would be at the country club. If she got herself together, she could probably...No, she suddenly knew she wasn't in the mood for either stairsteppers or socializing. But then another idea came. It was a good one. Joanna lifted her head, surrendered the ghost of a smile, and grabbed her phone.

"Villa Vista Care Community. This is Irene."

"Hello, Irene. This is Joanna Gritzner, Mattie's daughter-

71

in-law."

"Oh yes, Mrs. Gritzner. How can I help you?"

"Well, I know that it's almost dinner time for the south wing and I know that dinner guests are supposed to reserve spots long before this but I was wondering…Well, actually I was hoping that I could still get a place at Mattie's table tonight?"

"Certainly, Mrs. Gritzner. We'd love to have you."

"I was just looking for a seat, Irene. I know they probably already have the meals allotted but…"

"Nonsense, Mrs. Gritzner. John, our evening chef, always plans for a few extra and he might be hurt if he couldn't serve you something. Let me see. The features tonight are baked chicken, meat loaf sandwich, or spaghetti. But John can just about always whip up anything else you'd like."

"Thank you, Irene. The meat loaf sandwich will hit the spot. Please thank him for me and I'll thank him again when I get there."

"Okay, I will let the guys in the kitchen know right now. And, come to think of it, the Trinisis came by a little earlier and picked up their mom to take her out to supper, so there's already a free seat at your mom's table."

"Great. Thanks again, Irene. I'll be leaving here real quick and I'll be there just about the time they start serving."

"Okay then. Drive careful though, Mrs. Gritzner. We don't mind you being late but we do mind you not making it at all. So long."

Joanna laughed at Irene's exhortation. She was such a pleasant lady. But then most of the Villa Vista staff were like that. Not all, that's for sure. But most. And, as she washed her face and applied a bit of fresh makeup, Joanna was deeply thankful she would be among such people tonight. Friendly. Patient. Able to put every crisis in perspective and carry on. She could sure use a dose or two of that tonight. In fact, she decided she would hang around after dinner too. For if there was anything that might help her sense of loneliness tonight, it probably would be spending some time with Mattie and

Grace in the Christmas Room.

And on the drive over, something quite unusual happened. It started with Joanna thinking things through and then somewhere along the way, she started talking to herself, speaking aloud into the silence of the car as she tried to understand what was happening. But as she left the highway and drove into the neighborhood where Villa Vista was located, her mood lightened considerably. She realized she was looking forward to the meal, to seeing her mother-in-law and Grace Trinisi, to having tea in the Christmas Room. And suddenly she realized she wasn't talking to herself anymore. She was speaking, as she had begun to do lately, to God.

Chapter 16
Door Number 1 or Door Number 2?

Overcoming the energy costs from the sizzling heat was not the only special challenge facing Carolyn Kovacs and the Villa Vista staff this summer. Sudden vacancies in two key positions had to be filled. A major plumbing project was underway in the kitchen. The ever-expanding mess created by government rules and regulations that were expensive, frustrating, and counterproductive was worse than ever.

And then there was the lawsuit.

The lawyers had explained to Carolyn that it was a frivolous suit with no chance of success. But it still meant depositions, interviews with health officials, and money. And it had produced no small amount of frustration in her staff.

The charges made against Villa Vista were very serious ones – medical malpractice, breach of contract, patient endangerment, and causing needless pain and suffering to family members. Quite the response for simply sending an 81-year-old woman to the hospital to be treated for a urinary tract infection! The resident in question, Mrs. McGullin, had a history of UTIs and when it struck in the past, the infection had created real havoc in her body and mind: fever, delirium, profound anxiety followed by listlessness, and low vital signs.

But this time, Mrs. McGullin skipped the first two symptoms altogether. The staff noticed some slowing down and a little slurring of speech just after supper one night. This was put in her chart with an alert noted for night staff to keep a close eye on her. And, sure enough, in the early morning hours, the resident was discovered to have produced discolored urine…and not much of it. Worse, she couldn't wake up.

The charge nurse called the doctor who ordered Mrs. McGullin to be transported to the emergency room. It was the right call. Within 18 hours, she was her regular self. Walking. Talking. Knitting. Working the *New York Times* crossword. A wonderful outcome, right? Well, not to Mrs. McGullin's out-of-state niece who believed herself to be the patient's only heir. The complaining niece insisted that the medical treatment violated the DNR orders she had sent to the nursing home several months ago – "orders" that were without her aunt's knowledge, let alone consent. Therefore the document, like the niece herself, had no legal standing. Nevertheless, the resultant lawsuit was full of the common phrases: "prolonging the dying process," a prohibition on "heroic measures" and "extraordinary means," "doctors playing God," and so on.

Carolyn shook her head and sighed. All this grief just for treating a UTI? Carolyn believed the lawyers when they assured her the case would go nowhere. Yet she knew too well that society was moving in that ominous direction. Rather than treating the old and infirm with honor and compassion, the movement was toward disrespect, discrimination, drastically reduced care (under the banner of cost containment), and euthanasia.

Of course, having spoken to the resident about her interfering niece, Carolyn Kovacs knew something the niece didn't know. And it was a fact that, despite herself, made Carolyn smile. For Mrs. McGullin had explained to Carolyn earlier in the year that she had placed her entire estate into a trust that her lawyers insisted was cast iron. And the entirety of that trust was already parceled out to Mrs. McGullin's church, a foreign mission society, and the local symphony orchestra. The grasping niece was fated to receive nothing at all.

Carolyn forced herself to focus on the other tasks before her. It was going to be a long, challenging day. However, the next item on her schedule promised to be a cheery one. And, right on time, she saw Rita come to the door. She was obviously nervous and Carolyn wanted to put her at ease as soon as possible. After all, it's often scary being called to the boss's office. She motioned for Rita to come in and sit down even as she spoke into the phone.

"Tamara, could you please bring in a couple of Diet Cokes for Rita and me? And a couple of those brownies that Marsha Trinisi brought over; that is, if there's any still around! We've got something to celebrate here. At least, I hope we're going to."

"Good morning, Mrs. Kovacs. You wanted to see me now?"

"Yes, Rita, I did. And though I've set aside a bit of time to talk about it, I think it's best to let you know right away what I'm thinking about. Okay?"

"Sure. Uh, has my work been satisfactory? You know, has it been…"

"Yes, yes, and another yes, Rita. I couldn't be more pleased. Your work ethic, your efficiency, the way you relate to the residents, your willingness to do extra to help them out and to assist your fellow workers – everything has been really quite wonderful."

Rita's relief was profound. She took in a large breath and smiled wide. "Oh, thank you, Mrs. Kovacs. You don't know how happy that makes me because, well…you know, you took a chance on me and I've really wanted to be a success here. So, I'm really pleased to hear that."

Carolyn returned the smile. "Well, then, here's my offer. Actually, I have two offers for you and I want you to stop and think for a moment before you tell me which one you choose. In fact, you may want to think it over for a day or two. Alright?"

Rita straightened up in her chair and folded her hands in her lap. She took another deep breath and said, "Go ahead. I'm ready."

Carolyn thought that Rita, at that moment, was one of the cutest, most pleasant things she had seen for a long time. "Okay, here goes. Door number one is for you to continue the excellent work you've been doing as CNA with a raise of $1.60 an hour and a change to the 7-3 shift."

Carolyn noted with pleasure how Rita's eyes and mouth opened at that offer.

Carolyn continued. "However, to be honest, I'm hoping you will take door number two. It only involves a $1.60 raise for right now. But after eight weeks of training, if the job works out for us and for you, it will go up another $2.40. That job is the assistant activities director."

Rita was stunned and couldn't think of anything to say except, "Oh, my."

"Look, Rita, like I said, you can take some time to think it over. But you've probably heard Mike Boone has re-enlisted in the Navy and he'll be gone in a month. Angie Stewart, who has been here over three years as the assistant AD, will then take over Mike's job. And that means we'll need a new assistant. We have all seen the way you work with the residents and the way you've volunteered extra to help with the sing-alongs, the oral history interviews those home-school junior high kids are doing, even the Sunday worship service. Rita, we think you'd be a great addition to the activities staff right away. You might even see it as the start to a new career, maybe getting certification and moving on up. What do you think?"

The tears began to fall but the smile was wide. Rita swallowed hard...twice...before forcing out, "Do I have to think it over, Mrs. Kovacs?"

"What do you mean, hon?"

"Can I please choose right now?"

Carolyn grinned. "Well, yes, of course."

Rita stood up proudly and extended her hand. "Mrs. Kovacs, I am really honored by your offer. More than I could ever say. And, if you mean it for sure, I'll take door number two!"

Yes, Carolyn Kovacs' day had several difficult chores lying ahead, particularly cracking the whip on those plumbers, but it had certainly started out very, very bright.

Chapter 17
"The Yellow One with Some White"

Mattie Gritzner was in bed most of the day. She had been battling an exasperating cough for almost a week but they finally had it under control. At least enough for her to get some sleep. Across the room, Tony Trinisi and his mother talked in low tones.

"I'm glad to see Mattie sleeping so soundly, Mom. She's been pretty sick, huh?"

"Yes, poor thing. She's been coughing her fool head off. Even during the night. She got so tuckered out from coughing that she slept through supper."

"Not supper," Tony corrected. "They haven't started supper yet. You must mean lunch."

Grace frowned. "Oh, I don't know what I mean. You ought to know that. I get a lot of things confused and I never know what time it is anymore."

"That's okay, Mom. That's okay."

They sat in silence for a few minutes. They did this often nowadays, being content in watching the birds outside and thinking their own thoughts. But doing it together was a priceless gift for both. It was certainly different than in earlier days. The Trinisi household had always been filled with noise

— conversation, laughter, arguments, music, dogs, the sounds of girls playing, the sounds of boys banging away as they made stuff. Orchestrating it all was Grace Trinisi, the extroverted, pretty, and remarkably organized matriarch of the family. But that was then. Brief and sporadic conversation between Grace and her son was now the norm with great patches of silence mixed in. And, as Tony reflected on the difference, he decided this was okay too.

Tony reached over and grabbed his mother's hand. She looked up and smiled with such kindness that Tony's heart melted. It was nice to enjoy moments like this. "Tony," Grace broke the silence with a whisper. "Did you get your lawn mowed today?"

Tony whispered back. "I did it on Monday, Mom. When I leave here, I'll do some watering. With the rains we've been having, I've not had to do much of that this month."

"The yellow one?"

"What do you mean, Mom?"

"You know, the yellow one. The yellow one with some white too?"

Tony had learned to take on himself the blame for his mom's memory loss as much as possible. Rather than increasing the frustration and embarrassment his mother already experienced in not remembering things or not speaking as clearly as she'd like, he and Marsha pretended the weakness was their own. He tried the tactic here.

"Oh, the yellow and white one. You know, Mom, I've been so busy at work and with baseball that I had forgotten that. I'll ask Marsha."

The redirection didn't work this time. His mom was still puzzling over the matter. "Oh, Tony. The yellow one that I liked...the one that turned both ways. You know, the yellow one with some white too!"

Tony knew his mom could get worked up about this if he didn't figure out the mystery. And it didn't matter whether she got mad at him or herself, he wanted to save her from that. So he did what he frequently did throughout his day. He lifted up a quick, silent prayer for help.

And God came through.

"Of course, Mom. I'm so silly. You're thinking of that yellow water sprinkler. The one that followed the hose and squirted out water in a circle. And the wheels turned and, yes, the wheels were white. It was called a tractor sprinkler. I remember how cool you thought it was. How could I forget that? But, you know; Mom, it broke a couple of years ago. I'm sorry; I should have told you." He had told her but again, it was completely unnecessary to remind her of that.

His mother's relief spread over her face. She smiled and patted his hand. "That's alright, son. I forget a lot of things too."

There were another few moments of silence. They were both thinking of that neat sprinkler. And they were both thanking God that they remembered it together.

Tony looked up at the clock. "They'll be serving supper in about 15 minutes, Mom. Should I call one of the girls in to help you use the bathroom before you go down?"

"Yes, I suppose I'd better. Are you going to stay for dinner tonight?"

"No, I'd like to Mom, but I've got to get home and try to get that lawn watered before it gets dark."

"Oh, did you get the lawn mowed yesterday? I know you like to water after you mow."

Tony laughed. "You're right, I sure do. Actually, though, I mowed a couple of days ago so I'm a little overdue. But it's interesting that you would remember that."

"Remember what?"

"That I like to water right after I mow."

"Well, I haven't forgotten everything, you know. I still remember quite a bit." She grinned and Tony wondered if she was making a joke.

He got up and kissed her. "I know you do, Mom. Okay, I'd better book. I'll stop at the nurses station and have them send someone down to help you get ready for supper. And tomorrow you've got a lunch date with Marsha and the girls. I put it on your calendar. Marsha is going to take you to the eye doctor and then the girls will meet you afterward at the Summer Kitchen. And I'll be by again on Friday. Okay?"

"Okay, Tony. You kids are so good to me. And the people here are too. I'm glad I live here, Tony. It's nice and I have a lot of friends, don't I?"

"You sure do, Mom." He stood up and pushed his chair back into the corner. Then he bent down and kissed her cheek. "I love you, Mom. And I'll see you on Friday. Want me to turn on the Christmas lights?"

"No, they'll do it after I come back from lunch." She quickly thought that was wrong and, after a glance out the window, she corrected herself. "I mean, after supper. But thank you. And thank you for coming by. I love you too, son."

Tony started toward the door but Grace called out to him, "Hey!" He stopped and put his finger to his lips to remind his mom that Mattie was still sleeping.

"What is it, Mom?"

"If that tractor is broken, how do you water the lawn, honey?"

Tony grinned. "By hand, Mom. Just like you and Dad used to do at the old place. I grab a cup of coffee and a lawn chair and the dog. And then I water the lawn by hand."

Grace smiled broadly as sweet mental pictures emerged from the mist. "Oh my, Tony. Weren't those good days? Such very good days. Those are memories I pray to God I never lose."

Tony bent down and kissed her again. I pray the very same, he thought. I pray the very same.

Chapter 18
The Adventure Hour

David Youngville had told himself over and again that he was only imagining freer activity in his right arm. Still, he couldn't stop hoping. The doctors never made any promises, of course, and even their speculations had been bleak. David had accepted the reality of his condition (most of the time, anyway) and he was determined to make the best of it. Even in his dreams, he was in a wheelchair, paralyzed completely from the waist down with only minimal mobility in his arms and hands.

But this morning Zachary had, without any prompting, made the same observation. David's arm *had* improved and Zachary answered David's doubts with evidence from the detailed charts he kept on his progress. The therapist cautioned him to not read into this more change than there was. However, there was change. The range of motion for his right arm had increased. So had his strength. He was able to hold greater weight with his left hand. David was very grateful. And he was moved to see how delighted Zachary was as well.

"The work is paying off," Zachary said, a wide smile illustrating his pleasure. "I know it hasn't been easy but you've been patient and you've handled the work well, even when it's been painful and tedious. I'm really thrilled we're seeing some progress."

David noted the pronoun. Zachary truly did identity with his patients. And though he could be a tough taskmaster, it was obvious he had deep sympathy for the people he treated. He was calm, knowledgeable, and encouraging without being patronizing. He reminded David of Coach Musciano from his high school days and Pastor Cooke from the church he sometimes attended. All three were men whose friendship had meant much to him in the years since the accident.

Zachary had shifted his attention from David himself to his wheelchair and so David asked him, "What's the deal down there? Did your physical therapy training give you mechanical knowledge too?"

Zachary chuckled. "No, this I got from high school shop. That and maybe helping my dad keep his 1969 Mustang roadworthy. Just consider this an extra favor for a friend."

"Thanks. But is there something wrong?"

Zachary looked up. "I don't know, you tell me. Does this wheel turn okay? Have you noticed any wiggling or anything?"

David thought for a moment. "Well, I'm not sure now. I guess my mind has been on other things the last few days. It might be."

Zachary wondered if the little blonde with the big glasses who started to visit David had been among the "other things" on his mind but he said nothing about it. "It looks like the nut is kinda loose, certainly a lot looser than the one on the right front. And the washer behind it looks bent."

"Maybe I should have Ralph look at it."

Zachary pointed his finger. "Just the man I was thinking about. I saw him earlier out battling the moles but I'll call down and leave a message."

"Thank you, Zach. I appreciate it." He paused for a moment as he got a bit more serious. "And, Zach? I appreciate everything else you've done for me. More than I can say."

Zachary rose up and laid his hand on his friend's shoulder. "It is my distinct pleasure, David. I enjoy serving you as a therapist. You're a terrific patient who understands that the real success has to come from your own effort…with God's grace, of course. But I also enjoy having you as a pal. I can't tell you the ways in which you've inspired and blessed me since you've been here. So, the thanks goes both ways. But, hey, we'll have to continue this later. Here comes Lois with Mrs. Gritzner."

"Gotcha. I'll see you Thursday morning if not before. Have a great day, Zach."

"You too, man. And I won't forget to have Ralph take a look at that wheel."

David moved his stick in a sweeping motion that guided his wheelchair in a graceful arc away from Zachary's side and out through the door. He smiled and nodded to Lois and Mattie as they passed. He moved confidently down the hallway. But now that he bothered to think about it… yes, that left wheel *was* a bit uneven.

He looked at his watch and quickly calculated that he had a couple of hours before the kids came. It was one of the most fun parts of his week and he had been overjoyed when Mike Boone had expanded the program. They called it "The Adventure Hour" and it now involved five of the long-term residents of Villa Vista reading aloud to several groups of school kids. There were two groups that came from Ronald Reagan Elementary who were third and fourth graders involved in a volunteer program organized by the Rotary Club. Another two groups, fourth through sixth graders, came during school hours from a Christian school down the block.

And then just recently, Margie Trinisi, Tony and Marsha's youngest daughter, had recruited a home-school group who showed up on Mondays. It was a small group, maybe fourteen or fifteen in all with the kids ranging from third grade into junior high. They had quickly become favorites with both residents and staff because they were very friendly, respectful, and helpful. These home-school kids were always accompanied by several moms (and sometimes a dad or two) and, after the reading time, they stayed to eat lunch with the residents. They even stuck around after that to help with bingo.

David relished this activity and he had been greatly encouraged by the children's honesty, curiosity, and friendship. He loved doing something significant and being valued for it. And he loved the books. He read different things to the different groups but so far he had given them *Wind in the Willows*, *The Chronicles of Narnia*, *Treasure Island*, *The Borrowers*, and the first couple of books in the Freddy the Pig series. With the group today, he would take a chance by diving into some poetry. But he was pretty sure they would take to it because he had selected great comic poems from Ogden Nash, Robert Service, and G.K. Chesterton.

David was really looking forward to the event but he was also thinking he might get a nap in before he had to get down to the cafeteria. However, as he turned the corner at the top of his hall, he sensed that his nap would have to wait. For there in his doorway waiting for him was Clark Gritzner. And he didn't look happy.

Chapter 19
Tea at Jane Austin's

It was the 12th of July. Brenda Gritzner was enjoying a break in her nursing school schedule by having brunch with her sister at one of their favorite "chick cafes," a colorful place called the Jane Austen Tea Room. Well, given the nature of their conversation, enjoy wasn't the best word. But she was appreciative of the chance to see Reggie. It had, after all, become a rather rare event. They both ordered scones and tea, making small talk until their order was brought to the table. But after the waitress made her exit, Reggie got down to the business of the day.

"Okay, sis. Give me the latest. Exactly why do you think Dad may finally be getting his act together?"

Brenda stirred a little coconut milk into her tea. "Well, I didn't exactly say that, Reggie. All I said was things are a lot easier at home than they had been. At least, in the sense of Dad being home a lot more. And things seeming a bit more normal."

"Seeming?" Reggie asked with irony. "You mean, all on the surface, right? Nothing's really changed then. Our father has become a lout, a drunk, and a two-timer. And Mom is just letting it go without a peep of protest. If that's normal, then give me weird every time."

Brenda heard the pain in her sister's voice but was a little relieved to hear the humor in that last line. She looked up and was encouraged to see Reggie giving her a little smile.

"Yeah, I know. I can be a bit beastly at times, Brenda. But, for crying out loud, I have plenty of reasons to still be angry and worried and hurt. I mean, what's happened to Dad? We know he's always had a temper. For goodness sake, even on his best days, he was a bit of a grouch. But he could also be loving and kind. And he was always responsible. But now, good grief. What on earth happened to him?"

Brenda shook her head. "I don't know, Reggie. I just don't know. But actually, I think things may be breaking in the right direction. And that's the main thing I wanted to tell you. I think Dad's dealing with his drinking, for one thing. I don't know if he got a scare somewhere along the way or what. Maybe it was you moving out. But something got him. I'd like to think that he's experiencing some kind of spiritual conviction, but I don't know."

"You think Dad's getting religion, Sis? You've got to be kidding. You know him better than that. Remember how he reacted when you became a Christian at camp that summer? No, I can't see anything like that happening with Dad. Going to church for convention's sake or to make business contacts, yes. But to seriously worship God or something? Uh, excuse me, but I don't think so."

"I know, Reggie. But listen. Last night Dad sat me and Mom down and not only confessed to overdrinking, he actually apologized for it. He promised us he was done with it for good and that he had learned his lesson."

That did arrest Reggie's attention. "Dad *apologized*? And he's going to stop drinking?" She took a sip of tea and held the cup to her lips for several seconds. "Well, that is a bit of a surprise."

Brenda reached down and grabbed her purse and pulled out an envelope. "Dad thought you were coming to dinner last night too and he thought he'd be able to give his apology to us all in person. But since he didn't know when he might see you next he sent this along."

Reggie opened the note and read it. It was brief and simple enough. Yet she read it twice. "An apology. Wow. Who would have thought that of Dad?" She sat in silence for a while as she read the note yet again. But then her skepticism returned. "Still, it's not very detailed, is it? No mention of what started the drinking. No mention of the lies I've caught him in about those nights away. And certainly no mention of the other woman."

Brenda nodded her head. "Yes, I know, Sis. It's incomplete, sure enough. But shouldn't we be encouraged? Isn't it a start maybe?"

"Start *maybe* is right, Brenda. But it could also be a sham. You know, he gets caught; the routine of his life gets busted open, and so he says I'm sorry, let's all kiss and make up. Criminals do that kind of thing all the time. And addicts. And liars. Well, I don't feel quite like kissing and making up yet. I'm sorry, Brenda. I don't trust him. The letter could be a start, I guess. But I still don't trust him."

Brenda looked at her sister. Reggie had no smile now. Instead, tears had formed in the corners of her eyes. Reggie did care. Brenda knew that. But her unbelief made sense. The apology was pretty weak. Perhaps she had read too much into it because it was so out of the ordinary for her dad. Perhaps because she just wanted so much to believe. But then there were a couple of other items that she hadn't told Reggie yet.

"Sis, there are two other things, three actually."

"What three things? About what?"

"About Dad." She saw Reggie stiffen a bit. "No, it's not bad. In fact, it's more unusual things, things that might be an indication of something really going on inside him."

"Pardon my skepticism, Brenda. But go ahead."

"Well, number one, Dad has started to visit Grandma a lot more. He's over there two or three times a week. Two days ago he even brought Grandma a little Christmas tree for her nightstand. Think about that. After the fuss he threw last spring over the Christmas Room, he goes out and buys Grandma a Christmas tree…in July! The thing stands about 18 inches tall and is lit up from the inside. It's really pretty and Grandma is absolutely thrilled with it. How's that for a change?"

Brenda could tell that bit of news had jolted her sister a little. And, if that did, she knew the next two items would as well. So she continued, "Number two? Zachary tells me that when Dad goes to visit Grandma, he nearly always spends some time with David Youngville."

Reggie was perplexed. "David Youngville? You mean the nice guy down Aspen Hall, the guy who's paralyzed from being hit by a drunk driver?"

Brenda nodded her head. "Yep, that's him. How they met and what they're talking about no one knows. Mom doesn't. And Zachary doesn't. Well, to be frank, maybe Zachary does know something about it. But, even if he does, he's not letting me in on it. We may be in love but he still isn't going to tell secrets out of school. Anyhow, Dad and David appear to be involved in pretty serious talks when they're together."

The sisters sat silently for a moment, sipping the last of the tea. Finally, Reggie spoke. "Okay, Sis. You've got me so curious about number three that I'm not even going to press you about your use of the word 'love' in connection with Zachary. So, what's number three?"

Brenda reddened a little at the comment…but just a little. "Well, first about that word. Maybe I was a little hasty. We're not using the word between ourselves yet but still…"

"Yeah, okay. But you both know it. Big surprise. Everybody who watches you two when you're together already knows it. But we'll talk about that later. What I want to know right now is what's number three?"

"Number three," said Brenda, teasing her sister by drawing her revelation out, "is this. Dad announced last night that he sold the boat!"

Chapter 20
Why Isn't He Coming?

The rains were again falling, a cool blessing to the gardens and lawns of the city, let alone the farmers in the outlying regions. The weather forecasters had also promised the rains would bring in a few days of cooler temperatures. Any respite from the unusual heat they had experienced this summer was going to be appreciated.

The rain had caused Rita Costello some nervous moments driving to work and now, two hours later, it was coming down harder than ever. She was still working the 11 to 7 shift but it was her last week to do so. Beginning Monday, she would be on days as she began her training to be Villa Vista's next assistant activities director. Rita hadn't gotten over the thrill of being asked and she had already started her preparations by reading the dozen articles that Mike Boone had copied off for her. Also, for the past several days, she had stayed at the facility through the morning hours, shadowing Angie Stewart who would be taking Mike's place. Both Mike and Angie seemed pleased with Rita's promotion. And that meant the world to her.

She heard the bell down the hall and was reminded of the tasks yet before her. The light was blinking outside number

14. The Christmas Room. Rita smiled. That meant Mrs. Gritzner needed to use the bathroom. She motioned over to Leticia that she would handle it.

As usual the Christmas Room was aglow with the lights from the tree and the electric candle in the window. Normally, all lights other than the bed lamp were turned off at eleven out of consideration for the roommate's comfort. But, in this case, both residents had requested they stay on and, after Ralph had rechecked the switches, cords and lights, stay on they did.

As expected, Rita found Mrs. Trinisi sitting up in her chair. Grace rarely went to bed before midnight even though she was usually wide awake again when Rita made her early morning rounds. She knew that Mrs. Trinisi did a bit of napping throughout the day but still, it sure seemed like she didn't get enough sleep.

Mrs.Trinisi looked over as Rita entered. She smiled and whispered, "Mattie dropped off again but I think she needs to use the toilet."

Mattie Gritzner had indeed fallen back asleep but she was easily awakened. And at Rita's question about going to the bathroom, Mattie thought for a moment before answering, "Well, honey, since you're already here, maybe I'd better."

Rita helped her up and into her slippers. She then attached a support belt around her, a belt that allowed Rita to share the weight and keep her patient from falling. Both Mrs. Gritzner and Mrs. Trinisi required these devices now. Even when they were using a walker, Grace and Mattie required someone alongside to prevent falls. For the most part, both women got around in wheelchairs. Mattie wasn't heavy but it still required strength (and careful diligence) to get her up, get her to the bathroom, and then get her properly situated there. But Mattie gave no trouble. She knew she was weak and gladly accepted all assistance given.

Grace Trinisi was another case altogether. Her particular form of dementia had severely affected her judgment and she constantly forgot just how weak she was. She was forever trying to get up and go on her own. The staff and her family spoke to her about this every day but Grace couldn't grasp the idea – not for more than a few minutes anyway. And so she was a severe fall risk. Because of arbitrary and counterproductive federal laws, however, the Villa Vista staff could not use restraints to keep her safe. So the falls had kept occurring. Thankfully, those falls had lessened quite a bit in recent weeks. But it wasn't due as much to Grace accepting her situation as it was that she simply wasn't strong enough to even try and get up on her own. Thank the Lord for all favors, thought Rita, even the ones that come in much different forms than you expect.

While Mrs. Gritzner was in the bathroom, Rita sat down on Grace's bed. "Mrs. Trinisi, are you getting sleepy yet? Would you like me to help you get ready for bed?"

Grace shook her head slightly. "No, dear. Thank you, but I believe I'd better sit here for a bit longer. He may show up yet."

"Who might show up? It's after one in the morning. I don't think anyone's going to come by now, are they?"

Mrs. Trinisi looked up, a little perplexed. "After one o'clock, you say? Maybe he forgot all about me." She looked out the window hopefully.

Rita tried again. "Mrs. Trinisi, who were you hoping to see? Who do you think forgot about you?"

Mrs. Trinisi frowned at the question and Rita silently cursed the loss of memory that old age so often brings. She also hated how age tended to steal a person's confidence and judgment, their purpose and comfort, and the very presence of loved ones. Grace finally answered sadly, "You know. My son." Rita saw tears in her eyes.

"Was Tony coming back tonight, ma'am? Did he tell you he was going to stop in for something else?"

Grace swallowed hard and thought. Rita guessed she was trying how to tell her something sad, something that Rita might find painful. "My son. He…" Grace suddenly looked lost and afraid. Rita guessed what was happening. She saw it so often working with aging people. The panic (sometimes anger too) when they realize something that was once theirs in abundance is now gone. Grace Trinisi's heartbreaking panic was because she had forgotten her son's name.

Rita tenderly interceded. "Yes, Mrs. Trinisi, your son Tony. I really like him. We all do. And his wife Marsha. And their kids Albert, Ann, and Margie. You have a great family."

Grace's relief poured out in tears. "Oh God, yes! Tony! Tony and Marsha. And I have other kids too. They're in other places. But I have five kids. Dear God, thank You. Five kids. And their names are Tony and Laura and Michael and Vincent and Mary Ann. Five kids and I *do* know their names!"

Rita leaned over and embraced Grace Trinisi. And, as Grace weakly sobbed, she made a confession born of her sudden awakening of memory. "Oh, child. I was sitting here feeling so sorry for myself, so sorry that my son had forgotten me, that he never comes to see me, that he doesn't love me anymore. My heart was so heavy because I didn't know when I might see him again. And I worried about what I had done to make him angry. Oh, Lord, what is happening to me?"

Rita grabbed a tissue and was drying the tears on Grace's cheek. "But Mrs. Trinisi, your son was here just tonight. He took you out to dinner and when you got back you guys went down and worked on jigsaw puzzles for a couple of hours. Your son loves you very much. He's always up here. So is the rest of his family. Of course they love you."

Grace moaned and raised her hands to cover her eyes. "Yes, I remember now. Now I remember going to dinner and playing puzzles. And yes, honey, I remember now that he comes to see me. So how wicked is it that *I'm* the one who forgets *him!*" Mrs. Trinisi's body shook with another sob, a strong one this time as she almost shouted out, "And, oh my Lord. I couldn't even remember his name!"

Grace lowered her hands and reached over to Rita. For several moments they clung to one another, both crying but both finding some degree of comfort in the caring arms of each other. After a bit, Grace's crying lessened and she began to pull away. "That's enough of crying now, honey. Just wailing about my troubles isn't going to do any good although I sure appreciate your help, sweetie. Thank you." Grace took the tissue that Rita still held and used it to wipe Rita's tears away. "You poor thing, I've made you cry too. I'm sorry, dear."

"Oh, that's okay."

Grace sat up straight and patted Rita's hand. "Okay, that's enough of worrying over such things. I need to do some serious praying now and you need to get back to work too."

Rita held onto Grace's hand. "That's okay, Mrs. Trinisi. There's nothing more important right now than sitting right here with you."

"Oh, but there is, dear. There is."

"What's that, Grace?"

Grace raised her eyebrows and gave Rita a mischievous grin. "You need to go help Mattie off the toilet, dear. The poor thing has been tapping on the bathroom wall for a couple of minutes."

Chapter 21
Sentimental Journeys

Joanna wheeled her mother-in-law into the cafeteria where a musical program was set to start at two o'clock. Already several residents were there and more were coming in. In fact, in addition to the residents with their walkers and wheelchairs, Joanna saw several family members and other guests awaiting the program. She guessed that Villa Vista must have scheduled a particularly popular group for the day. Maybe it's a chorus of school kids and the guests were their family members called in to provide moral support.

Whatever the event was (the bulletin board had simply listed it as Sentimental Journeys), Joanna was very glad she was there with Mattie. With things in such disarray in her home, not to mention in her heart, Joanna had been feeling lost and alone. But in visits to her mother-in-law, in spending time with her and Grace in the Christmas Room, and in beginning to get involved in the social life here at the nursing home, she had discovered a welcome respite from her troubles.

With a surge of comfort, Joanna saw Marsha Trinisi and one of her daughters wheeling Grace into the cafeteria. Joanna waved them over in invitation. As she did, she searched her brain for the young girl's name. Annette? Annie? Something like that, she was certain. Mattie and Grace had spotted each other now and, like little girls, were waving enthusiastically to one another. How close they had become, Joanna noted with a sense of yearning. Everyone should have such a friend.

Marsha settled her mother-in-law next to Mattie and then sat down in the chair by Joanna. "Good afternoon, Joanna. And hello, Mrs. Gritzner. I love that ribbon in your hair. It's very pretty. Joanna, I don't remember if you've met my daughter, Ann."

"Hi, Ann. How are you?"

"I'm fine, Mrs. Gritzner. It's nice to see you again. I like your new hairstyle. It's very chic."

"Oh, thank you, Ann. You know when you try a new look, you're always convinced you look weird, if not outright awful. So, I appreciate the compliment." Everyone laughed, even the mothers-in-laws who didn't really get the joke. They just loved seeing people getting along. The cafeteria was filling up as more residents and guests entered, many of the residents being escorted by staff or family. The mood was clearly upbeat and expectant. Noting this, Joanna said, "Wow. This is the most people I've seen in here. Is it a special entertainment this afternoon? Something new?"

Marsha answered. "Well, yes to the first question but no to the second. It's certainly a special program. Maybe the most popular they have. No, I tell a lie. Bingo is the most popular. But Sentimental Journeys even gives bingo some competition." Marsha nudged her mother-in-law. "Hey, Mom, tell Joanna here what *you* think of the Sentimental Journeys show."

"You mean the old music?" Grace asked. "Oh, it's my favorite. They play the music from when we were young. It's really nice. And so too are those people that bring it."

Mattie, usually very quiet, spoke up too. "It's like going to a dance, isn't it?" Mattie's question wasn't just directed to Grace Trinisi but to the other residents sitting around them too. It prompted a flurry of conversation. There was plenty of agreement, more compliments and expressions of gratitude, and talk about the neat pictures that the program included. The ensuing chat among the female residents swirled around hairdos and hemlines of the 1940s, while the three men sitting behind them concentrated on the pictures *they* most loved – the cars, the street scenes, and people in various occupations from the past.

Joanna listened with relish, noting the enthusiasm the residents had for the program. After a while she whispered to Marsha. "Okay, you've all got me curious. What's this whole thing about?"

Marsha grinned. "Let me put it like this. I'd bet the music you listened to as a teenager has remained your favorite music throughout the years, right?"

"Yes, I guess so."

"Well, that's the basic trick of this program. They bring these guys the music of their youth, the music they listened to in the days when they first put on makeup and went to dances and courted their beaus. What's not to love about that? Plus, it's music they never hear anymore. The big bands that they danced to back in the day are all gone. The radio stations don't play that music anymore. And these guys have lost their phonographs and record collections. So Sentimental Journeys is the only way they can hear these songs they love, songs that meant so much to them."

"Wow. That's a great idea. But how can they reproduce a whole big band sound? Do they use synthesizers and computer-generated stuff?"

"Oh, no. They aren't musicians themselves. They play the original bands and singers – Glen Miller, Bing Crosby, Tommy Dorsey, Chick Webb, Helen Forrest, Artie Shaw, the Mills Brothers, Benny Goodman, and a bunch of others. I guess they do about a dozen songs each time."

Ann joined in. "But it's not just the songs, Mrs. Gritzner. They also show a PowerPoint program that has a couple hundred pictures from the same era. Those are really cool.

And they really get the residents thinking, and remembering, and talking. Mr. MacGregor also does a commentary where he tells things about the songs and the musicians...sometimes about things happening in the pictures. It's very interesting stuff, even for someone my age. But these guys," Ann waved her hand to indicate the elderly residents sitting around them, "they think it's the best program that Villa Vista does for them. They just love it! And it brings back the memories of brighter days."

Marsha added, "All the things Ann said are why Carolyn and the staff are so high on Sentimental Journeys. They see it as fun and wholesome, a great emotional lift for the residents. But even beyond that, they appreciate the fact that it improves people's health."

"How so?" asked Joanna.

Marsha motioned to her daughter. "You explain it, Ann. After all, you're the one who did the term paper on Sentimental Journeys."

Ann grinned. "And got an A on it, I might add. An A for which Dad took me out to dinner at the Parliament. Remember, Mom?"

"How could I forget?" Marsha turned back to Joanna. "Her father let her eat lobster that night and she's been asking for it regularly since then. I told her she could have lobster whenever she wanted *after* she becomes a banker or a doctor. But go ahead, Ann. Tell Joanna what you concluded about Sentimental Journeys in that A paper of yours."

"Well, first for my sources. I sat in on a lot of the Sentimental Journeys shows and watched people's reactions. Then I talked to residents about the program afterward and listened to the stories that the program drew out from them. I talked a lot to Colin and Mary MacGregor too. But then I also interviewed Carolyn and Dr. Marsh, and Mike Boone too – even Dr. Florence who is a professor of gerontology at the college. I learned that Sentimental Journeys was a special treasure because it stimulated their minds and memories; it reduced stress and boredom; and it improved self-esteem.

And, because the MacGregors visit the same facilities every month and spend time visiting people before and after the show, there's a *relational* benefit too that helps sharpen all of these things and keeps them more involved in life, more well-balanced emotionally. For all those reasons, Carolyn is really sold on the program. Plus, there's a couple of..."

"I'll tell you why *I* love it." Grace Trinisi interrupted her granddaughter. "The music and the pictures remind us of a time when we didn't need walkers or wheelchairs or oxygen tanks! Right, Mattie?"

Mattie smiled and nodded her head. "I hope he plays Lawrence Welk today. He's my favorite."

Joanna noted that her mother-in-law's comment started a new vein of conversation as others began sharing their own favorites. Dinah Shore, Duke Ellington, Frank Sinatra, Helen O'Connell, Guy Lombardo, and Harry James were a few of the names mentioned. She listened for quite a while until she reached over and patted Ann's hand. "Thank you for explaining the program, Ann. I'm *really* glad now that I came along. This should be interesting." She paused and turned to Marsha. "But your earlier answer to my question was yes and no. What is the no?"

"Oh, let me think. Oh, okay. The yes was that the program is a special one. But the no was to your question about it being new. Because it's not. The MacGregors do a complete show here every month and I think they've been doing it for a few years at least. And then, Villa Vista isn't the only place they go. They do it at a dozen or more nursing homes and other senior centers all over town."

"No kidding? Don't people get a little tired though; you know, seeing and hearing the same thing every month?"

Ann jumped back into the conversation to answer. "That's funny, Mrs. Gritzner, because Grandma says she wouldn't mind if they played the same show every week! But the MacGregors actually have 23 different programs. Except for the Christmas show (which is just outstanding), they don't have to repeat a program for two years. Oh, one more thing.

They do the show for free. There's never any charge to the facility – none at all. Cool, huh?"

"Yes," Joanna answered, impressed. "Very cool. But tell me then, just who are these guys?"

Ann pointed to an older couple coming right then through the door. The woman, long-haired and attractive, was carrying a computer case and a large speaker while her husband lugged in a large screen and a heavy suitcase. The audience saw them too and started applauding. Through the tumult, Ann told Joanna, "That's Colin and Mary." She said it with obvious delight and pride. "They used to teach at the tech school over on Front Street. But she retired and Mr. MacGregor started working with Naylor Construction. That's kinda a competitor to Dad's company but that's alright. We love them anyhow! They go to our church too. We'll introduce you to them after the program if you want."

Joanna watched the couple begin to work the room, shaking hands, giving hugs, and exchanging pleasantries. She thought of the work that must have gone into creating just one of the shows, let alone 22 more. And she wondered where the love and energy came from that sparked such a compassionate concern for people living in nursing homes.

"Yes, Ann. I think I would like very much to meet them. Thank you."

Chapter 22
"A Dead-End Job?"

"But Lois, this would be a great opportunity for you, a chance to get out of a dead-end job and back into hospital nursing. And though I don't know the particulars, I'm sure the package will be worlds better than what you're getting in that lousy nursing home."

There was no response from the other end of the phone. "Hello? Lois? Are you still there?"

"Yes, Renee, I'm here."

"Oh good. I thought my stupid phone had dropped another call. That's been happening a lot, especially it seems when I'm talking to my husband."

Lois Vendee rolled her eyes but suppressed a chuckle. It may not be the phone that's the problem, she thought. It's probably poor Herb just using it as an excuse to stop listening.

Renee started again. "Are you *sure* you're there, Lois? Are you thinking it over?"

Well, no, she wasn't. But Lois didn't know how to get through to her sister-in-law. It was exasperating how many times Renee had boasted about being a surgical nurse and the huge hospital system that employed her. And how many times Renee had mocked and criticized Lois' change of career? Lois was tired of it. In fact, she was so tired of it she decided it was time to push back a little.

"Renee," she purred.

"Yes, honey?"

"It so happens that sitting across from me here in the coffee shop right now is Carolyn Kovacs, the director of that 'lousy nursing home' where I work. That's right; she's my boss at that 'dead-end job' where I toil and suffer. Here, I'll hand the phone over and you two can talk over my situation."

"Don't you dare, Lois! Are you crazy? Don't you know Carolyn sits on the mayor's commission with me? What on earth are you thinking?"

Lois finally laughed out loud. "Keep your shirt on, Renee. Carolyn isn't really here. Well, not just right now anyway. But she *is* meeting me here in a few minutes. Do you want me to call you back when she *does* get here so you can talk about my 'dead-end job'?"

"Good grief, you had me going." Renee really did sound shaken. "But if you're dead set on staying there at...well, there at a nursing home, then all you have to do is tell me. I mean, it's none of my business and I'm not going to try and force you into anything. I'm not that kind of person, you know that."

Lois, of course, knew anything but. Still, she hoped this warning would keep Renee at bay for a while. Renee would carry tales to others, certainly, but at least Lois would be free of Renee's personal pushiness for a week or so.

"Well, then Renee. It's settled, okay? I appreciate your letting me know about the opening. But I would also appreciate you finally realizing that I like my job and I am not interested in going back to surgery or to the ICU. I'm happy and very fulfilled where I am."

True to form (and despite the disclaimer she made), Renee believed Lois' career *was* her business and she started right in again. "I completely understand, Lois dear. I only wanted to help you see things that you might be missing. For instance, if you returned to surgery, you'd..."

Lois interrupted her. "Renee, Carolyn Kovacs is just sitting down in the booth here. I'm sure she would find your comments interesting. Hold on and I'll hand the phone over."

"No! No, Lois. I have to go now. Sorry. Goodbye!"

Lois laughed again and hung up. She thought, "That was a nifty trick. I should have done something like that a long time ago." She looked up at the wall clock, a pretty art deco thing that she'd love to hang in her living room. Carolyn wasn't actually here yet but she would be here any minute now. They were going to enjoy a coffee together before heading over to the parade committee meeting.

Lois thought for a minute and decided against telling Carolyn about both the phone call and why she felt so secure and satisfied in her job. Carolyn would be pleased but she would probably be embarrassed as well. For Lois loved her job as Villa Vista's Director of Nursing primarily because of Carolyn's compassionate and enlightened leadership. Her boss set high standards for the staff and she required strict adherence to those standards. But she took great care to explain the *why* behind the rules and how those rules improved the lives of the residents. Despite the practical necessities related to profit, government compliance, the limitations of an older building, and so on, Carolyn constantly stressed that Villa Vista existed not for the owners, administration, or care staff. Villa Vista existed for the residents. And, as long as that priority was constantly applied, the owners, administrators, staff, residents, family members, and even the general community would find Villa Vista Care Community noble and important.

Carolyn set the tone herself. Her regard for the residents was sincere and eloquently demonstrated. Her political skills in dealing with the owners, government bureaucrats, residents and family members, staff, outside contractors – those were also superb. She was both a tireless worker and a selfless one, ready to set up chairs for an event, hand out meals, converse with residents, and, as she was an experienced registered nurse who kept her credentials up to date, to lend a hand in direct care of the men and women in her charge. Lois smiled, remembering how frequently Carolyn had to use the extra set of business clothes she kept in her office after getting her other clothes soiled through less pleasant duties.

There was yet another side of Carolyn Kovacs that Lois admired and that was the bold, creative genius she used in promoting Villa Vista. In so many ways, Carolyn developed a variety of critical resources for the facility: money, neighborhood interest, volunteers, new resident applications that would otherwise go elsewhere, and so on. The owners of the facility were thrilled with her success too because Villa Vista was making more of a profit than most of their facilities...even the newer and larger ones.

But what most fueled Carolyn Kovacs' initiatives wasn't a desire to make more profits but rather the knowledge that the business's success greatly enhanced the quality of care for all its residents. That was the purpose behind the connections with schools, recruiting volunteers from the Catholic seminary and the evangelical college, the bake sales, the pet shows, and the upcoming parade. One especially effective program that Carolyn had created was a partnership with local churches that "adopted" a Villa Vista room. The church members would help with the costs of renovation, furnishing and decorating a particular room. That was only the beginning though. After the room was ready, the church members made frequent visits to the occupants. The program had proved a real triumph.

But there were other notable successes. Under Carolyn's leadership, the resident's dining experience had been greatly enhanced: the food quality, an expanded menu, renovations to the dining room, and the encouragement of family involvement in meals. Carolyn had also pursued with great energy what she called a serenity strategy for Villa Vista. This had affected everything from the colors of the walls, to the lighting scheme, to the introduction of attractive aviaries and aquariums in each wing.

Every change was calculated to make residents more peaceful, more comfortable, and more at home. However, the emphasis in Carolyn's serenity strategy was the reduction of noise in the facility. Carolyn had presented to the Villa Vista owners an abundance of academic research showing how intense a factor noise could be in increasing a person's stress and confusion while decreasing their abilities to relax, sleep, and think.

Carolyn was most persuasive and, after wrangling a bit over the costs, they allowed her to implement several of the changes she had suggested. New privacy curtains were ordered that were heavier and better for deadening sound. Televisions were attached to the walls closer to each resident's bed. And they were turned on only when the resident requested. The televisions that had been in the common areas near the nurses stations were removed. Intercom announcements were reduced. Sound absorbing tiles were applied on the bathroom walls. A few rooms were put in reserve for single occupancy, providing temporary respite for residents dealing with special anxiety.

The result was a quieter and yes, more serene, facility. And both the residents and the staff were all the better for it.

Yes, Lois reflected, Carolyn was a very good boss and Lois was honored to work with her. She also knew there was a special pride in being part of a great team, working with skilled professionals who really cared about providing crucial services to people in need.

A dead-end job? Really? Her sister-in-law didn't have a clue.

Chapter 23
Hard Duty

It had been a rough night for David, one with little sleep but a whole lot of discomfort due to some painful and embarrassing intestinal problems. Ron Sylvano, the CNA working the south hall during the 11 to 7 shift, hadn't helped the problem. In fact, he had made David's woes even worse. Ron was new to the job. He seemed like a nice enough guy, David had thought, but it had become all too clear tonight that he found certain tasks related to the care of a partially paralyzed person difficult, even disgusting. The aide's lack of professionalism (and compassion) had been hard enough for David to bear but, to make it even worse, Ron had called in help more than once during the night to help clean him up. And the only help available had been female.

It had been a long time since David had wept over his condition but last night he lost control of his emotions. In fact, he did so twice. No, he blushed when he thought of it, make that three times. For along with the two times he cried in frustration and shame, there was another when his tears had flowed from anger and resentment toward the aide's inept and thoughtless care. He had managed not to say anything mean to Ron. But it wasn't because he hadn't thought those things.

The last couple of hours David had felt better. He was exhausted and his throat was sore from vomiting and his bottom chafed from the diarrhea. But whatever had been in David's stomach must be all gone now. The churning and nausea were over. Still, he didn't know what it might portend, so he was pleased that he had an appointment with the physician's assistant when he arrived later this morning.

During the long hours of the night, David hadn't lifted up any prayers other than quick, desperate ones for God to grant him some degree of relief. And he knew that was fine with God. But now, with his body relaxed enough to allow for other thoughts, he had begun to pray for the right way to tell the PA or Lois, or maybe even Carolyn Kovacs herself, that Ron wasn't cut out for this job. He knew it was a tough duty and he wasn't excited about getting anybody in trouble, even someone this incompetent. However, it was a prime directive for caregivers to put the needs of their patient before their own comfort, before even their own fears. Therefore, Ron's low tolerance for the nastier parts of ministering to a sick person, let alone the lack of sensitivity he showed for David's modesty, disqualified him. And Villa Vista needed to know this.

David didn't dislike Ron. He didn't want to get him fired. Yet, he had to speak up. He would explain the matter to both the PA and Carolyn. Because it wasn't just about him. David had to think of all the others who would be in Ron's hands. So David's mind was made up.

Until Ron came in the door.

"David? David, may I talk to you for just a minute?" Ron Sylvano quickly held up his hand as if to ward off an objection he expected to come. "I realize I might be the last person you want to see this morning but can I please have a moment before I go home?" Taken off guard, David didn't answer. "Alright," Ron said with sadness. "I understand completely." Dejected, Ron turned to leave.

Ron was almost out the door when David found his voice.

"No, Ron. Come on in."

The young CNA took a deep breath and a hard swallow before re-entering the room. He moved as if he was going to pull up a chair and then decided against it. He didn't feel that welcome. He stood a few feet away from the wheelchair and began. He spoke slowly, carefully and David had the impression he had already gone over these remarks several times in his head.

"David, I want to apologize to you. Really. From the bottom of my heart. I'm so sorry for the way I acted with you last night. I really like you and I admire you so much and yet...Well, last night when you were sick and...uh...when you were..."

"When I was sick and soiled and stinky," David inserted the words for him. "Isn't that what you mean?"

Ron hung his head and slowly nodded. "Yes," he sighed. "That's what I mean. I'm sorry, David. I thought I was getting used to things like that; you know, getting toughened up enough to keep my head and concentrate on taking care of the patient. But last night I started to get sick myself and I lost focus. I know I almost dropped you when we first got to the bathroom and I started to panic. That's when I pushed the button and got the ladies to help. Of course, they are professionals and they knew what to do and how to do it well. Me? I was like a kid, scared and sick. I suddenly wanted to run away and throw up."

Ron paused and lifted his head so that his eyes met David's. "I really let you down last night. I shouldn't have treated you with revulsion. I shouldn't have shirked my responsibilities by forgetting my training and my priorities. I shouldn't have called in Milly and Leticia unless I really needed the physical help. I'm sorry, David. I'm going to stick around until Mrs. Kovacs comes in this morning and tell her what happened and tell her that I'm quitting. People here deserve genuine compassion and they deserve practical help. I've shown I can't handle that. But I needed to come tell you myself. And to ask you to forgive me." At the end of his remarks, Ron lowered his head again and said softly, "Thank you for listening to me." He turned again for the door.

David's throat still felt raw. So too did his other end. But, in the few moments it took for Ron to make his confession, David's inner attitude underwent a dramatic shift. How powerful a game-changer, he reflected, is a sincere apology. He heard his raspy voice call out. "Ron? Thank you for your apology. I accept it wholeheartedly and without qualification."

Ron nodded. It was more than he hoped. Yet he was grieved that he had lost the friendship of a man he so respected. "Thank you." It was more than he deserved, thought Ron, more than he expected. Yet he decided to say one more thing. "David, if it's alright, I would still like to come by occasionally to visit. Would that be okay?"

"Well, let's consider that for a moment." He motioned with his head toward the folding chair next to the nightstand. "Will you have a seat for a minute and let me say a couple of things?"

"Sure!" Ron knew there were rebukes on the way but he far preferred that to the strong silence he'd been expecting. He pulled out the chair and sat down.

"Just two quick points, Ron. First of all, you need to realize that what you experienced last night isn't something even unusual, let alone proof that you don't care. Feeling revulsion at sights and sounds and smells that are, well, that *are* revolting is a natural thing. Sure, you're gonna have to work at dealing with it if you stay in this line of work. But just because things overcame you once or, for that matter, even if it's a recurring problem, it's not necessarily grounds for you to give up altogether. I'd bet everyone on the staff here could tell you stories of how they reacted badly in certain situations. I've personally seen a couple just since I've been here. For crying out loud, my sister has five kids. And one time, the littlest one, Shana, got sick. And while Kerry, that's my sister, was trying to take care of her, she was overcome with nausea herself and made a big mess. That kind of thing sometimes happens, no matter how much you think it shouldn't affect you. But you know what my sister *didn't* do? She didn't go to her husband and say, 'Honey, I have to quit being a mom because one of my kids just made me sick!'"

Despite himself, Ron chuckled at the story.

David went on. "You see what I mean. Don't make more out of it than what it was. Secondly, realize that if you quit today, you're going to make it a lot tougher on the staff and therefore on the residents themselves. You know how hard Carolyn works to get good people, people who have genuine compassion, who are selfless and kind, who have a good work ethic. And, of course, nursing homes are always especially short staffed when it comes to male caregivers. So, what do you say? Would you do yourself and Villa Vista *and me personally* a favor by at least taking more time to make a decision?"

Ron was nodding...and smiling. But then, a sudden thought changed his countenance.

"But what about Milly and Leticia? I let them down too."

"Okay, perhaps so. But I'm almost sure they wouldn't be giving it a second thought. They're pros, Ron. Just like what you're going to become. Still, to make sure, I'd suggest you go tell them the same thing you told me."

Ron stood up. Relieved but resolute. "I will, David. I will. And thank you."

"Hey, enough of that for now. You'd better hustle or they'll be heading home before you get to them."

"You're right." He spun around and headed quickly out the door. But a second later, David saw Ron's head pop back into view. He was smiling broadly now. "See you tonight, David!" And he was gone.

David sat musing for a few minutes before lifting his gaze out the window toward the sun peeking through the clouds. "Well, Lord," he whispered, "that certainly worked out differently than what I was planning." Then he laughed out loud. "I think I might go ahead and risk a little breakfast after all. I'm famished."

Chapter 24
The Pre-Flight Program

Mary Harbison was 87. Diabetes, high blood pressure, and the loss of her left leg were among the physical challenges she faced. Nevertheless, her mind was clear, her spirits upbeat, her social skills quite active. Zachary O'Rourke knew a bit of her life's history but, even if he hadn't seen her photo album or heard her stories, he might have guessed she had been a basketball player in her youth. The way she was dribbling the orange exercise ball from her wheelchair would prompt the same recognition in any observer.

Zachary yelled over to her. "Mary, did I just notice a double dribble there?"

Mary snorted in response and kept the ball bouncing evenly. And fast. "If you did, sonny, you'd better get your eyes checked. If I did such a thing, Coach Wilson would reach down from heaven and smack my noggin! You just pay attention to Mr. Bones there and let me be. In fact, Mr. Bones probably knows a lot more about double dribbles than I do. Just ask him."

Zachary laughed. So too did Mary. And so did "Mr. Bones," the long and lanky gentleman Zachary was now working with. Ted Bonney had played basketball in his youth too. In fact, he had been an All-American when a senior on his college team. He had wanted to try and play beyond that (professional basketball was just beginning to be an attraction) but he followed his father's advice and enrolled in medical school instead. It was the right choice. Dr. Bonney had built a successful, even illustrious career as a pediatric surgeon with several breakthrough procedures among his achievements.

When possible, Zachary scheduled these two in the same hour because they enjoyed each other's company and their stories were so interesting. But more had come from this pairing than Zachary could have imagined.

About three months ago, Zachary had introduced Mary and Ted to Tayron Medube, a student from the local Christian college who served as a Villa Vista volunteer. Tayron was a history major who was looking for a career in teaching and coaching. He also played basketball and baseball for the school. Zachary had suggested to Tayron that interviews with Mrs. Harbison and Dr. Bonney would make a great oral history project. And they did. From that project, though, other things began. First, Tayron invited his basketball coach to meet his new friends. Then the coach brought the whole team for a visit. Next, Tayron's history project sparked some local TV coverage. And, before one could say Bob Cousy, Mrs. Harbison and Dr. Bonney had been invited to schools, a couple of civic clubs, and even an audience organized by the state historical society to talk about basketball's early days. The publicity presented yet another triumph for Villa Vista's reputation. More important, it was a striking reminder to the community of how significant and interesting were the lives of the elderly.

Later, when both Mrs. Harbison's and Dr. Bonney's workouts ended and they had been escorted back to their rooms, Martina Pinchuk, one of the other physical therapists on the Villa Vista staff asked Zachary about lunch. "Are you up for Chinese? The rest of us are heading over to Wang's for the buffet."

Zachary replied, "Well, it sounds good but I'm having lunch with my older brother. He's driving in to see me before I take off tomorrow. Thanks though."

"When do you go?" asked Thom, the occupational therapist who split his time between Villa Vista and two other facilities.

"My flight takes off at 5:45 in the morning."

Thom groaned. "5:45? Please tell me you already have a way to the airport."

Zachary laughed. "Don't worry. That's already set. My brother is spending the night and he's going to drop me off on his way back home." He winked at Thom as he walked out the door. "But I wouldn't do that to you anyway. You're too nice a guy."

The journey Zachary was to begin the next day started with a flight to New York, a much longer flight to Paris, followed by another few hours before landing at Accra on the Atlantic coast of Ghana, and capped off by a fairly short flight back north to Ouagadougou, the capital of Burkina Faso. Even if everything stayed on time, it would be 28 hours before he arrived at his final destination. Along with three other physical therapists, two Americans and a Swede, Zachary would be helping out with a Wheels for the World team, part of the international outreach of Joni and Friends. He had already made two trips with the organization, once to southern Poland and last year to the Dominican Republic. Both trips had been only two weeks long (this one would be a couple days longer), but the impact had been profound. Zachary had found the experience emotionally challenging, physically exhausting, but remarkably enriching. He would miss his friends here at Villa Vista, both staff and residents. And he was especially going to miss being with Brenda. Nevertheless, he was looking forward to the trip.

Zachary would meet the other therapists in the Paris airport but the whole team wouldn't be assembled until Ouaga. That team would then include the therapists, three men who had experience with adjusting wheelchairs, and a pastor from Great Britain who served as organizer, translator, chronicler, counselor, and whatever else was needed.

The basic purpose of Wheels for the World was to take donated wheelchairs and walkers, have them repaired and refurbished by American prison inmates, and then freely give them away to adults and children who desperately needed them. The job of the physical therapists was twofold: to make sure the wheelchair was adjusted for the particular needs and body shape of the patient and to provide counsel to the wheelchair recipients (and family members) regarding ongoing treatment, exercise, diet, and so on. The wheelchair mechanics also took part in these sessions sometimes, instructing people how to operate and maintain the devices. On each of the previous trips, Zachary's teams had handed out more than 200 wheelchairs along with several dozen walkers. The number would be a bit higher this time around.

Zachary had arranged his schedule so his last afternoon at Villa Vista would be light. He also wanted to enjoy a leisurely lunch with his brother and still be able to cut work a couple hours early. He planned to grab a nap before heading over to Ollie's Steak House for a nice dinner with Brenda, Reggie, Albert Trinisi, his brother, Jack, and several other friends. Sometime after dinner he'd find a couple of hours alone with Brenda. He had important things to talk over with her.

Chapter 25
Painting Fingernails

Room 14 in Villa Vista's south wing had been part of the structure built in 1958. But in the past year it had become better known (and loved) as the Christmas Room. The reasons for its popularity were clear. The beauty of the decorations. Novelty in the midst of drab sameness. The emotional power of Christmas symbols. And the testimony of joy and spiritual triumph so meaningfully embraced by persons struggling with poor health, memory loss, loneliness, immobility, pain, and impending death. The Christmas Room was enhanced further by the individuals who had occupied it: Grace Trinisi, Rosie Madigan, and now Mattie Gritzner. And not to be overlooked were the charming and gregarious members of the Trinisi family. Tony, Marsha, and their kids had become favorites of staff and residents alike. And, in recent weeks, new attractions had come on the scene: Joanna, Brenda, and Reggie Gritzner.

On this late summer Saturday morning, Regina Gritzner was in attendance at the Christmas Room. Reggie's life had gained considerable speed since she left home a few weeks earlier. She had picked up six credit hours in two intensive-study courses, plus she had found a part-time job doing data entry at the college library. She had dropped Todd for good, finding the company of Albert Trinisi much more wholesome and stimulating. And finally, Reggie had joined her mother and sister in volunteering time at Villa Vista.

Joanna Gritzner had become involved in several of the facility's organized social programs. And Reggie could see that it had been excellent for boosting her mother's spirits and confidence. Reggie, more introverted than her sister and her mom, preferred more individual-oriented activity. Therefore, she spent most of her visiting time with her grandma and Mrs. Trinisi in the Christmas Room and serving as a kind of hostess to the people who dropped in there. However, Reggie also enjoyed taking the ladies down to the game room where they would put together jigsaw puzzles. Then Reggie made one other exhilarating discovery. She had started to read poetry aloud to them. It was an activity that soon spread to other residents.

Reggie quickly realized that it wasn't her reading skill or even the intellectual content of the poems that her listeners most loved. It was the rhythm, the imagery, and the texture of the words themselves. For some, the poems awakened memories of their youth. They had studied some of the poems in their school days. They had memorized them. They had read them to their children. *The Highwayman. Thanatopsis. Lepanto. Evangeline.* There were also Shakespeare's sonnets, the Psalms and Major Prophets from the Old Testament, comic verse and nursery rhymes. In the beginning, most of the poems she read came from two poetry books that Tony Trinisi had brought to his mom. But Reggie started trolling the Simpson Street Library for others, finding personal delight in the poetry of G.K. Chesterton and Phyllis McGinley. She was thrilled too in finding this unexpected bridge between her grandma's generation and herself.

On this overcast morning though, Reggie was comfortably ensconced in the Christmas Room where she was painting Grandma's and Mattie's fingernails. This was a service available on Monday and Thursday mornings at Villa Vista but Reggie had taken on the task for these ladies…and occasionally Mrs. Harbison too. They listened to music. They had tea or Cokes. And they discussed a wide range of subjects – growing up on the farm, the home front during WWII, stories of kids and grandkids, gossip about the nursing home, girl talk.

But this particular morning, girl talk was off the agenda because Albert Trinisi, Grace's grandson, was hanging around. Albert was a personable and spirited young man who worked for his father since he was fourteen. Now, at twenty-one, he was already a foreman of his own crew. He was a conscientious and hard worker but there were other interests in his life too. He possessed a bachelor's degree in Spanish, a pilot's license, and an admirable collection of early rock and roll records. And, as Reggie appreciated, he was also a very nice and good-looking fellow.

Reggie and Albert had first met here in the Christmas Room and, though they had started dating, it was here at Villa Vista they saw each other more than anywhere else. They tried to coordinate their weekend visits to their grandmas for the same time and had a standing dinner date every Wednesday night with the grandmas, Brenda, and Albert's two little sisters, Ann and Margie. After dinner, they would all take their desserts back to the Christmas Room where they finished the evening in the glow of the window candle and the Christmas tree lights.

This morning Grace and Mattie were both feeling pretty good and were a bit more alert than usual. Tony had once noted that seemed to be the case whenever the grandchildren were present. "I guess the presence of their children is old news," Tony had once remarked. "Or perhaps there are just too many memories when their kids are involved. It's harder to select and relate, easier to be confused and overwhelmed. And so they tend to check out a little more. But when the grandchildren show, there's a special joy and freshness. And anyone can see how they light up."

That's why Tony cleared Wednesday nights for his kids to

spend time with their grandmother and why he'd made a habit of going over to Albert's on Saturday to mow and water his lawn. He knew Albert's work schedule was especially hectic nowadays and he wanted to help free up time for him to spend with Grace. That Albert genuinely enjoyed that duty was a great blessing to his dad. And that Albert had, on his own, invited his sisters to participate in the activity...well, that meant the world to Tony too. Reggie, whose home life had never been particularly warm or loving (even when it wasn't as dysfunctional and mysterious as it was now), found this a very attractive feature of Albert's personality too.

Reggie was finishing her task by putting a clear protective layer on Grace's bright red fingernails when Lois Vendee looked in. "Hey, Albert. Thanks for bringing the donuts in this morning. Unlike most Saturdays, I actually grabbed one before they were gone. Even more surprising," she laughed, "it was a chocolate glazed one! Those always go fast. So thanks a bunch. You guys are way too good to us."

Albert raised his hand as if to deflect the compliment. "Hey, Lois. It's my pleasure. And for the excellent care you give to these two magnificent ladies, it's the least I can do!"

"Well, thanks for that too. But, no kidding, with you bringing donuts and your mom always bringing in cookies and your family helping out with activities like they do – hey, yours too, Miss Gritzner – it means an awful lot to us all. It's a *delicious* encouragement." She laughed again. "Of course, you know here in the health professions we're not supposed to be so crazy over donuts and cookies. Leticia was just reminding us of that a few minutes ago – just after finishing her second glazed cinnamon twist!" Lois waved goodbye. "See you in a little while, ladies. I'll have your medication then, Mrs. Trinisi."

"She's one of my favorites," said Reggie as Lois' steps echoed from the hall. "I think Brenda is going to be a nurse very much like her when she's done with the school."

Albert agreed. "I think you're right, Reg. She'll be terrific."

"Is she a nurse now?" asked Mattie. "I thought she was a

school teacher."

Reggie smiled at her grandma and then at Albert. He knew what it was like to cover the same ground over and over with his own grandmother. But she learned valuable lessons from observing just how well he did it. For instance, she no longer used phrases such as "Don't you remember?" or "I've told you this many times already." No, she answered each of her grandmother's questions as if each were brand new and put excitement and full detail into her reply.

Also, like Albert did, Reggie would look directly into her eyes and give her complete attention as they talked. He had once told her that effectively conversing with people with Alzheimer's or other dementia required several things. Patience. Clarity. Animation. Sincerity. No small amount of acting skills. And a very large amount of humility and love. As Reggie noted Albert's wide smile, she knew he was delighted with how she had taken his advice to heart.

Chapter 26
"Three Mary Alices"

Sometimes Rita Costello felt overwhelmed in her new position as assistant activities director. The change in duties had been even more challenging than she imagined and her body hadn't caught up yet to working days instead of nights. And then there was the sheer number of people she was now involved with! In her previous position, Rita worked a skeletal shift in which she was responsible for no more than fourteen residents, most of whom slept peacefully through most of her shift. Her new job involved her with almost the whole population of Villa Vista. Added to that were all of the day staff she had to coordinate things with. And family members. And volunteers.

Was it *too* much? No. In truth, Rita loved every hectic, confusing, challenging minute of it. And things were getting a little easier with each passing day.

Rita had spent much of the morning sitting in on two of the reading groups. David had read an original Hardy Boys adventure story to the class from Lincoln Elementary and Ellen Gutiérrez had gone through a section of *Journey to the Center of the Earth* for the home-school group. Also, the audiences for both included a few residents as well, people who liked to be read to…and maybe just liked to be around kids.

Rita didn't have much to do with the activity except rounding up residents and then escorting them down to the red auxiliary room for the programs. Well, she also had paperwork to do. There was always that. But by watching Mike and Angie, she learned you could do quite a bit of that while you were in attendance at the programs themselves. That was one of Mrs. Kovacs' hard and fast rules – a staff member had to be always present at the various social activities. They were there to provide oversight, protect the residents, respond to emergencies, and help volunteers. But Carolyn didn't mind a little multi-tasking if you remembered that your priority was to keep everyone safe and on point.

But unlike her predecessors in the position, Rita wasn't very good at handling paperwork during the events because she usually found them too absorbing. She couldn't fill out forms and keep activity reports up to date if she herself was wrapped up in the program. During this morning's readings, for instance, Rita was the most interested person in the room. Her own education hadn't gone so well and she found reading laborious. The very idea of reading for pleasure had been beyond her. But listening to these wonderful stories convinced her that she had really been missing something and she promised herself she was going to improve her reading skills. But that didn't mean she was going to go out and buy these particular books. She was having way too much fun listening to David and Ellen read them out loud.

The rest of the morning she had spent in a discussion with Angie Stewart about how to boost the morale of those residents at Villa Vista who were bed-bound or otherwise reluctant to come to organized programs. Mrs. Kovacs had even stepped in for a while with a few ideas of her own. But there had been a little time before lunch in which Rita made a few "get acquainted" visits in the north wing. Among the people she met was Mr. Jeffers, a city councilman who had once been caught in some kind of scandal. She didn't know any details (it was way before her time) but it must have been a pretty big deal because Amy told her he was one of the few residents who never, ever had a visitor. Well, until recently, that is. That changed dramatically when he became one of the gentlemen "adopted" by the members of a local Baptist church who had previously repainted and redecorated his room. So now even Mr. Jeffers had a few people coming by throughout the month. And, on the first Sunday of every month, a big family from the church came and had lunch in the blue auxiliary room with Mr. Jeffers and his roommate, Mr. Chan. From what Rita had been told by Angie, the improvement in Mr. Jeffers' attitude and even his general health – made from these new social engagements – had been remarkable.

That morning Rita had also met a lady named Mary Alice O'Neill. Rita had given the lady a thrill when she explained that Mary Alice was also her mother's name. "Why, dear, that's so nice to hear. You know, when I was growing up there were three of us Mary Alices in our school. But I left that town when I finished school (I only went to the eighth grade, I'm afraid), and I have very rarely met another. Where is your mother from?"

"Atchison, Kansas."

"My, my. Atchison, Kansas. Who knows? Maybe she was one of *my* Mary Alices. Do you think so?"

"Well, perhaps," Rita answered. "Where were you from?"

Mary Alice looked quizzically at Rita for several moments. "I'm sorry, dear. What did you ask me?"

"I asked where are *you* from?"

Rita saw the same blank look. "I live here, dear. I'm in Room 10."

"Oh, I see. Room number 10. That's a pretty nice room I hear."

"Oh it is, dear. It is. And I always eat at the restaurant here too. And I take a bath in that room there." She pointed across the hall. "They always close the door so that no one can look in. That's good, I think."

123

"Oh, I agree. I think that's a very good idea. It certainly would make me more comfortable."

"Yes, me too. So, isn't that something, that you and I are both named Mary Alice. You know, when I was in school (I only went to the eighth grade) there were three Mary Alices there. Isn't that something? Three in one school. And now there's two right here! My, my. Or wait. Is it three? Did you say your mother was a Mary Alice too?"

"Yes. But it's only my mother with that name." She pointed to her name tag which Mary Alice carefully peered at. "My name is *Rita*."

"Oh, I see. And you are from Topeka, Kansas? Or, no...what was it?"

"It was *Atchison*, Kansas where my mother was born. I was born here."

Mary Alice nodded in understanding. "Okay, dear. I see. Sometimes I get things muddied up. It's your *mother* that's a Mary Alice, not you."

Rita smiled. "You've got it." She pointed to her name tag again. "My name is Rita."

Mary Alice extended her hand and gave Rita a big grin. "Well, it's nice to know you, Rita. And thanks for coming to visit me."

The two shook hands and Rita then bent down and gave her a hug. "I'll be seeing you soon, okay? Maybe I can come by later and take you to pet day. What do you say?"

"Yes. I like that day. The last time a lady brought a white dog. All white hair. Just as white as mine. It so reminded me of a dog my poppa had when I was a little girl."

"And where was that, Mary Alice? Where did you grow up?"

"I'm from...let's see...where did I grow up?" Mary Alice looked away from Rita and, for several seconds, gazed down the hall. Then suddenly, she lit up. "I remember. I came from Atchison, Kansas. I think that's it. And, you know something – I was one of three Mary Alices in my school. Three! Can you imagine that?"

Chapter 27
Confessions

David Youngville rarely spoke of the accident that had taken away all but the smallest fraction of his mobility. For the rest of his earthly life, he would be stuck in this wheelchair. He was trying hard to make his life yet count, to continue seeing the beauty in the world, and to embrace the spiritual joy that was still very much available to him. David had talked about the accident to Clark Gritzner but not until they had spent several conversations together. Even then, it was only because Clark had specifically asked him about it. There was in this case, however, another motivation. David wanted his story to serve as a warning. Very early on, David suspected that Clark had a drinking problem and that he might likely try to drive while intoxicated too. One of the compelling purposes of David's new life was to do whatever he could to keep such moronic menaces off the road. So when he told his story to Clark, he spared no details about the accident, the harrowing difficulties of recovery, or the plight of living in his condition.

David sensed he had scored points in that conversation but it wasn't until today that Clark let him know how seriously he had received the message. Clark had been speaking about his boat and the disappointment he felt in having to sell it when he suddenly stopped and asked David, "You knew that first time we talked about your accident that I was guilty of driving drunk myself, didn't you?"

"Yes," David had answered. "I guess I did."

"Well, of course, I was guilty. And even when I was aboard the *Blue Wave*." Clark paused and shook his head. "And so that's why you gave it to me with both barrels, huh?"

"Yes, I suppose so. Like most people, I don't suffer fools gladly. But when it comes to fools who turn an automobile or, for that matter, a boat into a deadly weapon, a terribly destructive weapon that puts innocent people, even little kids, in the crosshairs, then I won't suffer them at all."

"You told me all those things expressly so I would stop. Is that right?"

"To be honest, Clark, I don't know all the reasons why I talked about it that day. I'm sure I had several motivations going at once. I probably told you in part to express my rage for everyone who drives under the influence of drugs, or booze, or any kind of inattention. And I did it in the most effective way I can. And I may have told you to win sympathy too. I wish I was above that but I'm not always. And, maybe you can understand this and maybe you can't, but I also told you in hopes that you might open up and tell me what tragedy *you* were dealing with. There was obviously some burden, some kind of guilt, something you feared. And I guess I wanted to be of help to you if I could. So, it was all those things. But there's no doubt that my main concern was to keep you from killing someone through your drunk driving…or even doing to someone what that drunk did to me."

Clark Gritzner listened hard to David's explanations, challenged and intrigued. David was considerably younger than Clark and, in the days they had known each other previously, he had been but a small cog in the machine in which Clark was a big wheel. But though David was now crumpled up in a wheelchair, a pitiable figure who had absolutely none of the trappings of power that Clark had previously respected, he possessed more moral strength, spiritual freedom, wisdom, and even more of a love for life than Clark did. And the conversations they had engaged in these past several weeks had only intensified Clark's admiration for him.

"Thanks for letting me have it that afternoon, David. Though I hated hearing it, and I felt more ashamed and hopeless than I ever had in my life, I also knew I needed to heed what you were telling me. And I need to let you know too that your honesty and courage *did* pay off. I didn't just stop drinking and driving that very night, I stopped drinking…period." He looked and saw David's inviting smile. "But I think you may have guessed that too, didn't you?"

"Well, let's say I hoped that was what was going on. And I certainly have been praying for that response. But with your confession, I can now say something I've wanted very much to say to you, Clark."

"What's that?"

David looked intently into Clark's eyes as he answered him. "I want to thank you for listening to me, for carefully considering your crimes, for being honest enough to weigh them in the balance. And thanks most of all for quitting. You may very well have saved lives by that decision. And, without a doubt, you have encouraged me more than I can tell you. God has used you to stress a lesson He's constantly on me about. And that is that my life still has purpose, still has value."

Clark hadn't expected anything quite like David's response and it left him a little stunned. The conversations with David had been deeply meaningful to him. They had been both fascinating and comforting, sometimes encouraging and sometimes infuriating. They had covered innocent enough topics like business and sports and politics, but also morality and the Christian religion. David had proven to be an extremely intelligent and well-informed person. He was persuasive but never pushy. In fact, several times in their talks about Christianity, Clark had expected David to turn into an evangelist and try to close the deal. That's the way it had been when his daughter Brenda had come home from that Christian camp when she was a teenager. David didn't do that. He argued well and, in points of disagreement, Clark felt he always ended in a corner. But David didn't go for the knockout. He was gentlemanly, acting almost indifferent to whatever decisions Clark eventually made about religion. But that calm confidence of David's was actually more unsettling than if he had insisted on Clark's immediate conversion. Clark had felt pushed by his daughter. Here in his talks with David, it was more like he was being drawn…and with his own will going along with it.

Still, nothing that David had yet presented in the course of their talks had touched Clark's soul as did this moving thank-you and compliment. He didn't know what to say in response. And, after several very uncomfortable seconds, that's exactly what he said. "David, I don't know what to say."

"Well, that doesn't matter. What was important was that I said it and that you heard it. Our conversations, and I certainly hope they continue, might actually be even more interesting and mutually helpful now that we've cleared some things up."

Clark especially felt the significance of two of David's words and he wanted to know more. "David, you said 'mutually helpful.' Is that true? Have you *really* found these talks of value? Because I've always feared I must be a bore to you. You're so bright and well read. And you have experience and an insight into human nature that astounds me."

"You were worried about being a bore to me?" David laughed out loud. "Just how many chances of interesting conversation do you think come my way? Remember, I'm a guy confined to a wheelchair with said wheelchair confined to a nursing home where most of my neighbors are fifty to sixty years my senior. You'd be surprised at just how boring things can get, my man!"

At that Clark laughed too, a rare experience in his conversations with David. He suddenly realized that laughter had become a rare experience in his life. David changed the subject. "By the way, it's almost three. Your mom will be getting out of therapy any time now so you'll need to get down there. But, before you go, did you get a chance to read that book I mentioned?"

Clark brightened. "Yes, I did. And I read it all. I even went back and read again some parts I had underlined. And, you know, I still can't agree with everything and I've got a lot of questions too. But I did find it helpful. It does clear some things up I had been bothered by."

"That's cool. Maybe the next time you drop in we can talk about it."

"Yes, I'd like that. I would." Clark got up to leave. "Uh, I know before you let me walk out, you're going to ask me the same thing you always do."

David grinned. "And what's that?"

"You know full well what it is. You always ask if there's anything specific I'd want you to be praying about."

"Oh, that. Okay, what about it?"

Clark paused, knowing this was a step he might not really want to take. "Well, when you ask that, I always say something flip like world peace or Phil Mickelson winning a tournament or something."

"Not always," David corrected him. "You've sometimes said your job and twice you've said getting tighter with your family."

Clark nodded. "Yes, I guess I have. But generally, David, I feel like I've been disrespectful. To you…and maybe to God as well. So I wanted to apologize for that. And finally, I wanted to tell you that, if you really think it might make a difference…I'd like you to pray for my family and for a way out of some very deep trouble I'm in."

David saw his seriousness and, though it took an effort not to inquire further, he left it alone. "Of course I'll pray for those things, Clark. And yes, you can bet your life that prayer makes a difference."

"You truly believe that, don't you?"

"My first prayers for you have been answered, Clark, and they definitely required a miracle."

"What do you mean?"

"Do you think you stopped drinking all on your own? If so, think again, Clark. Tell your mom I'll see her at dinner."

Chapter 28
Christmas Room Conversations

As summer gave way to autumn, there were fewer times when the lines of Grace Trinisi's memory, judgment, and cognitive abilities seemed tangled and far away. Whether it was the socialization created by the Christmas Room, a feeling of responsibility she had developed toward Mattie, a better balance in her medication, or simply the loving prayers of her attentive family, the demonstrable effects of her frontal lobe dementia had lessened. Grace realized this too. She was more thoughtful, more careful about herself. For instance, most days now she remembered that her physical weakness kept her from safely getting out of bed or trying to make it to the bathroom on her own. Same thing with her mental faculties. She understood (most of the time) that when her husband appeared, it had been in a dream and not in reality. This pleased her to no end, providing evidence that, as she put it, "I'm not always goofy!"

But most important to Grace's family was that the anger, denial, and frustration that had been so frequent in the earlier years of her dementia had been largely absent for months. Grace was so much more peaceful and accepting. She was complimentary and concerned for fellow residents and very grateful for every tenderness shown her. And the best parts of Grace's personality – kindness, generosity, sense of humor, love of God – these sparkled perhaps more brightly than at any other time in her life.

Mattie Gritzner had reached a similar plateau in her mental condition but she was more naturally introverted and docile. And her physical condition was even more precarious than her roommate's. Mattie's bouts with UTIs were recurrent and she was on oxygen most of the time. She was also more heavily medicated for pain which caused her to spend a lot of time sleeping. Yet Mattie was richly blessed by living with Grace Trinisi in the Christmas Room. Grace had become her best friend and she found great comfort in Grace watching over her, prompting the staff to intercede for her needs, encouraging her spiritually, making her laugh. Mattie also loved the color, cheer, and brightness of the decorations. Plus the soothing ministry the Christmas music provided to her soul was wonderful. This was a very difficult time of life for both widows but there was no doubt that they enjoyed a special blessing from being roommates here at Villa Vista.

Earlier in the evening, both women had received visitors. Mattie had dinner with Joanna and Reggie while later on, Grace entertained Tony, Marsha, and her granddaughters with Cokes and cupcakes. But it was now an hour after all the company had left and while Grace, as was her custom, sat in her chair with a quilt over her, Yoki Takahashi had prepared Mattie for bed. Yoki had a nifty way with the sheets that kept residents comfortable but decreased the possibility of their rolling out of bed. Carolyn had heard of the technique and applauded it. In fact, she called in-service meetings for the nurses and aides from all shifts so Yoki could teach them her technique. Carolyn also rewarded her with a day off with pay for coming up with such a good idea.

As Yoki was tucking Mattie in, she looked up and whispered, "Do you think Grace would like to stay up and talk to me a little?"

Yoki nodded to Mattie. "I just bet she does. Let me ask

her."

Grace very much wanted to do that and so Yoki helped her over to the stuffed chair that was beside Mattie's bed. She got her situated comfortably with a pillow on her left side and a warm blanket draped over her. "Are the lights from the tree going to be enough for you girls?" They both said yes, that would be very nice. "Okay, then. You both have your buttons so let me know when you need anything. I'll be sure and look in a couple of times before my shift is over."

Yoki stepped back and took in the charming scene. Mattie had taken to asking for her companion to be close beside her two or three nights a week now. Grace was always happy to comply. Having checked on them regularly, Yoki knew how it went. Grace told stories of her life with Mattie dropping in only occasional comments or questions. Grace sometimes would hold Mattie's hand and say prayers or recite poems and Scripture passages. All of this was delivered in a dreamy stream-of-consciousness style, all the genres of talk flowing in and out and among one another. And it was punctuated too by periods of silence, the women sometimes trying to recover murky memories. Or dozing. Yoki smiled and closed the door just enough to block the hallway light from shining across the bed.

It was the task of the Villa Vista caregivers to give concentrated, skilled, and compassionate service to every resident. And most of the staff did their very best in carrying out those duties. Nevertheless, as Yoki was changing the linen for Major Lindstrom after an accident, she reflected on why some residents stood out, in a nice way, from the others. The most obvious reasons were a resident's pleasant personality, the expressions of gratitude, the ease of care. Grace Trinisi was one of the treasured cases in that she exhibited all of these winsome traits and more. Mattie Gritzner wasn't as magnetic a personality but she was kind and patient. Plus, Mattie benefited from being so close a friend to Grace. And, not to be discounted, Mattie lived in the most popular place in Villa Vista, the Christmas Room.

Yoki loved the charm of the Christmas Room and she knew it provided a warm and wonderful atmosphere for the women and their guests. But she suspected that Tony Trinisi was well aware of another truth; namely, that the uniqueness and color of the Christmas Room helped draw special attention to his mother. It set her apart, brought her to the forefront of staff members' attentions, and made people more naturally inclined to befriend her and dispense a particular excellence of care.

In thinking it over, Yoki figured that the Trinisi family's desire to ensure the best care possible for Grace helped inspire their countless acts of friendship toward the staff. The cookies and donuts. The constancy of visits. The bird feeders. Volunteering for so many of Villa Vista's events and services. The cheerfulness and compliments they bestowed on everyone in the place. Yoki had no doubt that the foundations of these acts of kindness were pure and genuinely altruistic. But she knew that Tony Trinisi was a very bright guy too. He had to know that the ripple effects of their involvement at Villa Vista and the uniqueness of the Christmas Room created greater incentive for the nursing home staff to give their very best to Grace. It was a smart plan, a loving plan, and she wished a lot more families would follow the same course.

Back in the Christmas Room, Mattie had fallen asleep. Her bedtime meds had kicked in and she would sleep soundly until needing to use the bathroom around one o'clock. Yet Grace continued to talk, lower in volume, but just as sweet and engaging. For her remarks were not just intended for Mattie but for herself too. And anyone else who might be listening. Her mother and father. Her husband, Frank. Her younger brother, Billy, killed in the first wave of air attacks on Pearl Harbor. Her friend Rosie. And, of course, Jesus.

Tonight Grace was remembering more than usual the years of her marriage. Years of intense happiness. She spoke of the weeks of her courtship by Frank. (They had married three months after their first meeting.) There were the hours of conversation on the porch. Frank rescuing the horse and cows when lightning set the barn on fire. Fishing at the river. Going to the movies at the Kennedy Theater – only fifteen cents if you went to the matinee, but a whole quarter if you went after supper.

Grace also shared the sweet clumsiness of Frank's proposal of marriage, the awkward talk he had with her father, and the pretty dress her older sister had made for the wedding ceremony which was held in the front room of the farmhouse. Grace also remembered the excitement of the honeymoon and, after all these decades, still blushed at the sudden vividness of the memories. "Well," she softly patted Mattie's hand, "I don't need to talk about that, do I? You had your man too and so you know what I mean."

The romantic reflections elicited more somber thoughts that Grace then spoke about. And it was in these minutes that she was speaking more to God than she was to Mattie sleeping beside her. Grace talked of the tragedy of her first miscarriage and then the second. At the first, she was able to lean upon the strength of her husband. But with the second baby she lost, Frank was somewhere in the South Pacific fighting his way from island beaches to the jungles beyond. "That's where You and me got a lot better acquainted. You remember, Lord. My prayers got a lot more grown up in those days."

Gracie's thoughts might naturally have moved to her next child (born ten years later) but she never had remembered much about that. Birthing Anthony had almost killed her and not only on the night of delivery – following almost two days of labor – but at another crisis with a blood infection when the boy was just five weeks old. No, those memories were buried forever, graciously so. As were most of the troubles that Anthony eventually got into. Grace did recall those sad, difficult times. She knew Anthony had got in bad with the police and had even gone to jail for a while but she had forgotten the specifics. She did remember Frank crying on the way as they took Anthony to Boys Town way out in

Omaha, Nebraska, a place where the judge had insisted he go to school. She also remembered the train trips back to Omaha when they visited him the next summer.

That's where Grace's memories perked up, probably because the changes in her son had been so dramatic, so wonderful. Anthony seemed taller and he was a lot bigger and healthier too after just that first year at Boys Town. He was well-groomed and polite and affectionate. By the second year, Frank and Grace began noticing how his letters expressed regret for his past actions. He wrote of how he was sorry that he had shamed his family and broken their hearts. He wrote also of great changes in his life, about becoming serious about the Christian teaching he had received in his youth.

The change in Tony was authentic enough that Monsignor Wegner contacted Judge Halifax and arranged official permission for Tony to return home. Frank and Grace took the trip back to Boys Town, traveling part of the way on the *Nebraska Zephyr*, in order to pick him up. It was the best Christmas present of their life.

Mattie was still sleeping but Grace told her the story anyway. "I'll never forget Frank taking Monsignor Wegner aside to ask him how we could work a Catholic into our home. You see, we were both Baptists. Well, Monsignor Wegner just laughed at Frank's question. 'Not to worry,' the priest said. 'You know, Mr. Trinisi, we produce pretty good Protestants here at Boys Town too!' It turned out that Tony had been faithfully attending a Baptist church over in Omaha for several months. Sometimes Tony even drove the Boys Town bus that dropped boys off at a Lutheran church and a Pentecostal church along the way. Isn't that interesting?"

Yoki had come in a few moments earlier and had listened with great interest to Grace's story. Grace saw her standing in the doorway and motioned to Mattie. "She's asleep now," she said softly, "but I guess I've been rambling away anyhow. I've been talking about my son Tony. But it's okay if she's asleep because I probably tell everybody the same things over and over anyway."

Yoki came over and pulled the blanket back up where it had slipped from Grace's shoulders. "Well, what you were saying about your son was all new to me, Mrs. Trinisi. It is a fascinating story, one that gives a lot of hope. I would never have guessed that your son had ever been …well, in trouble with the police. And I thought Boys Town was just a Catholic thing."

Grace nodded. "Well, it kinda is, I suppose. But it's more too. You'll have to ask Tony about it. He is still a Baptist, you know. So am I. Tony is an elder in the church but he's still a big fan of Boys Town. He gives them money and goes to the reunions. Maybe you have seen him wear a baseball cap that says Boys Town. So you ask Tony about it."

Yoki shook her head. "Oh, no, Mrs. Trinisi. I wouldn't want to embarrass him for anything in the world. I'll just pretend I never heard about that stuff."

"Goodness sakes, child. He wouldn't mind that. You can even ask him about the times before he went out there. It's funny but he doesn't seem to mind telling people about his past. Maybe because God worked things out so well for him in the end." Grace then motioned for Yoki to come closer. She looked over to make sure Mattie was still asleep. "You know," she whispered, "that's why I keep telling Mattie about Tony's troubles and how God answered our prayers because, I'm afraid, her son has got into some serious trouble too. And I want to make sure she keeps praying and doesn't give up on him."

"I'm sure that's a good thing to do, Mrs. Trinisi. But, of course, Mr. Gritzner is a little too old to enroll at Boys Town, don't you think?"

"Yes, he sure is, honey. But that probably doesn't matter to God. He has His ways of getting to you wherever you are."

"Yes, I suppose He has, Mrs. Trinisi." Yoki looked over at the candle shining in the window, then at the lights in the big Christmas tree. She also noted the green and red lights glowing from within the small Christmas tree on Mattie's cabinet. "I'm sure He has." She noticed then that Grace seemed a little more tired so she asked, "Mrs. Trinisi, would you like me to help you get ready for bed now?"

"Yes, dear. That would be nice. I am getting a bit sleepy. But I've enjoyed reminiscing with Mattie tonight and it's been good talking to you too."

"Thank you, Grace. For me too." It took a few minutes before Yoki got Grace through her bathroom routine and snugly tucked into bed, her sheet technique being particularly important for Mrs. Trinisi. And when Grace asked Yoki to lean down so she could give her a goodnight kiss on the check, Yoki happily allowed it. It seemed the most natural thing in the world. "Goodnight, sweetie. And thank you for your help."

"It's my pleasure, Mrs. Trinisi. It really is." Yoki turned to go but a sudden inspiration stopped her and she turned back to the bedside. "Mrs. Trinisi?"

"Yes, dear?"

"If you ever think of it, Mrs. Trinisi, could you say a prayer for my boy? He...well, he has troubles too."

Grace smiled. "Of course I will, honey. What's his name?"

"Lee."

Grace repeated the name twice. "Okay, honey. Now, of course, I'm probably going to forget a lot. So you need to make sure to be regular in *your* prayers for him, alright?" Yoki nodded her assent and turned to go before hearing Grace whisper her name. "Honey, please take one of those sheep from the manger scene there. It will be a reminder to pray for your son. In fact, please take them both. Tony brings me a lot more whenever I need them. Maybe it will remind your boy too about the important things – Jesus, family, faith, and courage to look up for God's light."

Yoki wiped a tear from her eye as she reached over and took the little sheep that had been resting beside the Holy Family in the stable. Under regular conditions, Yoki would never accept a gift of any sort from a resident but Carolyn had informed the staff that they were free to accept certain things from Grace Trinisi, things that her son specifically provided so that his mom could give things away. Cookies and other dessert treats. Diet Cokes. Christmas ornaments. And the manger sheep.

"Don't worry, Mrs. Trinisi, I would be honored to take a sheep for me and my son. I'll give him his tomorrow and I'll tell him what you said. I'll also tell him all about how you inspired me tonight. Thank you so much."

Grace Trinisi beamed. "Has your boy ever come by and seen our Christmas Room? You tell him he can come by anytime and meet us." She yawned and pulled the covers up to her neck. "Yes, you tell him to come for a visit someday."

By the time Yoki turned off the Christmas lights and pulled the door halfway closed, Grace had joined Mattie in peaceful slumber.

Chapter 29
Molly's On the Green

The Gritzner home was a bit calmer than in previous months, at least on the surface. But the calm didn't mean that the tension had been eliminated or the mystery resolved. Joanna was still heartbroken and perplexed over the erosion of her marriage. True, Clark was around more. There had been no more out-of-town excursions, no more disappearances to taverns, and, with the boat now out of their lives, no more hours spent out on the water or puttering around the *Blue Wave* while dockside. But even though Clark was home, he and his wife were not talking much. Joanna could tell he was trying harder to be civil, even thoughtful, but she knew there were secrets still being protected.

Joanna also missed having her daughters around. Brenda was busy with nursing school and with her handsome physical therapist. And Reggie's break had been dramatic. She sometimes came for Sunday dinner but otherwise she carefully avoided coming home. But she wasn't completely avoiding her mother. Well aware of her mother's loneliness and unhappiness, Reggie had been meeting her for lunch at least once a week. They also saw each other frequently at Villa Vista.

That had started when Joanna, Reggie, and Brenda had begun coordinating their visits to Grandma Mattie. These little parties began as a wonderful diversion from Joanna's worries, but the visits to the Christmas Room led to even more productive pursuits as they all became involved in some of the social activities at the nursing home. It was great for all of them but, in particular, Joanna had found an increased sense of purpose and a new confidence. Her new friend Marsha Trinisi called it "soul satisfaction."

Brenda had tried to help her mother as well. She made sure she was in attendance at Sunday dinner and at least a few other meals during the week. And on Mondays when she didn't have a class until the afternoon, Brenda and Reggie and Joanna all met for brunch at Molly's on the Green. There they ignored their diets and splurged on a full English breakfast as they shared girl talk and watched golfers play the 12th hole.

The conversation this morning had been especially charming as the girls shared with their mom stories involving their new beaus. Brenda was definitely in love, so definitely that she now openly talked about a future with Zachary. Reggie was far less committed than that but she too was aglow with pleasure in finally finding a man she liked and admired. But, in a brief lull in this happy conversation, there was a sudden and rather alarming moment in which it seemed both daughters remembered the plaintive predicament of their mother's own romance...if romance it could still be called.

Joanna realized the significance of the awkward silence. "Girls, it's alright. I couldn't be happier for you both. And I love hearing you girls talk this way. Really. So please don't start feeling guilty because things aren't quite the same with your father and me right now. We're just going through a rough patch. But I think it's been getting better these last few weeks."

Brenda nodded sympathetically, "That's good to hear, Mom."

Reggie, always the bolder of the daughters, asked. "How so, Mom? Did he ever tell you about those so-called business trips?"

There was a lie on Joanna's lips but it died quickly. Reggie wasn't a girl to be fooled even by a good liar. And Joanna was far from that.

"Yes, Reggie. It is better."

"But not good, right?"

Joanna looked down at her teacup and then out to the putting green before she answered. "No, not good."

"But he really *has* stopped drinking hasn't he, Mom?" Brenda asked hopefully.

"Yes, I'm sure he has. And he's home a lot more and he's tackled several of those jobs that had stacked up. I guess he has all that energy that he used to spend on the boat. And then, girls, I know you may not feel this to the extent I do, but your dad seems to have a new softness about him. He's visiting his mom more. He talks a lot with David Youngville. And he appears to be trying to fix some things up with me too. He brought flowers home a few times and he has even started helping me with the dishes."

Reggie asked, "Do you think he's sorry for anything in particular? You know, besides the drinking."

Joanna smiled. "I don't know, Reggie. I think maybe he is." But she quickly added, "I'm sure it doesn't have anything to do with another woman." She saw Reggie's skepticism. "Yes, I know you're still thinking about those supposed business trips – and so am I, believe me – but I'm pretty sure I could tell if it was that."

Reggie nodded. "Okay, Mom. I guess you're right. Maybe I was wrong about that but there's still so much to be explained."

"I know, honey. I know."

Brenda hadn't wanted to insert herself into this topic but she heard herself saying, "Money. It's got to be some kind of money thing, don't you think? That would fit with Dad selling the boat, right?"

"And you know what else?" Reggie set her cup down as a new idea struck her. "Remember Mr. Clossing telling me when I called that second time that Dad had gone to Chicago?"

Brenda said, "Yeah. So what?"

"Well, that's where Uncle Durward lives, right? Remember, we talked about that?"

"Yes, we did. And so you'll remember I suggested then that maybe Dad had gone to see him for some reason. But, Reggie, I thought you weren't buying that idea."

"I wasn't...then. But think about this. Say Dad is in some kind of financial bind. Wouldn't it make sense that he try and convince Uncle Durward to give him a loan or work something out with Grandma's properties there in Chicago?"

Joanna shook her head. "I don't think so, Reggie. I'm not sure that your dad's brother is any better off than we are. He certainly wasn't in years past. Plus you know how badly they've got along over the years. No, I can't imagine that Uncle Durward has anything to do with it."

Reggie wasn't ready to give up on the Chicago angle just yet. "What about Dad's share in Grandma's inheritance? Isn't the hardware store still Grandma's? And that big house of hers on the lake?"

Joanna thought that one over a bit. "I don't know how that all works. It would all be up to however Grandma set up her will. With the house and all that land – oh yes, and the store – I suppose your dad will receive some inheritance if Mattie still has him in her will. But that would only be when and if Durward sold any of it."

"There you go." Brenda had latched onto the idea now and was trying to put the best spin on things. "Maybe you're on to something, Reggie. Maybe that's where Dad was in those absences, up in Chicago to check things out, make up with Uncle Durward, and plan out what they'll do with the estate. And the reason he didn't tell us was that he didn't want us to get our hopes up in case nothing came of it."

Was this possible? It wouldn't have seemed likely a few

weeks ago but now the Gritzner girls, even Reggie, were looking for some reason to hope for their father's reclamation and the restoration of the family. They all knew that, even if true, this didn't completely clear up the unexcused absences, let alone the drinking and spikes in anger. But they all wanted to believe something better about Clark than what had plagued them in recent months.

It was Joanna who finally shifted the conversation to a more pleasant topic. "Hey, I've got to get over to Villa Vista by 10:30. There's a high school choir coming in to entertain and I volunteered to help set up and bring residents down. I think we have enough time though to hear about Zachary's trip to Africa."

And so Brenda did tell them some stories of Zachary's time in Burkina Faso. Some sad. Some inspiring. But all engaging. It was a good way to end their breakfast conversation. Yet later, as the women went their separate ways, they still wrestled in their minds with what was going on with Clark. And where would it all end?

Chapter 30
Danger from Within

It was the first day that actually *felt* like autumn. Or, at least, that proved autumn was surely on its way. The temperature had dipped into the low 40s the night before, certain trees had begun to shed a few leaves, and the morning dew lingered on the lawns long into the morning. It was the kind of day that Carolyn Kovacs would have loved to spend at her father's cabin on the river, snugly ensconced with tea and bagels and a Rafael Sabatini novel. Yet here she was checking in early at Villa Vista with a very full day ahead of her. She entertained high hopes that, though busy, it would be a lot easier than the previous day. That day had been a monster.

It had started with news that the plumbing problems in Aspen Hall in the south wing had erupted again. Carolyn almost shuddered with the memory of just how apt the word "erupted" was in this context. Four rooms had eventually been affected. She had the residents removed and put elsewhere while she helped Ralph remove the furniture from the rooms. As they hustled with this task, Lois, Leticia, and a couple of the CNAs fought to keep the water from coming into the hallway. They had managed pretty well but it took several hours before the plumbers got everything fixed.

Carolyn knew that the fans and dehumidifiers had run all night but she wouldn't move the residents back until the rooms were thoroughly cleaned and the furniture (all of which she had ordered thrown out) replaced. She had made the furniture order yesterday but it wouldn't be delivered until two this afternoon. All of this had been a major hassle but the residents had taken it in stride, in large part due to the staff's responding quickly, calmly, and efficiently to the flood. Carolyn had shown her appreciation by springing for sandwiches and pie from the deli for everyone who helped out.

However, the worst part of yesterday hadn't been the near inundation of Aspen Hall. Not by a long shot. The worst part was the midnight meeting in her office in which she had fired Edith, an aide who had been working in the north wing for just three weeks. Carolyn reviewed the affair in her mind – from the beginning. The young woman had come with excellent references from a nursing home and a day-care center where she had worked in another state, references that had been thoroughly checked out. She had also been interviewed by Lois, by Grant Katulka, and then again by Lois and Carolyn together. All signs had been positive and they thought they had made a good hire.

They were so wrong.

The very first week there drifted up to Lois a couple of complaints about Edith's bedside manner. Lois made a note of this and even asked the charge nurses to keep an eye on the new employee. They did. And they weren't pleased. It wasn't that Edith did anything overtly wrong when she was caring for residents. But she did show impatience and a lack of team spirit toward other staff members. And, when her temper flared, she was abrupt, even churlish. One incident prompted a direct rebuke from the charge nurse. That seemed to help, for the second week brought no complaints and Lois believed Edith was developing more positive relationships with her co-workers.

But then came Tuesday night. Zemi Chukwu, a college

student who worked part-time on the kitchen staff, was passing out nighttime snacks to designated residents and picking up dinner trays from residents who had eaten in their rooms. As he was approaching Room 19 in Willow Hall, he heard a voice harshly say, "You say that again and I'll *hurt* you again." Zemi stopped still but he heard nothing more except what he thought was subdued sobbing. He started to enter the room and almost collided with Edith who was storming out. He tried to excuse himself but Edith was already heading down the hallway. He looked inside the room. Mrs. Lancaster's bed was empty. Zemi remembered hearing that she'd been sent to the hospital for surgery earlier in the week. But Sister Bernadette was there in her bed looking wide-eyed with pain and fear. And yes, she was crying.

"Sister, what's wrong? Do you need something?"

The little lady shook her head. "Oh, please, don't send *her* back!" She looked over Zemi's shoulder to the door. "Please send me someone else. Don't let her hurt me."

Zemi reached down and held her hand. "Okay, Sister. It's okay. Just ring your bell and I'll stay here until someone comes. No one is gonna hurt you, I swear to that."

Sister Bernadette continued to cry and to look with fear toward the door. Zemi pushed the button himself and promised her that he would stand by and protect her. He then asked, "What happened, Sister? What's wrong? Are you in pain?"

"I have to use the bathroom and I need help. Oh, Lord; please help me!" She looked up at Zemi, shameful tears wetting her cheeks. "I can't help it. I try to hold it but I have to go to the bathroom. But she wouldn't help me. And then...then she hurt me! Oh, Lord, please don't let this go on!"

"Sister, don't worry. I'm here, and help is on the way. We'll see you get to the bathroom really quick now."

Sister Bernadette squeezed his hands. "Oh, thank you! Thank you! I try to hold it but I just can't. Really, I try!"

"It's alright, Sister. That's a natural thing, nothing to worry about. I understand."

"But she'll be mad if I go again. She'll hurt me."

Zemi felt his face flush with anger. "Who will be mad, Sister? Who do you think will hurt you?"

"That girl." She shot a glance back to make sure no one was at the door. "That girl gets so mad at me but I just can't help it. I try to hold it but...please don't let her come back."

"That girl hurt you? What did she do?"

Sister Bernadette started sobbing hard again and lifted up her arm. Zemi saw two purple bruises on her forearm.

Zemi was heartbroken and mad but he was a bit scared too. After all, he worked in the kitchen, for crying out loud. He wasn't a nurse. Only rarely did he have contact with the residents. He had been carefully warned about touching residents, even helping them from wheelchair to table. He wasn't even supposed to hand out food or drinks to anyone who wasn't on his list. He didn't know if he was overstepping his bounds now or what sort of trouble he might get into for interfering.

But Zemi knew one thing – no matter what happened to him later, no one was going to hurt Sister Bernadette while he could help it. So he stayed his ground until Trudy Nelson answered the bell and started helping Sister Bernadette to the bathroom. Even then, when Trudy saw how strongly Sister's hands had been holding onto Zemi, she asked him if he would stick around for a few moments. Zemi nodded.

Trudy assured Sister Bernadette, "Sister, Zemi here is going to stay in the room for a while but I'll help you into the bathroom. Alright?"

"Oh, bless you, child. And bless you too, young man. I do have to go awfully bad."

Within two hours from the moment that Zemi stepped into Sister's room, even though it was nearly midnight, Carolyn Kovacs, Lois Vendee, Dr. Carlton, and John Sprague, Villa Vista's primary attorney, were sitting in Carolyn's office. So were Edith, Zemi, Trudy...and Sergeants Martinez and Flynn of the local police.

There was no question of what had happened. Edith had been arrogant and defiant to the Villa Vista officials, believing that all she had to lose was a job she hated, a job that she coarsely decried with offensive expletives. She admitted pinching Sister Bernadette for "carrying on like a baby" about going to the bathroom. Edith insisted she was being "worked to death" in taking care of these old fools, most of whom "would be better off dead." How could they expect her to give an old nun who wore diaper pants so much attention?

It was only when the police arrived that Edith cooled off and tried to change her story, blaming everything on an old lady who must have hallucinations and was just making up lies to get her in trouble. It was too late. She had made her earlier statements in front of several witnesses. And Lois had taken photographs of the ugly bruises on Sister Bernadette's arm, bruises that would show up even more cruelly in a couple of days.

Carolyn had known that her decision to call in the police might be second-guessed by the company officials who owned Villa Vista. They would absolutely hate the inevitable publicity. She could imagine Roland Harvell, his large brows upturned and his thin lips frowning as he asked, "What *were* you thinking, Mrs. Kovacs? Deliberately advertising that there is elder abuse going on at Villa Vista? Do you think that was a wise business move?"

But Carolyn already had her answer. She would carefully tell her boss, "Yes, Mr. Harvell, I certainly do. It was much better for Villa Vista to show that elder abuse, whether by inattention or overt action, is treated with swift and unalterable justice here. It's crucial that we announce to anyone listening that we don't ignore such crimes or cover them up. God forbid that we care more about protecting our business interests than we do about protecting the people in our charge. And there's one final reason, though I certainly don't need it to prompt my action. Reporting this crime to the police as well as to the other appropriate agencies is what both federal and state law requires me to do."

Carolyn applauded these laws because they helped create layers of protection for people who were so vulnerable to bullying and exploitation. And she was pleased that experienced investigators would now intervene in the case. No reputable facility would ever make the mistake of hiring her again.

Carolyn didn't really think she'd have much difficulty with the Board of Directors. Despite Mr. Harvell's critical spirit, she was sure he would see that her move was the correct one. And with Mr. Stephens, Mr. Goldstein, Mrs. Covey, Dr. Petrovsky, and the others, her decision would not only be accepted, it may even be applauded.

There were way too many nursing homes around whose sole concern was profit. Quality medical care, life enrichment, cleanliness, keen attention to needs – these critical matters were, in some facilities, underrated to despicable levels. Patients in such places were disrespected, neglected, over-drugged, and poorly fed. So Carolyn was pleased and proud to work for a company that strove hard to provide a patient's basic needs and beyond. But that wasn't enough for her. She cared about improving the industry as a whole. That's why she promoted Villa Vista in the way she did. She wanted to set an example for others to follow, to show that quality care was the best way to win business profits. And it was the best way for the people behind those business desks to retain their humanity.

The next few days wouldn't be easy for Carolyn or for Villa Vista. But Carolyn knew she had done the right thing.

Chapter 31
A Problem Solved

Money wasn't an issue for David. The problem was booking the medi-van for a round trip to the wedding. There were so few transportation vehicles that could accommodate the size of his wheelchair and both of the companies that had them were notorious for lack of punctuality. But David really wanted to go. After all, Thomas Matson was one of his best friends, one of a very small group who had remained his friend after the accident. That situation had angered and hurt David quite a lot in those first months after the accident. But though the hurt lingered, the anger was gone. David had forgiven his friends for retreating when they found it too uncomfortable to be near him. People tend to hang around those who are like them – who can do the same things, go to the same places, and dream the same dreams. But that had all changed in a horrifying split second for David. He was even sympathetic with his former friends now for, after all, in the weeks following the event, hadn't David experienced the same desire, namely, to establish distance between who he once was and who he had become?

It had been a painful time for David – in mind as well as body – a tormented period bouncing from denial to absurd hope, from a hatred of the drunk driver who had maimed him to a hatred for himself, from religious conviction to the most awful doubts and fears. So, no; David had empathy for those (even in his family) who had abandoned him after the accident. He understood their weakness. But more important, he had learned that forgiveness created a healthier, happier state of mind. And he desperately needed that to go on.

Nevertheless, David cherished and delighted all the more in those few friends who had remained solid and true. And, among that select group, none had proved as steady and encouraging as Thomas. David *had* to make it to his wedding.

The solution surfaced one evening at a performance of Sentimental Journeys. The music of the big band era wasn't what David grew up on, of course, but he had started going to every presentation. He was initially attracted by the program's unique flair and the enthusiasm it generated among the residents. But the photographs and the commentary were very interesting and appealed to David's interest in American history. And he really liked Colin and Mary MacGregor, the couple that brought the show to Villa Vista. They were interesting, caring, and generous with their time. David had learned that the MacGregors created the Sentimental Journeys program all on their own and presented it free of charge to a dozen senior care facilities every month. He admired that. And, truth be told, David had got hooked on the swing music itself. His musical library now included Artie Shaw, Chick Webb, Tommy Dorsey, and a bunch of other swing-era stars alongside his Beatles and Abba.

Still another draw for David's attendance at Sentimental Journeys was the opportunity to be around younger people. He had learned much in the past eighteen months about intergenerational friendships and he realized how limited his socialization was before he came to Villa Vista. He had established wonderful friends among the seniors here: Ralph Yarborough, Horace Jones, Grace Trinisi, Rev. Gonzalez, Grant Katulka, Sarah Truelove, Ted Bonney, Ethel van Dorn. The list went on. But David desired the fellowship of younger people too. And the Sentimental Journeys programs had become a regular date night for Zachary and Brenda, for Brenda's younger sister, Reggie, and her new boyfriend, Albert Trinisi, and often for a young adults group from Albert's church. David had been fully accepted into their company and he found it a bracing, fulfilling experience.

Somewhere in the conversation with his new friends following the show, David had shared his frustration about getting transportation for the wedding that was coming up in just two days. Out of the blue, Albert said he could take off a couple of hours and would be more than glad to drive him over.

David smiled. "Thanks, Albert. That's a nice thing to offer and I really appreciate it. But it's not quite that easy."

"How come?" Albert asked innocently. "I'm driving Dad's truck anyway for the next few weeks. I've seen how Zach lifts you outta that chair and I'm sure I can do it easy enough too. I can haul it in the back of the truck until you need it at the church."

David looked over to Zachary and motioned with his head as if to say, "You explain it to him." But Zachary only looked back at him with a grin. "What's the problem? I think that's your answer, brother."

David was silent for several moments, his gaze shifting from Zachary to Albert and back. He realized suddenly that this was a test, the kind Zachary had put before him before. As both his physical therapist and his friend, Zachary often challenged David to risk leaving the safe haven that was his deluxe wheelchair. But David's standard response was resistance. It had taken almost three months for Zachary to persuade David to leave the chair for aquatic exercise. And so far, that was about the only thing David would risk.

Was this the moment to take a new chance? To deal with the embarrassment, discomfort, and fear? To risk having a problem with his internal plumbing in public? To surrender, even for a brief time, the security of his white cocoon?

Zachary finally spoke with a calm confidence. "It's up to

you, David. I can teach Al how to transfer you safely. That's no big deal. In fact, I'm working Saturday so I can do it myself when you're leaving here and coming back. I'm sure that I can rig something up for the trip over there. All you'll need to do is sign a waiver and anybody could take you. Personally, I think it's a great idea."

"Me too," chimed in Albert. "And, no kidding, I'd love to help you out."

Albert's grin was sincere and infectious. Zachary's was more mischievous. But together they provided David the incentive he needed. "Okay. Let's give it a try."

With the decision made, the men wasted no time in preparing for the event. They finished their drinks, said their goodbyes to Marsha and Joanna who had also been in attendance at the show, and headed down to the rehab center. Albert's strength proved to be more than sufficient for the task and he was appropriately careful in lifting and positioning David. No problem there. And no problem with the truck either. Albert took them all outside (Brenda and Reggie were there too) and explained how easy it would be to use an aluminum ramp to get the wheelchair in and out of the truck. He showed them how he would use sandbags and bungee cords to keep it secure on the road. For his part, Zachary rigged an additional safety harness for David besides the seat belt itself. He would also use pillows to keep David as comfortable as possible for the ride.

Zachary took it all in. Albert would do fine. And remarkably, David was content with the plan. Zachary was confident too that Dr. Carlton would sign off on the plan and let Albert take David to his friend's wedding. "Guys," Zachary said, "that's enough practice. It'll work just fine. And since I've already felt a couple drops of that rain they've been predicting all day, let's get inside before it starts in earnest."

They just made it under the long vaulted roof that overhung the front entranceway when the rain let loose with surprising force. Brenda and Reggie hustled in to grab Cokes and the last of the brownies to pass around. It was an exciting rainfall, complete with thunder and lightning crashes in the distant north. As they sat there, enjoying the sounds of the storm and the comfort of one another's company, Zachary was looking forward to Saturday almost as much as David must be. It would be a big day for David, maybe even a breakthrough day. For to get him to even consider leaving his comfort zone (if the term could be applied to someone who bore what David did) was a very important moment. Zachary reflected on the months of persuasion, the hundreds of hours of rehab work, and no small amount of prayer that had been invested to get David ready to make this move. But it took something else to finally give David the desire and the courage necessary. It took the power of genuine friendship – first through the welcoming wedding invitation from Thomas, then in the enthusiastic offer of assistance from Albert. Zachary smiled up at God, so movingly active in the stormy night sky, and thanked Him for this long-desired answer.

Chapter 32
Travels in the Christmas Room

The rainfall had softened but the night was still quite dark and windy. It looked cold but, through her window, Grace Trinisi could see Mattie's granddaughters sitting with their new boyfriends, one of whom was her own grandson, Albert. The kids didn't seem to feel the chill that she did. But that was natural – they were in love. The poor young man in the big white wheelchair had been with them for a time but he had gone inside a bit earlier. Dennis? No, she didn't think so. Dwight? No, that was her old neighbor. David? Yes, she thought that was it. David. She often prayed for that young man. For it was natural for old people to live in this place. That was in the inescapable nature of the world. As sad as it was, age eventually took away one's mobility and strength and mind. Grace sighed deeply. It took loved ones away too. But to have such a young man as David live here among all these old, tired folks like her seemed especially unnatural and sad.

Grace liked David a lot. He was kind and polite; he was smart and interesting; and even in his sad condition, his heart was cheerful. She enjoyed talking to him in the cafeteria and he had even started to visit her in her room. Maybe most important to Grace was that, like her, David faithfully prayed to God and looked forward to heaven.

Yes, the young man was one of her best friends here. So she was thrilled to see him make friends with other young people, kids who were wise enough to see beyond that big wheelchair to the nice young man who lived in it. She was proud that her grandson was one of those friends.

Grace looked back outside. Her grandson was sitting across the picnic table from Reggie and they were laughing at something. But Brenda and her young man, the doctor who worked down in the rehab room, had moved over to one of the iron benches. They sat close together holding hands and having their own moment together.

And right then, somewhere way off in the dark rain clouds beyond, Grace heard a whispering voice, a voice that reminded her of Frank. Maybe it *was* Frank, she thought, and she listened very carefully. Had she really heard him? Raindrops hit the window. The wind spun her bird feeder outside and she noted the little squeak it made. And then there was Mattie's breathing mask that she wore when she slept. But, of course, Grace was so used to that particular noise that it hardly mattered. No, whatever it had been, the whisper was gone. But not the effect. And so, whether it had been Frank's voice or simply the sight of young people in love...or maybe the memories stirred by hearing those big band songs earlier in the evening, Grace Trinisi began to think back.

"Good evening, Miss Landvik. My name is Frank Trinisi. My father is Carlo Trinisi, the man who drives the coal truck. I've helped him deliver to your farm a few times. I don't know if you've ever seen me. Anyhow, I'm home on leave before being sent out again, Lord knows where, and I almost didn't come tonight to the dance. But my pal Joey Sordano — that's him over by the bandstand, the sailor holding his cap in his hands — he told me you were going to be here tonight. You see, his sister works with your mother and she mentioned you'd be here tonight. And even if you don't remember me from delivering coal, I remember you because

I've seen you at least twice. Once you were still in school and you and two of your friends offered to help my brother and me unload a truck of peaches up at Vacey's store in Kirksville. You girls said you'd unload the whole truck for a dollar because you were trying to get money for hamburgers and a show. Well, we let you. For a few minutes anyway. Do you remember that? Then Vincent and I pitched back in and helped and we got it done in no time. It was fun. But we never told you that Mr. Vacey was only giving us *four bits each* to unload that truck. We had to pay you girls another four bits out of our own pockets! But, hey; we weren't complaining. We enjoyed being with you all.

"And then the second time I saw you was one day just a year ago last November. You were giving that speech about the Pilgrims and the Mayflower Compact at the Harvest Festival. You talked right before the mayor did but all my pals agreed with me that your speech was a lot better than his. It was very interesting, inspiring even. In fact, it was so doggone inspiring that I went out that next day and enlisted in the U.S. Army!"

"Okay," Frank said laughing. "I see you don't believe me. And, don't worry; I was only joking about that. But I *did* enlist the next week and even if your speech wasn't what sparked my decision, it didn't dampen it either. And, this is no lie at all, Miss Landvik, before I left home for boot camp, I borrowed a book from my sister called *Yonder Sails the Mayflower*. It was written by Honore Morrow and I read it on the train. I read it straight through, right to the end. I figured it was a grand idea for me to know more about the history of the country I was going to fight for. Well, I liked that book and I read it again just last month because, forgive me if I'm too bold, Miss Landvik, but I hoped one day to have a talk with you personally about the subject. My sister, Betty…you might know her. She was two classes below you but she quit at fifteen and now works on the farm and sometimes at the Woolworth's in town. Well, anyway, I had her read the book too and so if I called on you tomorrow evening, I could bring her along to allow for all the social conventions.

"So I must apologize, Miss Landvik, for not having a common acquaintance introduce us but I didn't know anyone but my sister Betty and she had to work the counter at Woolworth's tonight. So I have made bold to present myself to you. I hope you'll forgive me if I seem forward, Miss Landvik, but please try to understand that I've wanted to be on friendly terms with you ever since that day with the peaches. And then, after your speech that I found so excellent, I've wanted it even more. Because I believe you would make a fine friend, someone that would make me a better person. And finally, Miss Landvik, as my last excuse for being so forward, I only had nine days here at home before having to go back, and I've already wasted three of those days trying to work up the nerve to come talk to you."

Grace wistfully remembered it all. It was all so vivid tonight. But that awkward, shy moment had been the beginning of something quite lovely. Frank and Grace did become good friends. Lovers too eventually. And then parents. And then partners in a construction business they started from scratch. Along the way, they built many houses and garages and stores and churches and so much more. And they also built for themselves a house and an office...then houses for each one of their kids. But, always and throughout, Frank and Grace Trinisi were good friends.

Yes, memories flooded and filled to overflowing the Christmas Room that night. Sharp and sure memories. Some charmingly sweet. Some intensely romantic. Some funny and some heartbreaking. But they were all Grace's. They were the stuff of her life, whatever their flavor or meaning, and she cherished every single one of them.

Grace was grateful to God that time and the comforts of her trust in heaven had made the tragedies of her life more bearable. There had been her father's horrific accident, her mother's breakdown, her own miscarriages, all of Tony's troubles, the fire that killed the Wasserman family, Sheila's suffering, Frank's lingering illness, and other horrors of a sin-wrecked world too numerous to count. The memories of these things brought tears to Grace's eyes tonight. But they were cool and gentle tears, not the searing and violent ones that had poured forth when these tragedies first broke.

And Grace thanked God that those hard memories were nowadays outnumbered by the pleasant and hopeful ones she cherished. Frank's return from the wars, both Germany and then Korea. Dancing to Larry Clinton and Lawrence Welk and Freddy Martin and so many others. Taking sandwiches and lemonade out to the job sites. Nursing her children at her breast. Hymn sings at church. Evening coffee with Frank on the back porch. Picnics and swimming at the old river cut. Reading nursery rhymes and Winnie the Pooh stories to the children before bedtime. Card games and charades with friends and, later on, with the kids. Romantic nights with dinner at the Lighthouse or Mandy's, finishing off with Frank locking the bedroom door for an hour or so. The glories of the vegetable garden and the big canning projects. Drive-in movies with the kids in pajamas. Music of all kinds playing on the radio and then later on a hi-fi stereo made from blond wood purchased at Sears and Roebuck. Little League games. The kids gathering around Frank in his big brown chair while he told them stories from the Old Testament. Baking with the girls. The hikes in the forest. The toy theater. Picking apples for jelly and cider. Long Sunday dinners in which Frank led the family (there were almost always guests around the table too) in a discussion over Rev. Rawlin's sermon.

And then there were the Christmases! Those memories were particularly precious to Grace. The cloves stuck into oranges. Wrapping packages. Christmas music in the stores. Baking and decorating cookies. Frank playing Santa at Vets Hospital and the old people's home. Hot cocoa after snowball fights. Scouting Taylor Woods for just the right tree. Grandma Faltskog making *Juletid Kokosmakroner* and Grandpa Trinisi making walnut fudge. The kids' pageant at church. Sledding down Wannamaker's hill. Tinsel on the tree. Ghost stories told by the fire. Taffy pulls at Aunt Helena's.

Snowmen and snow forts. The nativity set under the tree and out on the lawn.

Grace's Christmas memories just wouldn't stop tonight and she spent several wonderful moments reflecting on each one. Mulling wassail using Grandpa Trinisi's recipe. The choir singing carols at church. Taking cookies to the old people's home and little presents to the unwed girls and their babies at the Wycliffe Home. Making eggnog. Attending *The Nutcracker* ballet at the Delphi. Gag gifts on Christmas morning. Upside-down pineapple cake. Pine wreaths with red-ribbon bows. The Christmas-themed shows on radio and then later on the television. The living nativity at the Presbyterian church on Lorraine Street. Chocolate-covered cherries.

Still more? Yes. Grandpa Landvik (and then Frank) reading Dickens' *A Christmas Carol* and the Christmas narratives from the Gospels. Trimming the tree after lovingly unpacking the ornaments that had been collected over the years. Cousin Paula's rum-drenched fruitcake. Hosting dinner parties throughout the Twelve Days of Christmas. Shopping downtown amid the crowds. Sassafras tea with honey. Ice skating on Willow Pond and at the ice rink downtown. Layaway plans at Montgomery Ward. Candles in the window. Christmas carolers coming to the front door and being "paid" with candy and apples and hot punch. Snuggling in front of the Christmas tree with Frank after the kids went to bed and thanking God for all the blessings from the year now nearly behind them.

"You remember still, don't you, darling?"

There was Frank's voice again. But this time it didn't seem to come from the clouds. It was right beside her. It was so distinct, so familiar that Grace turned from the window that she had been gazing through and looked around the room.

Grace whispered, "Are you here, Frank?"

There was no reply, no sound at all except for the steady rhythm of Mattie's CPAP machine. But that was all that Grace heard. No sleigh bells. No children's laughter. No lover's sighs. And no Frank. Nevertheless, Grace spoke a very loving answer, "Yes, I remember, dear. I don't always, I must admit. But I remember *so much* tonight and it has warmed my heart so. Thank You, Lord. And thank You for all those sweet Christmases. Thank You even for the ones that were hard. And dear Jesus, thank You also for Frank, and for our children and grandchildren. Thank You for a good life. Because, even adding up the bad times, it *was* a good life."

Grace noticed she was holding one of the little sheep from her nativity set, the one Tony had brought from home to complete the Christmas decorations in her room. And looking lovingly at that little figure, she was reminded of the supernatural and superseding effect of Christmas. Ah, yes. She remembered that too.

Grace gently placed the sheep next to the shepherd, the one closest to Mary and Joseph. The manger in between them was empty and that confused Grace for a moment. Then she remembered Tony telling her that the baby Jesus was still inside Mary's womb until Christmas morning. Tony would wait and place the baby in the manger only on Christmas Day. He had told her, "Mom, that's what *you* always did. And the wise men. Remember how you wouldn't put them in the nativity scene until Epiphany? Until then, you had them traveling from the kitchen cabinet to the bureau in the den then, a few days later, around the corner of the dining room table and then the fireplace shelf. Only on Epiphany did you put them next to the Holy Family. Remember, Mom?"

Yes, she did remember...tonight. Grace smiled broadly and breathed another prayer of gratitude to God. She was remembering an awful lot tonight. It was so nice. So very nice.

When Yoki slipped into the room a few minutes later that smile still adorned Grace's countenance. But Grace Marie Landvik Trinisi was fast asleep.

Chapter 33
Santa's Helpers

In the wake of the news coverage dealing with the Edith business, three families notified Villa Vista they were no longer considering the facility and wished to be taken off the waiting list. Carolyn Kovacs wasn't surprised. But, on the other hand, eleven families *had* signed on, several of them specifically mentioning Carolyn's published statements to be major factors in prompting their decisions. Carolyn didn't need vindication. But, if she did, she had plenty. The Villa Vista ownership and its board members were more than pleased at how things turned out.

A welcome side effect of Carolyn's action had been a boost of morale for the staff. From the administration to the caregivers and all of the support positions, the employees of the care center had been forcefully reminded of the extreme seriousness and value of their work. They enjoyed knowing they were part of a team that was increasingly known to the public for its compassion and integrity. The staff knew better than anyone that there were plenty of bad nursing homes out there, places that tended to make the very name a thing of disgust and dread. Many of the staff even had personal experience working in such places. It was hard to decide what were the worst features in such businesses: indifference, neglect, unsanitary conditions, lack of training, overcrowding, noise, overmedication, sloppy business practices, theft, bullying, or the calculated schemes to cover up these horrors? So, to now work for a nursing home with such a high reputation as Villa Vista, a place that made resident care a priority, was wonderful. And to have your family and friends *know* that you were part of such a nursing home? Well, that was great too.

This wave of good feeling came at an important time for Villa Vista in that it guaranteed the owners' decision to pursue an expansion of the facility. Adjoining land was purchased and architects hired with instructions to create 30 private rooms, 40 double rooms, two large activity rooms adjacent to a small kitchen, additional storage space, and a maintenance headquarters with a triple garage. The basic needs had been laid out by Carolyn herself after a lot of study and innumerable conversations with her own staff and others in the industry. It was a dream come true for Carolyn, a chance to better serve the residents already at Villa Vista as well as to open up to many more individuals and families the high-quality care that had been established there. True, it was a dream that was still a long way off. The groundbreaking wouldn't be until next summer and the construction would take anywhere from ten to fourteen months after that. But the dream was taking its first steps toward reality.

Carolyn had a full day ahead but she worked out her schedule to be free for Mrs. Zann's "graduation" from rehab at ten o'clock and for a late-afternoon meeting with a representative of a company specializing in computer technology that helped people with speech disabilities. Carolyn had witnessed a display of the company's products at a medical convention last month and had immediately asked for a visit from a sales rep. She knew how devastating it could be to a person's spirit (and overall health) when he or she lost the power to communicate to others. It went beyond frustration. Indeed, it frequently led to despair. For such a person to discover that a tablet-sized computer with a keyboard could help them *speak* their thoughts...well, that was a lifesaver that Carolyn wanted to learn more about. She had already obtained permission to purchase as many as she felt necessary but she wanted to get the whole story on the products, the prices, and the learning process it would require of her staff who would then coach the residents.

Carolyn had also planned into her day a luncheon with Tony Trinisi and a gentleman named Roger Mazurak, one of Tony's colleagues. Ralph Yarborough would be there also. So, when 12:30 came around, the four had started in on sandwiches, cucumber salads, and lemonade on the back patio of Villa Vista. Ralph was already deep in a conversation with Mr. Mazurak about the facility's lawn problems which, not even counting the damage done by a very hot summer, were severe. Crabgrass. Weeds. Nutsedge. And the ongoing battle with moles. Ralph had exhausted his best efforts and had eventually hired professionals, but the critter problem was still far from under control. He hoped that Roger, the award-winning landscaping director of Trinisi Construction, could provide some answers. Carolyn was sitting in on the meeting because she held the purse strings for any expenditure necessary.

It turned out to be a very helpful meeting. Mr. Mazurak had brought along relevant advice, albums of photographs and blueprints, and a lot of charm. His ideas were exciting yet eminently practical. Both Ralph and Carolyn were impressed. Mr. Mazurak proposed that Villa Vista use sod to start the lawn fresh in the fall. But he also explained how shrinking the amount of grass in favor of rock gardens, berms with flowering bushes, and oasis areas with covered porches and paved walkways would create more beauty, increase resident use and appreciation, and yield a lot of financial savings in upkeep. And it would create incentive for the moles to find new homes.

Ralph thought it was an excellent plan. So did Tony. But it was Carolyn who needed to be convinced because she was the one who would have to sell the plan to the board members. "Okay, guys. This was a great meeting. Thanks, Ralph, for setting it up. Mr. Mazurak, I'm impressed with the plan and the layout you've drawn up. I'm sure it would create a dramatic and beautiful change the residents would love. And I'm especially pleased to see how positive Ralph is about your proposal. We like to keep him happy around here!"

Ralph smiled broadly. "Well, Carolyn, I think it would solve a lot of problems, that's true. But, if it ends up looking even a *little* like these pictures Roger worked up, everyone is going to treasure it. Just think of the folks who'll want to sit out in those oasis areas."

Carolyn nodded. "I agree. That certainly is a selling point." But Carolyn then took a deep breath and arched her eyebrows as she looked over at Tony. "The question I've got to ask now is how much is this going to cost, Tony?"

Tony shrugged his shoulders and motioned to Roger. "I've no idea. That's Roger's department."

Carolyn turned and was encouraged by the man's wide smile. "Mr. Mazurak? Can we afford you?"

Roger laughed. "Yes, ma'am, I think you can. At least, Tony here thinks it's a deal you won't be able to refuse." He handed her a sheet breaking down the numbers. "We're offering you the whole package at Tony's cost. And all the labor will be free of charge if, that is, you don't mind some of the work crew being kids from the tech school that we're helping break in. Consider too that Villa Vista can probably recoup its full investment in a few years just from the savings in water and lawn care."

Carolyn certainly hadn't figured on this. A fair offer, perhaps even a sweet deal? Sure, that's what she had expected from Tony Trinisi. He had, after all, already proven to be a gracious and generous friend to Villa Vista. But this? Wow. This was remarkable.

"Tony, I don't know what to say."

"No need to say anything but yes, Carolyn. And the same offer goes for the landscaping of your new building if you end up hiring us for that project. Believe me, it's a good deal for us too. The before-and-after photos will make great advertising for the company. And I'm pleased to be able to do something for the folks who are doing such a great job taking care of my mom."

Carolyn felt overwhelmed. Mr. Mazurak's creativity combined with Tony's amazing generosity would create a prettier, less expensive, and more resident-friendly Villa Vista. What wasn't to love? "Well, perhaps all I *can* say then is thank you, Tony. Thank you from all of us at Villa Vista. And thank you too, Mr. Mazurak. Your ideas are terrific."

"Make it Roger, ma'am, and that will please me fine. And one more thing. If it would be okay, we'd like to jump into this thing right away. Maybe get started next Monday?"

"Monday will be fine, Roger. Just fine." Carolyn looked out to the east where the new structure was going to be built and then to the west where Roger's pictures filled her mind. Imagine. That patch of weedy, mole-traveled lawn was going to be transformed into something quite lovely and inviting. "Thank you again, Ralph, for pursuing this idea. Villa Vista owes you big time. And Tony, I know it's your mother who lives in the Christmas Room, but I wouldn't be at all surprised to discover that you and Mr. Mazurak...uh, I mean, Roger, are among Santa's best helpers. God bless you."

Chapter 34
Storytelling

Ron Sylvano was tired but the heavy sleepiness that had hit him just before noon had subsided. He was working a double shift for the second day in a row, taking both his normal 11 to 7 and then sticking around to take Bob Jr.'s duties from 7 to 3. Bob and Bob Jr. both worked at Villa Vista. The son was making his way through college by living with his folks and working here as a CNA. His dad, not the friendliest guy in the place, but dependable and efficient, was Director of Cooperative Finances. When asked what that meant, Bob Sr. would simply frown and say, "I'm the Medicare-Medicaid man."

Bob and Bob Jr. were gone on a combination fishing trip/family reunion out west. To Ron, who never had much of a family life, such a thing sounded super. But when Ron had expressed his envy and told Bob Sr. how lucky he was to get everyone together like that, Bob had curled his lip and growled, "You don't know my kin, son. The fish in that river will have more personality than my family does. I already can't wait to have it all over and come home." Bob Jr. told Ron later that his dad didn't really mean what he said; he was only pulling his leg. But Ron still wasn't sure.

It was dusk and Ron was sitting at the dinner table with Mrs. Trinisi, Mrs. Gritzner, Mrs. Hayes, and Sister Bernadette. His mealtime duties were ended. Well, almost ended. He had helped some of the male residents dress and get ready for supper. Then, one by one, he brought them and some of the ladies in his hall to the cafeteria. He took meal requests and waited on tables – not just his own people either but anyone nearby that he saw in need. He enjoyed the activity, especially those few minutes of rest when he sat down and shared coffee and dessert with residents before beginning the individual treks back to their rooms. Many of the staff preferred taking these minutes in the staff break room with one another. But Ron, Suzie, and Griff thought sitting with the residents more rewarding. Sometimes there were family members or other guests who came along for meals and it was nice to spend a few minutes with them as well.

"Are you married?" Sister Bernadette suddenly directed a question to Ron.

"No, Sister. I'm not."

"Why not? Don't you *want* to get married? So many young people seem to avoid it nowadays." The last part was directed at the other ladies at the table, making Ron feel a little uncomfortable for being used as an example of what Sister clearly thought was a bad thing.

"No, Sister. It's not that I don't *want* to get married. I just haven't found the right girl yet."

"Well, you'd better start looking harder, young man. You're not going to get any handsomer, you know."

Ron didn't know if she meant to be humorous but he laughed anyway. "Okay. I'll take your advice very seriously, Sister."

"Well, I hope you do." She said it with firmness and without a smile.

"Let the boy be. There are a lot worse things than not being married." Ron looked over at Mattie Gritzner with no small amount of surprise. Mattie's socializing had become rare in the past few weeks. One sometimes caught her whispering something to Mrs. Trinisi but otherwise she was quiet and withdrawn. This was the first time he had heard her speak for days.

"That's true, Mattie. That's certainly true." Mrs. Hayes reached over and patted Mattie's hand as she spoke. "And handsome isn't always what it's cracked up to be either." That prompted a chuckle from her friends, even Sister Bernadette. Mrs. Hayes then followed her observation with a robust and colorful tale about her first husband. She told very funny stories.

Ron listened politely but his thoughts also traveled to memories of his own grandmother. She was a good storyteller too. In fact, so many of the elderly people he knew excelled in the art. He had once commented on this to Mrs. Kovacs and she readily agreed. "You know what their secret is?" she had asked Ron. "It's the fact that they've lived interesting lives. Younger generations don't have as much to talk about, at least as far as personal experience is concerned. Sure, they've seen a lot of movies and watched a lot of TV and they've played more video games than you can count. But they're only spectators of these things. They're looking from the outside in on things that aren't real. But older people have played the protagonists in their own real-life stories. Their knowledge and experience, all of their heartbreaks and joys – these haven't come vicariously. These older people tell great stories because...well, because they've personally *lived* great stories."

Ron well understood Mrs. Kovacs' point. In his circle of friends, conversation was dominated by the movies or television shows they watched. There was very little talk about personal adventures or achievements. Ron knew he would be hard pressed to convince his friends but, the fact was, he believed that senior citizens, even the ones living in places like Villa Vista, were flat out more interesting than people of his own generation. He smiled to himself as Mrs. Hayes came to the punch line of her story and promptly began on another one. Yes, he was pleased very much with his job here. It was sometimes difficult, sometimes messy, and sometimes very sad. Yet it was worthwhile and significant. In a culture that constantly sang about compassion and love and serving the needy, Ron was engaged in something quite rare. He was *doing* it! And, in the process, he was learning how to live life well and to the full.

"More coffee, ladies?"

Chapter 35
Brothers Again?

As Mattie Gritzner's medical condition grew worse, greater amounts of medication were needed to keep her free from pain. And that meant not only long hours of sleep but also a general drowsiness in those few times she was awake. Mattie was most alert in the early morning and her loved ones had begun to concentrate their visits in those few hours. Joanna and her daughters frequently came to have breakfast with her. And Clark, showing signs of both his grief and his guilt, had begun to visit his mother before he went to work. In these visits, Clark would sit close to his mother's bed and they would talk of earlier times, of that golden age of Mattie's life in Chicago when her two sons loved their parents, loved their animals, and loved each other. There were certain stories that Clark told over and over because his mom asked him to. Those stories were almost always about things involving Clark and his brother, Durward. Stories of helping their dad, camping trips, family pets, summer jobs.

Clark believed his mother asked for the same stories time after time only because of her advancing dementia. He was wrong. Mattie Gritzner asked for the same stories, those stories which starred both of her sons, for two very clear-headed reasons. The first was that she loved the feeling those stories brought her. The images were sharp and full of comfort. They even sweetened her dreams in those long hours when everyone around her mistakenly thought her mind was dormant. But the second reason was even more purposeful, perhaps even a bit devious. For in these last days of her life, she wanted to help Clark remember that he *had* a brother, one to whom he was once close. Mattie hoped that Clark's remembering some of the good times would provoke more positive feelings between him and Durward. Maybe she might even spark a reconciliation. This was one of two constant prayers in her waking hours. The other was that God would free Clark from whatever terrible burden he was carrying, whatever it was that had made him so irritable and distant and unhappy. Grace had taken on Mattie's burden too and every day they tried to find a time to pray together for that reunion.

The breakthrough came one morning in mid-October when Clark decided on making a phone call to his brother. He told himself he was doing it for his mother's sake, but he also knew that his longstanding animosity towards Durward had softened through the reliving of those memories of their youth together. But he was still very nervous about making contact. In fact, he almost lost his courage when he suddenly remembered David's frequent reminder that he was praying for him. That was the stimulation he needed. He pulled into the Villa Vista parking lot, and in a moment of unusual resolve, took out his cell phone and hit the number he had programmed in the previous evening.

It only rang twice before a gruff voice answered. "Hello."

"Hello, Durward. This is Clark."

There were a few seconds of silence and Clark had to fight the urge to hang up. But finally his brother's voice came on the line again.

"Yes, Clark. I'm here."

"I hope I'm not calling too early but I remembered you used to meet with that group of guys for coffee."

"Yes. I still do. I'll be leaving in about 20 minutes."

"Okay, good. Well, let me tell you why I called…"

Durward interrupted him. "It's about Mother, right? Did she die, Clark? Just tell me."

"No, no, Durward. No, she didn't die. In fact, I'm here at the nursing home right now getting ready to go in and see her. She's most alert in the early morning so that's when I usually come by."

"That's what I heard. That's good, Clark."

"Where did you hear that?"

There was another uncomfortable silence on the line until Durward said slowly, "Just because I don't talk much anymore to *you* doesn't mean that I don't talk to Mother."

Clark was surprised, so surprised that he couldn't help release a bit but of anger in his voice. "She hasn't told me anything about that."

"Well, she wouldn't now, would she?" Clark could almost see the smirk he figured was on Durward's face. "I mean let's face it, Clark. Past experience has shown Mother that even bringing my name up with you can spark explosions."

Clark winced. And not only at the memories his brother had kindled but at the realization that his whole plan was unnecessary. He had hoped to give his mom a special gift, a chance to talk to her wayward son. Only to discover she had *already* been talking to him.

"So, Clark, tell me. Why *did* you call?"

Clark felt like a fool. But it would be even worse if he tried any dissembling now. "Well, apparently I've been operating on a false assumption. But it's all my own doing. I understand that, Durward. It's my own fault. But here's what I was thinking. You see, Mom has slowed down quite a bit and, to be quite frank, I think the end is getting near. The doctor tells us…"

"I know what the doctor says," Durward broke in. "I'm in pretty regular contact with Lois Vendee and Greg Kwan. Before that last turn for the worse, when she was still in rehab, I kept in touch with Zachary O'Rourke too. So, until lunchtime two days ago, I've been pretty much up to speed on Mother's condition."

Clark let that sink in. But in place of his first reaction – anger and a desire to justify himself – he found himself being pleased and grateful. "I didn't know," he said quietly. "And I know, Durward, that's my fault too that I *didn't* know." Clark paused as he felt a wave of conviction sweep over him. "Durward, had I only taken the time to put aside my hatred and pride, I would have realized that, of course, you *would* make the effort to stay in touch with Mom. It was foolish for me to not remember that. Despite all that I've held against you, your heart toward Mom and Dad was always tender, always considerate." Durward heard a deep sigh before he heard his brother conclude. "Way more tender than mine."

Durward didn't speak and Clark concluded his brother's silence was fueled by those years of rejection. It wasn't. It was only because, for the first time in decades, Clark had genuinely surprised his brother. And he didn't know what to say.

So Clark continued. "Mom has been asking me to tell her stories from the old days on Decatur Street and even earlier like when we lived on the south end of town. And most of the stories she wants to hear are about things you and I did together. Anyway, I thought this morning I could give her a nice present by asking her if she wanted to talk to her older son and when she said yes, I'd call you up and hand her the phone. And so that's why I called you now, to see if you would go along with it. So, I'm sorry, Durward. I just didn't know."

Clark knew he wasn't feeling disappointment only because his surprise gift to his mom had fallen through. He was disappointed too because he had wanted to connect somehow with his older brother, to put aside for a few minutes all the bad feelings of the past years and be the kind of friends again they had been in those long-ago stories.

"Clark?"

"Yes, Durward. I'm still here."

"You say you're outside Mother's place right now? You were going to call me when you got inside and hand her the phone?"

"Yes, that was the plan. But, like I said, I thought…"

"Yes, well, that doesn't matter much now. Your idea was a good one. A very good one. And Mother will be absolutely thrilled. We both know that. So, of course, let's do it."

There, in the pre-dawn that shadowed the Villa Vista parking lot, Clark Gritzner almost broke down. He had been carrying so much pressure and shame and fear in these past several months. Yet he was being given so much grace. From Joanna. From David Youngville. And now from the most unexpected source of all, the brother that he had long vilified as a drunk, a thief, and a jailbird.

"And, Clark?" Durward's voice came on the line again, distinctly friendlier than just a few minutes ago. "Maybe you could call again this weekend and tell me some of the stories you've been remembering for Mother."

"I will, Durward. I will. And I'll enjoy that very much."

Chapter 36
All Hallow's Eve: Daytime

On the morning of All Hallows' Eve, Lois Vendee came into the foyer with a big grin and an open newspaper. "Hey, did you guys read about Ralph? He saved a guy from choking last night down at the Lakeland Ballroom! There's a neat write-up on the front page. The reporter even dug up stuff from way back when Ralph was in high school. Did any of you know that he worked summers as a lifeguard out at Croft's Lake? The story says he saved dozens of people from drowning back then. How cool is that!"

The office staff gathered around to read the account. It described Ralph's application of the Heimlich maneuver to a choking man after the fellow's wife started screaming for help. Ralph had made one quick glance around the room to see if anyone else was making for the fellow. He was hoping for a doctor or, better still, an off-duty firefighter. But no one was moving so he took charge and, in just a few seconds, the obstruction had been cleared and the man was fine. Had that been all, the incident probably wouldn't have been considered news. But the choking victim turned out to be Errol R. Rutledge, the wealthy financier who owned a supermarket chain, two of the city's largest shopping malls, and maybe a third of the downtown district. It was the man rescued that made the rescuer big news.

"How about those pictures?" asked Mr. Nguyen, who had craned his neck over Lois' shoulder to see the paper. The pictures really were something. There was a nice portrait-style that the photographer had taken afterward with the lights reflecting off the lake in the background. And then, as a bonus, there was a photo of Ralph as a teenage lifeguard that the reporter had discovered in the newspaper's microfiche files.

"He was quite a handsome galoot in those days, wasn't he?" noted Lois. "A very dashing young man."

"But catch this part," Grant Katulka said and he read it aloud. "Yarborough was credited with saving more than 25 swimmers from life-threatening peril during his summers as a lifeguard. A remarkable achievement for a young man, to be sure. Yet when this reporter asked Yarborough if he was proud of his heroism, he only laughed and said, 'I was a lifeguard. That was my job. Plus, I couldn't compare with Ronald Reagan up there on the Rock River. They say he saved 77 people!'"

Everyone joined in the laughter but they soon let Grant finish reading the rest of the article. Immediately afterward though, Carolyn Kovacs spurred them to action. "Hey, we hardly have any time to get ready before Ralph shows up. Let's give him a hero's welcome, okay?" Carolyn remembered the pom-poms and went to find them, spreading the word to staff as she did so. Lois and Rita made signs. Grant started surfing the web for a recording of something relevant he could play over the speakers. Gloria spread the word to staff and grabbed one of the carrot cakes she had ready for lunch and began to decorate it appropriately. "Ralph Yarborough. Our hero!"

And it was a hero's welcome indeed that greeted Ralph when he came into work. The staff was lined up in the foyer to cheer and applaud him as he entered. So too were a few of the early-rising residents who had been given front-row seats.

Carolyn had handed out the pom-poms and they waved them with enthusiasm. Over the loudspeaker, the theme from *Superman* by John Williams played, the only song Grant had come up with. Ralph was smiling and giving obligatory little waves but he was as red as a beet.

Zachary O'Rourke was one of those greeting Ralph as he came in. And his was among the firmest handshakes when he delivered his congratulations in person. He could tell Ralph had mixed feelings about the surprise reception. There was, of course, pleasure in knowing you had friends, friends who were genuinely happy when something positive happened in your life. But Ralph couldn't help but be embarrassed too and he wanted the party to be over as soon as possible. Zachary leaned over and spoke in his ear, "The only way to finish this off is to go ahead and make a little speech." Ralph shook his head vigorously but Zachary was insistent. "No other way, I'm afraid. Just thank them for their show of support and they'll make you answer a few questions about what happened and then you'll be free and on about your day. Two minutes, maybe three at the most."

It was actually closer to twenty minutes before Carolyn closed things off by declaring it Ralph Yarborough Day at Villa Vista and reminding everyone that Gloria would be serving carrot cake at morning coffee or lunch, whichever you chose. And with a few closing pats on the shoulder, a few more attaboy comments, and several joking references to that old lifeguard photograph, things got back to normal.

Well, as normal as things were going to get anyway on a day when most of the staff wore Halloween costumes.

Zachary reflected on both Ralph's reception and the costumes throughout the morning. He thought about the irony in which fun and festivity took place in a facility where there was also pain and loneliness and fear, a facility where the rigors of old age, disease, and rejection made life such a difficult trial for many. Zachary could easily imagine an outsider concluding that frivolity of any sort, certainly the reception accorded Ralph this morning or caregivers wearing costumes, was incongruous at best, in decidedly poor taste at worst. But Zachary saw it differently. He was very glad to be working with the team Carolyn Kovacs had assembled. For he knew firsthand how effective festivity and novelty could be in the battle against tedium, loneliness, grumpiness...even pain. He knew too that residents of a nursing home *wanted* color and fun in their lives. They weren't dead yet and they resented being treated as if they were. They hated being unnecessarily deprived of things they had enjoyed all their lives. Yes, of course, there were limits. One had to always strive for appropriate sensitivity. But to introduce fun, music, change, beauty, humor, and other such things into caregiving was not something antithetical to quality medical care. Just the opposite.

And with that conclusion, Zachary hooked the sheriff's badge onto the pocket of his Western shirt, squared the Stetson on his head, and adjusted his fake mustache. It was time for his first group session.

Chapter 37
All Hallow's Eve: Nighttime

"No witches, Sis. Witches are definitely out."

Brenda was talking on the phone to Reggie who was parked outside the costume shop ready to go in. She had volunteered to help with the Halloween party at Villa Vista that night but had procrastinated badly about selecting a costume for the affair.

"What's wrong with witches on Halloween?"

Brenda sighed. "Well, most important of all, it's Carolyn's orders. No witches. No monsters. We are talking about little kids and older folks. So, scary and grotesque are out. Light-hearted and cute are in."

Reggie frowned. "I'm going to have a hard enough time as it is shopping this late but now you're telling me most of what Halloween is about is off limits? Great."

"Look, Reggie. It's not a big deal. We're not the stars of this thing. It's the kids who we'll be escorting through the rooms trick-or-treating. We just need to get into the spirit. There's no reason to go nuts or spend a lot of money. And I can guarantee you that picking up something down there is going to be expensive."

"Even if I'm shopping at the last minute?"

Brenda laughed. "*Especially* when you're shopping at the last minute! Listen, why not just do what I'm doing? Go homemade."

"Like what?"

"Like I'm doing. Heavy lipstick, big rouge circles on my cheeks, eyes like Liz Taylor in *Cleopatra*. Plus I borrowed a red, frizzed-out wig from Cassie Lincoln. I'll be really cute."

"Good grief, Sis. You'll be creepy! Are you sure *you* won't offend Mrs. Kovacs' rules?"

Brenda smiled. "You're just jealous! No, really, Reggie. You'll like it. Oh yeah, to complete the outfit, I've got a yellow scarf and one of Mom's old hippie dresses, that purple one with the madras print. And sandals. My old leather ones with the pink stripes. What do you think?"

Reggie purposefully groaned into the phone. "It sounds like a weird cross between Linda Ronstadt and Raggedy Ann. I don't know, Brenda. You say Zachary is going to be there, too?"

"Yes, he'll be there. Why, don't you think he'll like it?"

"Let's just say, I think your relationship must be tight indeed if you're not afraid to let him see you in that getup. But anyway, let's get back to *my* troubles. What could I use?"

"Well, let's think for a moment. You could go in and look around a bit but I'm pretty sure the prices will scare you – no Halloween pun intended." Both girls were silent for a few moments before Brenda had an idea. "Hey, why not use my scrubs? You could go...No, that's no good. Dressing up as a nurse in a nursing home isn't much of a costume, is it? Forget it."

Over the next few minutes the sisters discussed several options. A hobo with coffee grounds on Vaselined cheeks to suggest a beard? No. Someone might think that patronizing. A cowgirl? No. The Miss Scarlet persona she had adapted for the Clue party two years ago? No. A little too sultry. A clown? No.

"I've got it!" Brenda declared. "How about wearing your tights and tutu from ballet class!"

"You've got to be kidding, Sis. It may be true that I've lost a few pounds on this Paleo diet but I'm not ready yet for Albert to see me in something like that. What else can we come up with?"

They finally agreed on the idea of Reggie wearing her cheerleader outfit from high school. She would put her hair in a ponytail, hang a whistle around her neck, and wear Brenda's saddle shoes. Like the old days, she would even put a square of white paint under each eye with a player's number on it.

Brenda asked coyly, "So...what number will you use, Reg?"

"Anything but 23, Brenda. Anything but 23! That's one handsome headache I'm really glad to have out of my life...forever!" She then laughed. "He did have me dancing to his tune for a while though, didn't he?"

"Uh, no comment. Anyhow, Albert is worth ten times his kind. And then some."

There was a long pause before Reggie answered. "You are so right about that, Brenda. I think I found a treasure. And Brenda?"

"Yes?"

"I know you have too. I'm happy for both of us. See you tonight."

The trick-or-treat event that night turned out to be more successful than anyone had imagined. A gang of kids participated – ages 4 through 12. They had responded to invitations delivered throughout the neighborhood, to the school down the block, to the other schools involved with Villa Vista activities, and to families of volunteers and staff. The residents passed out treats, many of them getting help from staff or volunteers. That's the duty that had been assigned to Brenda and Reggie. The children paraded in their costumes through the halls and cafeteria where a substantial portion of the residents had gathered to greet and treat them. And there were a few rooms where small groups of kids were escorted inside. Carolyn was making sure that even the bedridden residents who wanted to get a kick out of seeing little kids in costume could do so.

A lot of staff and volunteers were needed to oversee such an activity. Kids had to be calmed, directed, and kept well behaved. Accompanying pets had to be controlled. Residents had to be kept from giving too much candy away or, if diabetic, to keep from sneaking any for themselves. There were a couple of minor episodes but they were quickly and deftly handled. It had been a great evening for kids, for families, and for the residents.

As a side point, Zachary and Albert considered Brenda's and Reggie's costumes to be fun and very attractive. And, because they were still in the Halloween spirit, they decided to continue the evening after the trick-or-treat party at Villa Vista had ended. After all, it was only a little after eight and they had skipped dinner to help out at the party. So, with Nick's Ristorante having become their default hangout, that's where they headed. They were all driving their own vehicles and it wasn't until they climbed in and were alone that they realized they were still in costume. Reggie and Zachary as cheerleader and cowboy wouldn't make much of a scene. Nor would Albert who had just exaggerated his regular work clothes, complete with a tool belt, hardhat, and a Trinisi Construction sweatshirt. But Brenda was going to make quite a fashion statement.

But Brenda didn't care much about that. It was Halloween and they wouldn't likely be the only ones in the restaurant who wore costumes. And, even if she *was* the only one, it was fine. She was going to be with people she loved, respected, and enjoyed. Brenda was also hoping that she and Zachary might have a little time alone tonight. He wouldn't care about her crazy getup.

***

While the young couples enjoyed the pasta at Nick's, Villa Vista was coming back down to earth from its triumphant Halloween party. Several staff members and a few volunteers from resident families stayed to clean up the cafeteria and take down decorations throughout the facility. By that time, residents were going to bed and almost everything was back to normal. The memories that had been made that night, however, would linger.

Carolyn and Rita had decided to end their long day with a cup of cocoa down in the Christmas Room. Mattie was in bed. She had been all evening. But she was awake, feeling comparatively well, and still joyful about seeing the children in their cute Halloween costumes. Mattie had been more comfortable staying in her room than going down to the cafeteria so Grace stayed with her. Their daughters-in-law had been with them too in order to help out with the trick-or-treating. However, things were a little different with these ladies. And why wouldn't it be? It was the Christmas Room!

A few days earlier, when Marsha had explained the trick-or-treat angle to the Halloween party, Grace had suggested an alternative. Instead of just handing out candy to the children who came into their room, Grace wanted to hand out Christmas ornaments too! It was an idea that Mattie liked as well and so, after Mrs. Kovacs gave her delighted okay to the project, Marsha had purchased several dozen Christmas tree ornaments from a couple of the dollar stores in town. Giving out the Christmas tree ornaments *and* little packs of M & M's turned out to be a big hit with the parents escorting their kids through the facility. It was an even greater thrill for the children. They were fascinated by the Christmas Room. It was so pretty and unusual, and it provided such an interesting contrast to the other rooms they had seen. They loved the candy, of course, but receiving an ornament from these dear old ladies in this wonderful room was a special bonus. It wasn't just a gift; it was more like a souvenir.

Carolyn was pleased with the success of the evening and yet she was pleased to have it over with too. She was thus in a relaxed mood as she sat between Marsha and the Christmas tree, sipping a minty cocoa drink. Marsha and Joanna talked about the costumes worn by the children and the interesting responses they had to the Christmas Room. Then Carolyn and Rita filled them in on the apple bobbing that Tony, Albert, and Ralph had set up for the older children out on the patio. And when they mentioned Ralph, they were reminded to tell Marsha and Joanna all about his heroics of the night before.

Grace and Mattie did nothing but listen. But they did that with intensity and joy. This had been a big night for them. Seeing all of those children. The fun of the costumes and handing out gifts. Mattie feeling better. And now the enjoyment of listening to some of their favorite ladies having fun together.

And for Mattie there was one more blessing of the evening, one very special to an old woman who knew her time on the planet was fast coming to a close. And that was the way her granddaughters had looked when they brought their boyfriends in to say goodnight. She could see they were happy. She could see they were in love. That reassured Mattie a great deal and, along with the changes she hoped were happening with her son Clark, made her think that the prayers she and Grace had been saying for their families were making a difference. And so as Mattie began to drift toward sleep, the soothing sounds of her friends' conversations moving more and more into the background, she said one or two more prayers. And then, even without putting her CPAP on, Mattie eased into a pleasant, comfortable sleep.

Chapter 38
The Debut

For two reasons, November 5 was going to be an important day for Rita Costello. First of all it was her birthday. She was looking forward to the delicious cupcakes Gloria always baked for staff members on their birthdays – cupcakes that were charmingly decorated too. There would also be a nice dinner that evening with extended family, including her cousins from Ohio who were in town. But the second matter? That was something quite different. For at 11:45, Rita was going to address a luncheon meeting of the local Kiwanis Club. And since the only public speaking she'd ever done had been to fellow offenders at a halfway house, it was no surprise that she had a bad case of nerves.

Rita had known about the speech for two weeks. Angie Stewart had called her in after one of the oral history sessions and asked her if she was ready to take the reins of the whole oral history program. Rita had been flattered and encouraged. And she took only a moment before saying yes; she'd be honored to do so. It would be a little intimidating to actually be in charge but Rita loved the program and had become quite involved already. Plus the basic procedures were already in place and working well. The school teachers, students, and church youth leaders who were involved knew the ropes. So did the representative of the state historical society who was cataloging the interviews.

Rita would now be the one who would set the schedule, recruit residents to participate, assure residents' families, do the paperwork, provide general encouragement and oversight to the young men and women doing the interviews, and handle the occasional public relations service. Like this luncheon talk to the Kiwanis group. Could she do it? Rita thought so but she was greatly encouraged by Angie who *knew* she could. "In fact, Rita," she had said, "I think you're just the person to take it to the next level. Even spreading the program to other facilities."

This particular invitation had come from a Kiwanis member whose mother-in-law was one of the first to participate in Villa Vista's oral history program. Winifred Battle had great fun having tea and cookies with two youngsters as she told her life story. Winnie's family listened to the audio recordings and were enthralled. They hadn't heard half of the stories and they found it gave them a deeper appreciation of Winnie's life and character. Winnie's son-in-law, Jack Drayton, had become a real cheerleader for the oral history program and he wanted his Kiwanis colleagues to know about it too.

Rita understood that this was a serious responsibility and she had been praying she wouldn't mess it up. She had worked hard in preparing her fifteen-minute speech and had delivered it twice for David Youngville. He had also helped prep her for the questions that might follow. Rita was a little shaky about the task but David had convinced her that was a good thing. "You're ready. Just be honest, humble, and let your natural enthusiasm for the program show through. You'll do really well."

Rita deeply appreciated Angie having confidence in her. And David? He hadn't only been a cheerleader and coach, he had provided Rita helpful inspiration. Just last week David had accepted his own public speaking challenge, to address an all-school assembly at his old high school. Zachary O'Rourke and Dr. Carlton had set it up. But it was David who found the courage to drive his wheelchair up on that stage. Once there, he spoke for 50 minutes – reliving the accident, describing the agonies afterward, and then sharing his pursuit of a meaningful life despite his physical limitations. David's bravery put Rita's speech in perspective and made her duty much easier.

Rita would never have thought a few months ago that David would ever tackle such a challenge. But he had changed so much since then. The most important factor in that change, Rita knew, was David's rediscovery of the Christian faith he had first accepted as a teenager. There was still an awful lot he had to struggle through and that would never change in his life. But the new friendships David had formed with Zachary and Carolyn and Ralph had started changing things dramatically. Spending time in the Christmas Room helped too. And recently David had become even more positive and confident as he connected regularly with Albert Trinisi, his sisters, and the Gritzner girls.

There was another element too but it was more mysterious to Rita. And that was those private conversations David frequently had with Clark Gritzner. No one really knew what was going on with that. Well, Rita thought that Zachary might know, but he certainly wasn't passing anything along. No, those closed-door meetings were a riddle. After all, two less-likely people couldn't be found for such intimate conversations. But something seemed to be happening for both men seemed different, especially Mr. Gritzner. He had become a model citizen in comparison to the short-tempered ingrate he had introduced himself to be. He now visited his mother frequently and treated her with affection. He showed respect and appreciation to Mrs. Trinisi and her family. And he had become a serious confidant to David.

What *was* behind it all? Rita smiled as she remembered Lois' conclusion. "What's to account for the change in Clark Gritzner? That's obvious, isn't it? Even Scrooge himself couldn't withstand the magic of the Christmas Room! The tree, the lights, those Christmas carols, the warm heart of Grace Trinisi. I'm telling you, they've all done their work. Without his knowledge, maybe against his will, old Clark Gritzner has been regularly breathing in the atmosphere of the Christmas Room for weeks. He can't help but be a changed man!"

Rita looked up at the clock and stopped her daydreams. She had to get going. She grabbed her blouse, a new frilly one she had bought herself as a birthday present, and went to the staff bathroom to change. She would wait to change into her heels until she got to the restaurant. As she emerged back into the hall, she saw David and Carolyn near the front desk. They were there to see her off, Rita was sure. Angie would have been there too but she was tied up in family meetings nearly all day.

"There she is," Carolyn said as she spied her. "We thought maybe we missed you. David and I wanted to wish you well."

David, sitting higher in his chair in recent weeks, a combination of his improved posture and a new form-fitting shell Zachary had ordered, was smiling broadly. "You'll do Villa Vista proud, Rita. We're all sure of that. Your only problem may be that Winnie's son-in-law will steal all of *your* time in bragging about the program himself."

"No," Carolyn offered. "I think he'll behave himself. I heard Winnie warning him yesterday to just introduce Rita and then get out of the way!"

David grinned and slightly shrugged his right shoulder, a new ability he had developed in the past couple of weeks. "Oh, in that case, he won't give you any problem. I can't imagine anyone crossing Winnie. Not even her son-in-law!"

David had become very fond of Winnie Battle. Every Friday afternoon at 2:30, the 92-year-old purchased a small packet of Hob Nobs, a British sweet biscuit that the Villa Vista residents' canteen sold. She then wheeled herself to David's room where she, David, and Dr. Bonney were waiting. The gentlemen would then escort Winnie to the

Christmas Room where Marsha Trinisi "played mother" and served tea and Hob Nobs to the gathered company. It was interesting to Rita that, even in Mattie's decline, weeks which were spent mainly in sleeping, she always managed to be wide awake for this half-hour tea ceremony. Was it the promise of good fellowship? The unique and delicious taste of the Hob Nob biscuits? Or, as Lois might suggest, was it just another example of the powerful magic of the Christmas Room? Rita wouldn't bet against it.

"I won't be gone long, Carolyn. I'll be back in time to hand out the Avon purchases after bingo. See you guys then."

Chapter 39
Blessings

Clark Gritzner had avoided talking with David Youngville for nearly three weeks now. Clark had continued to visit his mother but, because he came so early in the mornings and because he used the rear entrance that kept him away from the cafeteria where David often sat in the early morning, Clark could more easily miss seeing David. On those occasions when they did make contact, Clark had some excuse as to why he wasn't coming by. Clark had developed the habits of a liar, but he wasn't a very good one with David. But his embarrassment with David was the least of his worries nowadays. Whether it was from the sheer weight of his lies or the disgust he felt from lying to the people he loved, Clark was beginning to crumble. He realized the peace he had bought with a change of behavior and sale of the *Blue Wave* was both precarious and temporary.

David was well aware of Clark's deliberate avoidance. Yet he didn't worry too much about it. He cared for Clark and never stopped praying for him. But he knew the solutions to Clark's problems lay with Clark alone. Worry wouldn't help. Nor would further attempts at persuasion, entreaty, or coercion. Clark knew the answers. He now needed to act.

There were other reasons that David wasn't preoccupied with Clark Gritzner. In recent days, David's time and attention were increasingly spent elsewhere. Dr. Carlton and Zachary O'Rourke had arranged additional speaking engagements for David. One involved another high school where David would talk about the devastation caused by drunk and stoned drivers and, to be properly inclusive, drivers who were distracted by anything else. The second audience was a service organization at the university medical school. To that group David would tell his story of rehabilitation providing a vivid example to these students (all studying to be doctors, nurses, therapists, or pharmacists) that the disabled are fully persons with incalculable significance, beauty, and spiritual dignity. Thus they are persons deserving the highest quality of medical care.

There was another project that took much of David's time lately, an even more personal one. Patty Efron was a newcomer to Villa Vista and though she was 15 to 20 years older than David, she was still 25 years younger than most of the other residents. Patty had been brought to the city by her husband when her muscular dystrophy made life at their rural ranch home (some 300 miles away) very problematic. But it turned out that her husband had something else in mind for Patty besides a nursing home admission. On the very day he signed her in, he confessed that he had filed for a divorce.

"Patty, dear," he had explained. "I'm truly sorry about this and it doesn't mean that I haven't appreciated our 27 years of marriage. Well, except for the hell of these last couple of years. But, Patty, it isn't fair that this disease ruins two lives. So I had to do something. I need to get on with my own life. It's hard, I know. It's going to be hard on both of us but, when you think it out rationally, it's the best way. It's the way we can best express our love for each other. Otherwise, you would feel awful for, you know, forcing me to live shackled to your disease. No, it's better to make a clean break now. I know it's rather sudden but I talked it out with Reverend Sommers and he understands. It's better to do it quick and complete so we can start adjusting. You may not agree with my decision right now, Patty. That's okay. Because I still love you, I'll accept that. But, trust me, it's the best thing for both of us and I know you'll understand that some day."

And then, after a final kiss on the cheek "for good luck," he walked out on her.

Patty hadn't heard from him since. She didn't know where he was. She knew nothing about her financial situation. She didn't even know if she was still married or not. She was alone, helpless, very near despair.

And that's when the mission of Villa Vista began. First, Carolyn Kovacs reassured Patty that she wouldn't be abandoned nor would she go without any assistance that could be given. Carolyn explained in detail the various services they would provide for her – both for body and soul. Grant got her financial affairs in order along with the details regarding insurance, Medicaid, and her pension from the county school system where she had been a teacher. He even brought in the lawyers to persuade Patty's husband to provide extra financial help for her care. Other Villa Vista staff members stepped into the gap too, going the extra mile for Patty's needs. But Patty was so wounded and fragile that Carolyn doubted for a while whether she would come around. The final link in Patty's safety net, however, turned out to be another resident.

Zachary O'Rourke had introduced Patty to David Youngville the second week of her stay. Patty had refused to consider the aquatic exercise that Zachary knew would be calming and therapeutic for her. In fact, she was reluctant to pursue any treatment at all. Zachary was therefore hoping that David's testimony might change her mind. And David did just that. He explained to Patty how the pool had become a major part of his therapy – relaxing his mind and emotions, stimulating his self-esteem by offering a sweet taste of freedom and weightlessness, increasing the tensility so invaluable to his physical improvement. He urged her to give it a try. She could always say no to subsequent offers. David's manner intrigued Patty right from the start. For his physical limitations were far greater than hers at this stage of the disease. Yet he was amazingly confident, emotionally balanced, and other-directed. She agreed to try the pool and, after her very first experience, she knew she wanted to do it over and over.

That conversation was just the first offer of friendship from David to Patty and, along with the attentions from staff and a few other Villa Vista residents, she began to adjust to the new realities of her life. David in particular was a tower of strength to Patty, a role model and sincere friend. In those first few weeks, she leaned heavily upon David, finding inspiration in his spiritual perspective and hope, his patience and gratitude, his humor and kindness. But David wasn't content to be a *model*; he was more intent on being a *mentor*. And, under his influence, Patty began to find in her own faith those very virtues she needed to overcome the tragedies she had encountered.

Of course, David wasn't Patty's only friend. Indeed, it took a team effort to provide an adequate safety net for Patty Efron. She had been struck hard by MD but, as severe a test as that was, she could probably have passed that. But to be so callously discarded by her husband, the man she trusted, the man she loved so deeply? Well, that had come close to destroying her. Thus, Patty's help had come at the critical time and David wasn't the only one thanking God for bringing her to Villa Vista instead of a less caring nursing facility.

So it was that David, though well aware of Clark's absence, wasn't spending much time fretting over it. Nor was David all that surprised when he returned from one of his reading sessions to find Clark Gritzner sitting in the green chair by the window waiting for him.

David was careful to keep any condemnation or irony out of his voice. "Hello, Clark. It's good to see you. How's your mom today?"

Clark closed his eyes and sadly shook his head. "She's not

doing good at all, David. I don't think she has much longer."

David didn't want to exploit the emotional intensity of the moment but he felt it necessary to remind Clark of things they had spoken of before. "Clark, your mother will die. If not today or tomorrow, then next week or next month or who knows? But the sting of death has been removed from your mother's future because she has trusted in Christ as her Savior. And, among many other wonderful things, that means she has a glorious and happy life with Christ ahead of her. A forever life. Yes, death will take your mom, Clark. But death cannot hold her."

Clark never lifted his head. "You say that with such confidence. I just can't see how you can."

"We've gone over it again and again, Clark. It's not fantasy. It's not wishful thinking. It's simply common sense faith in the record of history and the revelation of God in the Scriptures."

Clark took a deep breath and finally looked up at David. "Yes, I know, David. And, as I've admitted, it does make sense the way you explain things. I suppose I'm even ready to believe it for someone like my mom. If anyone deserves heaven, she certainly does."

"But she *doesn't* deserve heaven," David interrupted. "And that's not slamming your mother. It's just telling you what she has tried to tell you herself a hundred times. The fact is that *none* of us deserves heaven. We're all sinners against God; we're short-sighted, self-centered traitors against the Creator. And yet Jesus paid the price for us all; He died in our place. He was the only One Who was sinless so He earned the right to be the perfect sacrifice, to take upon Himself the penalties of our sins."

"Yes. Yes. I remember, David. And I get it, really. I understand the concept. And I see that's how the Bible lays it out. I just…oh, I don't know."

David was silent. Clark was right. He had sufficient understanding of the gospel. Their talks had covered a lot of ground but the primary ideas had been stressed over and again. Clark had the information. David could do nothing to force him to trust in its truth.

Clark was silent for a long time too. He then looked out the window. He could see a crew from Trinisi Construction finishing up their fall efforts on the new landscape. It looked great.

"Want to know why I came by today?" Clark finally asked. But he didn't look at David as he talked.

"Of course."

"Zachary O'Rourke was in my office yesterday. He invited me out to lunch but I told him I couldn't take the time out of the office right then. He just smiled at me and said he thought that might be the case so he had planned for that very contingency. Then he sat down across from my desk, reached into his backpack, and pulled out a couple of meatloaf sandwiches, carrot slices, and Cokes. I didn't have a choice but to have lunch with him."

"He's a resourceful fellow." David smiled slightly. "Were the sandwiches any good?"

Clark shook his head impatiently, "Don't make jokes. You know that's not important. Don't you want to know *why* he wanted to have lunch with me?"

"Clark, I'm no good at these guessing games. Obviously you want to tell me. That's why you're here. So, go ahead; just tell me what's on your mind."

Clark continued to gaze out the window. How long ago was it that he wanted to drive a bulldozer when he grew up? Forget it. That was another life ago. He turned back to face David.

"He wanted my permission to ask Brenda to marry him."

"Hmm. That's a quaint idea. I haven't heard of that in a long while."

"Well, me either. But he was dead serious about it. And very calm. Confident. Polite on the surface but I figured he was determined to do so no matter what I said."

David considered that. "Yeah, I can imagine that. So what did you do? What did you tell him?"

Clark arched his brows and scratched his ear. "I asked him if it really mattered what my opinion was. And if I said no, would he ask Brenda anyway?"

"Okay, you've got me curious. What did he say?"

"Yes and yes."

"What do you mean, yes and yes?"

Clark shrugged his shoulders. "That's what I said. And he just grinned, took another bite of his sandwich, and said, 'Yes, it matters very much to me what you say. I desire your permission, even your blessing if you'll be so kind to bestow it. But, of the second question, yes again. For no matter what *your* answer is, Mr. Gritzner, I *am* going to ask Brenda to be my wife. I love her. I can't live without her. And I pledge to you that I will be the best husband to her that she could ever find. I swear this before God.'"

David gave a little whistle. "Wow."

"That's exactly what I thought. It certainly made whatever I said rather anticlimactic."

"But nevertheless he wanted your permission. That's pretty honorable, I think."

"I do too. And I believe him."

"You mean when he said he'd make Brenda the best husband she'd ever find?"

"Yes," Clark admitted. "I'm almost sure that he would."

"So you gave him your blessing?"

Clark looked back out the window. "Not exactly. I thanked him for asking me and I told him I was impressed very much with him and I had been ever since I met him. I also told him that I trusted him and I thought he would indeed make Brenda very happy. However, I asked him to do me one very big favor."

"And that was?"

"I asked him to give me two days before asking her. I figured I would have to explain why but he didn't ask. He stood up, extended his hand and shook mine firmly. 'Two days it is, Mr. Gritzner. I'll ask her on Saturday night.' And then he thanked me, cleaned up from our little picnic, and left the office."

A long silence followed before Clark turned to David reclining in that big white wheelchair. "Aren't you going to ask me why the two days?"

"Do you *want* to tell me, Clark?"

Clark paused before answering. "I wasn't going to. Not just yet." He took a deep breath and then walked over to close the door to the hallway. "I need a little space to take care of things long undone, David. They are things that might well cause the end of my marriage and I'm scared to death to do them. Zachary didn't force anything on me that shouldn't have been done on my own way before this."

David ventured no question. He had no guesses as to what was on Clark's mind. He would wait, as he had throughout these past several months, for Clark to state his own mind.

"I have confessions to make, David. I can't hide them anymore. I can't lie anymore. I won't even get the credit of confession from my own will. I'm confessing because I'm ready to get caught anyhow." Clark walked back to the window, his back to his friend. "I have a confession to make to my wife, Joanna. And to my daughters. And to my mother. And, God spare me, I suppose to my brother too." Clark slumped back down into the chair and let out a few heavy sobs before saying with a heavy heart. "And, David, I'm going to have to make a confession to the police as well."

Chapter 40
The Storm Breaks

Zachary was awakened early – way too early – by the ringing of his cell phone on the bedside table. It was Brenda.

"Hello?"

"Zachary, I'm sorry to call you so early. I'm sure you were asleep."

Zachary avoided the standard denial and openly admitted, "Yes I was. My alarm doesn't go off until…" He looked over at the clock radio, the one memento he possessed of his father's. It read 5:10 and he had to stifle a groan. "Until 7 o'clock."

"I know, I know. And believe me, I am really sorry but, Zach, I've wanted to talk to you since late last night but I've been trying to process everything. And I hoped to talk to you without crying."

Zachary sat up quickly. Brenda had his full attention now. "What do you mean, Brenda? What's going on?" He was aware there was a tightness in his chest. Processing? Crying? What was he about to hear?

Brenda suddenly realized she was sending the wrong signals. "It's not about you and me, Zach. Well, not directly. At least, I hope it's not."

"What then, honey? Is it your grandma? I looked in on her before I left yesterday and Lois said she was doing okay. Did something happen during the night?"

"No, no. It's not Grandma." Brenda paused but there was no easy way to break her news. "It's about my father."

"What about your father?"

Brenda thought she had cried out all her tears in these last sleepless hours but now, at the moment she had to tell Zachary her news, she found she still had more. Plenty of them. "My mother called Reggie and me late yesterday afternoon and asked us to come home by five o'clock. Neither of us thought we could make it but Mom begged us to come. She said it was very important and she needed us to come no matter what. And so we did. I think we both were thinking that Mom was going to tell us that she and Dad were splitting up. So, we both changed our minds and went over. And when we got there…" Brenda took a deep breath and tried to control her crying. "You see, Reggie had come by and picked me up from school and so we were together when we drove up. We had seen as soon as we turned the corner that both Mom's and Dad's cars were in the driveway but it wasn't until we got close that we saw a 'For Sale' sign stuck in the front yard."

"They're moving? Is that what the deal was?"

"Oh, Zachary." Brenda gave a sobbing sigh. "If that's all it was. No, it's a lot worse than that."

"Sickness?"

"No."

Thank God for that at least, Zachary thought to himself. Brenda remained silent on the other end and Zachary didn't feel like turning this into a guessing game. "Look, Brenda. I can be out of here in fifteen minutes. Why don't we meet for breakfast and we can talk in person."

Brenda had been hoping he would make such an offer. But she wasn't up to putting on a public face yet. "Zachary, I'd love to see you. Thank you so much. But could you come over here instead of us going out? No one is here except me and, if you have time, you could drop me off at school before you go to work."

"No one is there? Where is everyone?" Zachary had thought it would be better to talk this thing out in person but the mystery was getting to him. "Never mind that. You can tell me all about it when I get there. Give me forty minutes or so."

"Okay, Zachary. Thank you. I love you."

That tag line did wonders for Zachary but his mind continued to race through possibilities as he showered, dressed, and drove across town.

***

In the sorority house just a few miles from Zachary's apartment, Reggie Gritzner was unpacking her suitcase. She also had gone all night without sleep but she hadn't let a single teardrop fall. Reggie had taken the news as hard as her sister but her reaction had an angry, bitter edge. Reggie loved her mother and pitied her. But she had lost whatever respect she once had for her. It had been all she could stomach to see her mom and dad sitting close and holding hands as he made his confessions. "We'll get through this, girls. We'll stick together because we love one another and God will help us get through this. Don't worry." If what her dad had admitted hadn't already been enough to make one sick, her mom's naive, enabling pep talk did the job.

Reggie had sat there and taken in the whole scene. Her dad's disloyalty and secrecy and crime. Her mom's misguided dedication to "stand by her man." Even Brenda's spiritual strength. Or was it just a convenient retreat into religion, a retreat that kept the dishonor and meanness from touching her? No, that was a catty response. She knew Brenda had been heartbroken and ashamed too. But Reggie didn't have Brenda's sense of balance, her independence, her anchor to God. All that Reggie had was pain and rage. And a blazing desire to call it quits with her family. And so, when her dad was through telling his sordid story, Reggie had got up from the kitchen table where they were all sitting and walked out. Without a word. Without a sign of understanding or sympathy or, most definitely, forgiveness. Without even thinking of Brenda needing a ride home.

Reggie drove home with plans to make her emotional distance from her parents a physical one too. She packed two boxes and two suitcases of her stuff and carried them down to her car. In one part of her mind, Reggie knew this was a self-destructive act. She would lose her work for this whole semester. She would be endangering her future. And she would be losing Albert, the best chance she ever had to find love and happiness. But Reggie wanted to dramatize her disgust with her parents and somehow mask her own hurt and helplessness. Brenda could look to heaven for comfort. Reggie would have to settle for California.

Before heading west, however, Reggie wanted to say goodbye to her grandma. She could always see Brenda sometime in the future and there were cell phones, texts, and social media to keep in touch with her. But Grandma couldn't use these things very well anymore. Plus grandma was going to die soon. Everyone realized that. Reggie had to see her once more before she left town. She needed to hold her hand, kiss her cheek and say a personal goodbye. Reggie also wanted her grandma to give her one more blessing, to tell her once more that she loved her and would pray for her.

It was nearly two o'clock in the morning when Reggie drove into the well-lit Villa Vista parking lot. Familiar with the routine, she decided to knock on the nurses station window to let them know who it was that needed the front door open. Yoki Takahashi saw her and gestured for her to go on around.

"Good morning, Yoki. Is it okay if I slip in to sit with my grandmother for a few minutes? I'll be very quiet."

Yoki smiled and re-set the alarm. "Of course. She's sleeping pretty soundly tonight and she may not wake up before 5 or so. Even Mrs. Trinisi is sleeping good tonight so it's awfully quiet down there but I know she'd love to have you near." Yoki gave a little laugh. "And, of course, you know as well as anyone that it's always good for people to spend a little time in the Christmas Room!"

And it *was* good for Reggie. As it always did, the room radiated charm and peace. What a beautiful irony it was, thought Reggie, as she walked in. A spot of beauty and cheerfulness in the middle of a nursing home. A haven from the storm. An oasis in the desert. Reggie sat down near Mattie, the reflections from the Christmas tree lights making her grandmother, even with her wrinkled skin and her CPAP mask, look festive.

Reggie took Mattie's hand in hers. It took a few seconds for that gentle touch to register but it did. Mattie's eyes opened slightly and, after a few more seconds, she realized who was visiting her. Her eyes opened wider and she squeezed Reggie's hand. Then they closed again. But her grip on Reggie's hand stayed. In that slight pressure, Reggie felt anew the love and pride her grandma felt for her. And Reggie's tears finally fell.

Reggie sat there beside her grandmother for a little more than an hour. And in that hour, much changed for Reggie. The atmosphere of the Christmas Room calmed her and took away the most violent part of her anger. It stimulated memories of past Christmases with Grandma and Grandpa Gritzner too. And her Grandma Peterson. And Brenda. And Mom. And yes, even nice Christmases with her dad. The Christmas Room also reminded Reggie of the Trinisi family...one of them in particular.

Also, for a substantial part of that hour, Reggie was focused on Grace's nativity set on the windowsill. The electric candle in the window above lit it up brilliantly. It was pretty in a way yet provocative in another. Once, when she and Albert were sitting in the room, Albert had pointed to that nativity set and said, "That's Christmas right there. The tree, the lights, the music, and all the rest are terrific. But they're only decorations. Christmas itself is the historic event that little nativity set represents. God humbling Himself to be one of us and eventually dying for our sins. Christmas is the promise of forgiveness and redemption."

There in the early morning hours, enjoying the sweet glow of the Christmas Room, Reggie pondered those words of Albert's. At one point, she smiled at her own prejudices. For her sister had been talking like that for years. But it was only when it came from Albert that she had really listened. And in doing so, she saw it made sense. Forgiveness. It's a precious thing to receive. And also a precious thing to give.

And that's why the breaking of dawn found Reggie back in her room unpacking. She wasn't going to desert Grandma in this, her final trial. Nor was she going to drop out of school and lose everything she'd been working so hard for. And she certainly wasn't going to do something totally dumb like running away from Albert Trinisi.

But there remained, however, the huge problem of facing Mom and Dad. What course Reggie was going to take regarding *them* was still unknown. But she had decided on one thing at least this morning. Prompted by that little nativity scene, Reggie had determined not to add *anything else* to the list of things she needed to be forgiven for. No, she would stick this thing out.

***

At the time Reggie was doing her unpacking, Brenda was frying bacon and eggs in anticipation of Zachary's visit. A few miles away, Clark and Joanna Gritzner were both in the Christmas Room. They were waiting as Yoki helped Mattie from the bathroom and back into her bed. Mattie had slept well and, though still unsure if Reggie had actually been with her earlier or only in a pleasant dream, she felt rested and in good spirits. Clark felt terrible, knowing that he would soon change that.

"Mother, I've got something very important to tell you."

Chapter 41
Good News and Bad News

The excited talk of Villa Vista on that cool November morning was the news report that the Errol R. Rutledge Foundation had announced its decision to give a grant to Villa Vista Care Community totaling $1.7 million! It would be used specifically for the construction of an exercise pool and a combination greenhouse/sunroom, the plans to be grafted in to the Trinisi Construction blueprints for the already scheduled expansion. The Rutledge grant would also allow enough to buy Villa Vista a new medi-van of its own and to re-do the plumbing in the existing building. Carolyn Kovacs and her staff were overwhelmed. And the residents shared in their joy.

The feel-good spin emphasized by most of the news stories was that Mr. Rutledge's generosity had first been provoked because it was a Villa Vista staff member who had saved his life earlier that autumn. In the days following that near tragedy, Rutledge had contacted Ralph Yarborough and asked if there were any charities he liked to support. Rutledge had expressed his desire to show his appreciation to Ralph in some tangible way – besides the offer he had already made for Ralph's use of his Hawaii home for a vacation. Ralph said

sure and before the day was out, Rutledge had brought
checks for substantial donations to Joni and Friends,
Samaritan's Purse, and a local pregnancy care center to
present to Ralph Yarborough in person.

But the story hadn't ended there, for upon arrival at Villa
Vista, Errol R. Rutledge graciously accepted Ralph's
invitation to take him on a tour of the place. And Rutledge
had been very impressed. He talked to staff members and to
residents, one of whom he discovered was the mother of an
old college girlfriend. He even made an impromptu decision
to stay and have lunch at the cafeteria where he enjoyed
Gloria's take on mac and cheese with bacon. Rutledge told
Gloria later that it was one of the best meals he'd had in
years. And then, following lunch, Rutledge had a long
conversation in Carolyn's office with Carolyn, Grant, Lois,
and Greg. After that, he introduced himself to Dr. Bonney
whom he remembered watching play basketball when he
(Errol) was a kid. Finally, Dr. Bonney closed out Rutledge's
visit by taking him down to see the ladies in the Christmas
Room.

The photo op at the nursing home was originally supposed
to take 20 minutes of Mr. Rutledge's day. He ended up
staying almost four hours.

It was just the start. Mr. Rutledge was so intrigued and
challenged by what he had learned that he set up other
appointments with Carolyn, the Villa Vista board, Dr.
Carlton, Grant Katulka, Tony Trinisi, and Zachary O'Rourke.
He became convinced that Villa Vista deserved better
resources and that the business would use them wisely and to
a very good end. More than that, Errol Rutledge believed that
by helping the trend-setting Villa Vista Care Community, he
would be helping the industry as a whole.

There were, however, two members of the Villa Vista
community who, overjoyed as they were by the news of the
grant, had other things on their minds that morning. Indeed,
Zachary O'Rourke and David Youngville were aware of
another story, one that might well show up in *tomorrow's*

newspaper. If so, it would present no feel-good spin whatsoever. That story involved the confession Clark Gritzner had made to David the day before. To his credit – and Clark Gritzner now needed all the credit he could get – he had given a full account of his deeds, not bothering to hide or excuse things that were not only immoral, but also illegal. He was as brutally honest when, later that same day, he made his confession to Joanna and his daughters.

Clark Gritzner had committed fraud and forgery, maybe embezzlement too. He had faked the signatures of his mother and his brother on a contract. He had lied, and schemed, and cheated his family out of their inheritance. David wasn't a lawyer, but everything looked to him like Clark would soon be heading to jail – his reputation ruined, his pride destroyed, his family heartbroken and shamed. And, of course, David couldn't forget that in response to the moral guilt Clark experienced over these things, he turned not to his family, not to a minister, not even to a lawyer, but to booze.

As it turned out, Clark's story was not particularly uncommon, not in the first stages anyway. A dissatisfied man entering middle age starts living beyond his means. His ambition gets impatient, then desperate and he starts cutting corners, going further into debt. He buys a home on a golf course that he can't responsibly afford and then doubles down on his desire to impress his new friends by buying a luxury boat. Throw in a couple of poker games where he loses big and then a few disastrous nights at the casino where he was trying to recoup his losses and, no surprise, you've got a fellow in deep trouble who is ripe for being plucked. Yes, the get-rich-quick scheme that he eventually fell for did, at one time, look like it could help pull him out of his financial troubles. But union delays and other political obstacles to a riverfront development where he and two of his fellow employees invested threatened to destroy the whole plan. There would be, in the short run, no return at all on his investments. And he had bills to pay, very pressing bills.

Even at this point, however, Clark Gritzner could have

survived. He could have sold the boat, sold the house, sold one of his cars, and still saved something of his credit. But he didn't want to cut his losses. And when Arlen, one of his partners, suffered a heart attack, he and Glenn were forced to come up with Arlen's third or lose the whole thing. Clark wrote a check from his mother's account to cover his part, the account that was supposed to pay for her expenses until she passed away. Then the county changed the zoning code, creating a dramatic increase in the land price. Clark removed another chunk of Mattie's account to keep the deal alive.

That was when the drinking started. And the trips to Chicago where Clark attempted to secure a loan based on the expectation of Mattie's death. Clark hadn't seen the will. Mattie had made that when she was still living in Chicago. But he was sure he was in for a windfall after they sold the house, the extra land on the lake, and the hardware store. So, even though he couldn't touch that money now, he figured that someone from his old firm or even his college fraternity would be willing to make a high-interest loan for such a sure and imminent payoff. But he couldn't find anyone interested. And the pressure kept building.

There were two brief flickers of hope last summer, one from a cousin and another from a former client who worked for a multinational electronics company. Both responded positively to his offer and Clark signed promissory notes using the hardware store as collateral. He did this knowing all too well that it wasn't his to sell – now or, quite possibly, ever. But had either one of those big loans gone through, Clark would have been fine. He could have replaced the money in his mother's account, got caught up in his bills, and still had the money to swing the riverfront deal. True, he was risking a serious hassle with his brother and that could result in his losing a big slice of his inheritance. But that wouldn't matter. By that time, he would have secured his *own* future and then some with his shrewd dealing. Everything would be okay…more than okay. And even things at home would go back to normal.

However, both of those deals fell through in just one afternoon. In fact, the rejections came less than an hour apart. Both men had called him on his cell phone with terse, angry slap downs. His cousin had been the first. "Clark? You can count me out of that loan. And there's nothing more to be said except this – I've done you a big favor, cousin, because I've torn up that promise. Now, if I never hear from you again, that's going to be fine in my book." He had then hung up. The second call was similar in tone and he too gave notice that the document Clark had given as security had been destroyed. What had happened, Clark had no idea. But it put him in very deep trouble.

The rest of his mother's account was eventually drained in his efforts to keep creditors at bay and to keep Glenn from doing anything foolish like pulling out. Clark knew he was committing a crime with every check he wrote from his mother's account but he couldn't stop. He just kept hoping he could replace the money before anyone knew. With Joanna still completely in the dark, Clark sold off his guns and then his share in the country club. He went so far as to forge Joanna's signature in order to sell several shares of their railroad stock. But then, the day after the city council voted against the *very idea* of the riverfront development, Clark knew it was all over. He was finished. If he was lucky, he might get a quarter of his investment back. The sale of the *Blue Wave* was to buy him a little time. But when his mother died, Clark knew that his crimes would be exposed and he would lose it all – his family, his job, his freedom.

Yet, even during the desperation of these past months (perhaps because of them), David Youngville knew there were other forces working in Clark Gritzner's life. Their long conversations had revealed that Clark had not been a happy man for a long time, long before his money troubles began. But at least now he was a man made forcefully aware of how desperately broken and woefully self-centered he was. The tantrum he had thrown that first day visiting his mother in Villa Vista had been a searing moment of realization. And as the months wore on, he began to understand how disloyal and mean he had been to his mother, his wife and daughters, his employers, and yes, for many, many years, his brother too. The glaring contrast he now saw between himself and his family, even between himself and many of the people at the nursing home, especially David Youngville, was startling. It greatly disturbed him. Finally, the hours of reflection he had spent in the Christmas Room holding his mom's hand made him deeply desire an escape, not only from his financial troubles, but from the man he had become.

Clark had been surprised that his confession hadn't turned David Youngville against him. He thought for sure it would end their friendship and that such a religious, morally upright person would feel nothing but revulsion at Clark's litany of crimes. But David hadn't acted that way at all. His response, in fact, was perplexing.

David had listened quietly to Clark's long monologue and, at the end, said but a few words. "Clark, thank you for telling me this. Now, of course, you must immediately tell your wife and daughters the same. Your mother too. Hold nothing back, just like you did with me. And then listen to this, Clark. An honest confession to the people whom you have wronged may be the hardest thing you ever do but it will serve as an opportunity to begin to get things straight. No matter what else happens, keep in mind that getting things straight with those who love you, and that includes God, is more important than anything else. You may well end up in jail. You could lose everything you once thought was so desirable. But, as I know better than most, it sometimes takes the end of one's first life to give a second, richer life a chance."

Chapter 42
A Family Meal

The whole Trinisi family sat around the table at Nick's Ristorante enjoying their dessert, coffee, and each other's company. Grace sat immediately to Tony's right and they were deep in conversation, Grace relating to him stories of the cardinals that lived in the burning bushes outside her window. She credited their choice of homestead to her son and his birdfeeders. "You must be giving them special food because they come to eat there several times a day. I love having them; they're so pretty and entertaining. And you can tell they love each other. They get along so nice."

Tony loved evenings like this. His mom was feeling good. She had energy. And she was more alert and conversant even though they had really stretched her limits tonight. Tony had picked her up on his way from work. It involved more effort to get her up into the truck but a double step he had made just for his mom made it safe. It was always worth it because Grace loved riding in the truck more than anything. She said it reminded her of riding with Frank in the old days, days of hauling things to build their houses or even before the kids when a truck was their only vehicle. Grace had eventually learned to drive that first truck, a blue Ford with a long-handled gearshift coming out of the floor. But it had taken her a while. Frank used to tease her by telling his friends that Grace had learned to drive that truck pretty easy. All it had required was a new transmission, two new clutch assemblies, and four months of the patience of Job. Grace remembered that joke on the way home and told it to Tony with great gusto. Tony liked that story. In fact, he liked it every time she told it.

Marsha and the girls had dinner waiting for Tony and Grace when they got to the house. Albert and Reggie pulled in right behind them. The plan was to have a quick meal, divide into two vehicles, and follow the route Ann had laid out to look at the best displays of Christmas lights. That would take an hour or so and they would then drive over to Nick's for their dessert.

It seemed that every year revealed less enthusiasm for Christmas from people in the city. There were fewer houses and yards decorated. And even the ones that did try to demonstrate some Christmas spirit didn't select nativity scenes, angels, or even Santa Claus. Instead, they went for polar bears, snowmen, and giant Disneyesque creatures blown up with air.

"Weird." That was the word Grace used throughout the night to express her response to these untraditional displays. Yes, there was from her lips the occasional "beautiful" and "wonderful" and "lovely" as they drove through the most decorated neighborhoods. But "weird" seemed to be the word she used more often than any other.

Still, they had a lot of fun. Tony, Marsha and Grace were in one car with Albert, Reggie, Ann, and 13-year-old Margie in the other. Well, that was for the first half of the route. Then Marsha traded places with the girls. In both cars, there was Christmas music, Christmas trivia, and, as Andy Williams sang in "It's the Most Wonderful Time of the Year," "stories of Christmases long, long ago." Marsha and Margie tried to get video clips of the best displays but with limited success. Then, over the coffee, cocoa, and pie at Nick's, there were more stories.

But not all of the stories this year were about Christmas. Clark Gritzner was also on the menu.

Tony and Marsha had, of course, heard about Mr. Gritzner's troubles but not, as the Gritzner girls once feared, from any newspaper account. In fact, there had been no newspaper account. All the Trinisis knew was what they had learned from Grace over the months. And they had taken that with more than a grain of salt. For not only did Grace get things in parts – and those often confused – Tony and Marsha realized that what their mom learned mostly came from Mattie who was even weaker in understanding than she. They figured Albert probably knew a lot more, but Tony had expressly directed him to keep a lid on it unless and until Reggie gave him permission. And Albert had carefully heeded that command.

But still there was an expectation that something might come up tonight. It was the first time that Marsha and Tony would see Reggie (except for a couple quick contacts at Villa Vista) and Albert had dropped a couple of hints that she wanted to talk to his parents about everything that had happened. It was Grace, however, who brought up the subject as she suddenly looked up from her cocoa, a frothy whipped cream mustache on her lip, and said, "Did you kids hear that Mattie's boy isn't going to jail after all?"

Tony didn't embarrass easily but this question almost did the trick. "No, Mom. We hadn't heard that." He looked over at Reggie with an "I'm sorry" look. "But that's good news, huh?"

Grace gave her son a mischievous smile, made all the more endearing with that line of whipped cream. "Well, son, you oughta know more than anyone here that that's good news. Jail is no party, is it?"

"No, Mom. It sure isn't." Tony had never sought to hide his misspent youth from his family but it was rarely referred to. And it had never been fully detailed...except to Marsha before they married and to Albert when the subject came up on a hunting trip with just the two of them. Tony figured that Albert had maybe passed along the general idea of those things to Reggie. But he took it in stride. "And you're right. I oughta know."

Tony said that last line with a little hint of pain which his mother caught. "I'm sorry, Tony. I was trying to make a joke but it wasn't a very good one. It's all so long ago. God forgave you and we forgave you – and you became such a different man since those days. I'm sorry, son."

Reggie took the opportunity to redirect the conversation. She directed her first remarks to Tony but, as she got further into her story, she shifted eye contact to make sure she was addressing the whole Trinisi family. "It's true. Dad isn't going to jail. But he might have except that he ended up getting the strangest reprieve. I'll tell you about that part in a minute. Let me explain first just what happened."

Reggie proceeded to review the whole sorry tale – Clark's poor business deal, his gambling losses, his drinking. Nor did she leave out the embezzlement and fraud. Her mood lightened a bit when she described her father's confession to his family but before that, it had been very difficult to get through. In fact, to do so, Reggie's manner had been somewhat distant. Not angry. Not vindictive. Not excusing or blaming anyone else. But Reggie told her story dispassionately because it was the only way she *could* tell it, especially to the parents and sisters and grandmother of the young man she loved.

Albert helped her get through the ordeal by holding her hand. He admired her courage and he knew how tough and embarrassing it was for her to recount her father's deeds like this. But Albert also knew this was an almost easy task compared to the one she still struggled with. That was forgiving her dad for those deeds.

Having made it through the most painful part of her story, Reggie relaxed a bit when she started to describe the twists and surprises that saved her father from jail. "Before Dad made his confession to us, he had already told David

Youngville at Villa Vista. David had arranged to have his own lawyer accompany Dad to the police station the next morning. They were there for several hours, Dad giving statements, giving access to his records and accounts, detectives interviewing him, and doing a lot of waiting in between. I suppose the detectives were checking out the things he told them. Anyhow, it was almost three o'clock before they let him go home but even the lawyer told him it looked pretty bleak. The policemen had told them that they would be passing everything over to the city prosecutor for the next steps. Dad had expected to be put in jail right then and he felt that was what he deserved. And, at Dad's explicit instructions, the lawyer hadn't interfered much. My dad wanted everything that was coming to him. No more excuses. No more wiggling on the hook. I think it was because it had really sunk in just how harmful and selfish his actions had been."

Reggie paused and looked at Albert sitting at her side. She squeezed his hand and he could tell she was again near the breaking point. Tears were forming in her eyes. Albert asked gently, "Shall I tell them the rest?"

Reggie nodded. "Please."

Albert took over. "Well, as you can imagine, this was all agonizing to Reggie's father. But then again, telling the police hadn't been half the heartbreak that telling his wife and daughters and his mother already had been."

Without thinking, Ann interrupted, "You mean he told Mattie too?"

Reggie shook her head yes but it was Albert who spoke. "Yes, he did. In fact, Sis, Mr. Gritzner told Mattie early in the morning before he went to the police station. That was just a few sleepless hours after he told Joanna and the girls."

"Oh, my. That must have been awfully sad." Ann said. "Did she even understand him? What was her reaction?"

"That's the first of the surprises," Albert said with a slight smile, "the first of those miracles that Reggie hinted at. Her mom told us about it later because she had been there too.

Mr. Gritzner began by telling Mattie he had something important to tell her, something that he did that was very bad, something that was unforgivable. And Mattie – you know how she's best in the early morning – Mattie told him strong and clear as a bell, 'Clark, nothing is unforgivable. Now tell me, what did you do?'"

"That's when Mr. Gritzner started to cry. Joanna told us that she had *never* seen him cry. Well, not since Brenda disappeared from the playground when she was 7. They found out later she had followed a dog into the forest where she got lost. But before they found her, I guess he sobbed like a baby thinking the worst. Anyhow, I'm off track. Mr. Gritzner cried all the way through but he made a full confession to Mattie. And I mean full. He even told her how he had held it against her for having forgiven Durward so easily after he had gone to prison when he was a young man. He talked too of how he blamed her for his own ego problems. He even admitted he had resented her living too long because it kept him from getting his inheritance and being able to avoid all his troubles."

Reggie looked over at Ann. "So you can see how talking to the police was a lot easier."

"Wow." It was all Ann could say. Yet it expressed what the entire Trinisi family was feeling.

"But here's the miracle." Albert picked up the story again. "After Mr. Gritzner made it through all this, Mattie just asked him one question. She said, 'Are you sorry for what you did, son?' He answered that he was very, very sorry but he knew that didn't matter. What he had done was despicable and he had no excuse. He was ready to accept whatever punishment the law gave him but it would never be enough to cover what he had done to her."

"But then his mother reached over and rubbed his head, just as if she was remembering how she did it when he was a little boy. They both stayed that way for a long time, until Mr. Gritzner was all cried out. And when Mattie spoke again, she did so to Joanna. 'Take him home now, honey. He needs some rest and I've got to talk to his brother.' And then she told Mr. Gritzner, 'Clark, I forgive you, son. And I still love you…very much. Things will work out all right. You go on home now and I'll see you tomorrow maybe.'"

Reggie took a tissue from her purse and dabbed her eyes, then blew her nose. "Now for the next surprise. The police called Dad the next afternoon. They explained how the prosecutor, after obtaining statements from both Grandma and Uncle Durward, had decided the case wasn't worth bringing to court. A Lieutenant Romero told him, 'Quite frankly, Mr. Gritzner, I believe you. You're probably as guilty as sin of embezzlement and forgery. Maybe a couple of other charges too. But your mother's and brother's testimonies differ significantly from yours and, without their cooperation, there's no way to convict you.'"

"'What do you mean?' Dad asked him. 'I told you and your colleagues exactly what I did. There's no doubt at all they were crimes.'"

"'Mr. Gritzner, with what your mother and brother said, a judge would have a lot more than doubt. Your wife can't be forced to testify against you. You're safe from that quarter. And neither your mother nor brother has any interest in criminal proceedings against you. They insist it's all a matter of misunderstanding. You can't embezzle money from a person who gives you authority to take it. That's exactly what your mother told Sergeant Lajeck. And your brother up in Chicago verified it. He told us that he and your mother spoke of this several times when she was…shall I say, in more control of her faculties. Your brother says that you tend to be irresponsible and inept when it comes to money matters, but that's the extent of it.'"

"Well, that just floored Dad. He told Lieutenant Romero there must be a mistake. He explained that Durward would never have allowed their mother to let him spend her money. Dad told him, 'Look, Lieutenant. God knows I've never given my brother any reason to want to protect *me*. So, it must be to protect my mother from hurt or scandal. He's not telling the truth. I'm sure he didn't know anything about my wasting my mother's account.'"

"The lieutenant just laughed at Dad, not a friendly laugh either. He said, 'Mr. Gritzner, I don't know why your brother is standing up for you either. I sure wouldn't bother. But that's what he says and that's what he would testify to if he was ever called into court. By the way, your brother even gets you off the hook from the fraud charge. Somehow he discovered your claim to own a hardware store in Chicago and use that as collateral for loans. I'm sure he was the one that threw the wrench in the works to stop you. And then he went further to save your hide by having the evidence of your attempts destroyed. Like I said, Mr. Gritzner, I know you're guilty. But I guess family is family, and yours is willing to let you get away with what you've done to them. And man, if that's not enough to persuade you to get yourself together, I don't know if anything ever will. So goodbye, Mr. Gritzner, and I hope I never hear your name again.'"

There was complete silence around the table for a long time. Ann finally said again, "Wow. So it's all over?"

Reggie sighed. It was clear that she was relieved to have finally told the Trinisi family what had happened. "Well, I guess so. As far as the court is concerned. But there's a lot of other stuff. Mom and Dad are selling the house. Dad lost a promotion at work after he admitted to his supervisor about lying but, in another act of grace, his boss kept him on. Plus Dad has picked up an extra job working at a rental car agency four nights a week. He's really serious about paying back everything he took from Grandma and Mom. I think he's serious too about making a new start in other things, taking advantage of the miracles that were given him."

"And a new start is all that me and Mattie have been praying for!" All eyes turned to Grace. She had a broad smile on her face and her eyes glistened with happy tears. "And when God gives a person a new start, those miracles don't stop. They just keep coming." She patted Tony's hand, "Don't they, son?"

Tony looked around the table at the best miracles God had given him after *his* new start: Marsha, Ann, Margie, Albert, and now perhaps, Reggie. "They sure do, Mom. They sure do."

Chapter 43
The Busiest Month of the Year

December is the busiest month in a nursing home's year. For not only must the facility staff handle all the regular duties of caring for their residents, they also have problems of warmth, energy costs, snow and ice removal, and holiday scheduling. On top of all this, December is chock-full of volunteers who need to be accommodated. Eleven months out of the year, nursing homes go with hardly a thought in the general community. Loneliness and boredom, disillusionment and suffering, are year-round ills in a nursing home. Yet it seems that the consciences of church folks, civic groups, and high school choirs wait for the ringing of Christmas bells to remember the nursing homes in their neighborhoods. Then they show up in droves ready to do a program. And all too frequently, they are then impatient and demanding about doling out their generosity. Not that Carolyn Kovacs or Angie Stewart failed to rejoice whenever community volunteers asked to come in and serve the residents of Villa Vista. But, to be honest, December volunteers often provoked more headaches than blessing.

Angie and Rita Costello were explaining a few of those headaches to their boss this morning. Most of them involved scheduling and weren't too much of a problem but Angie did have some more serious complaints. For instance, one of the captains of a civic organization's caroling crew (there are a stocking full of carolers every December) had insisted that the Villa Vista staff assemble all the residents in the cafeteria for a "program" that would last three songs only. Well, two songs actually. The third was the men singing, "We Wish You a Merry Christmas" as they exited and headed back to their bus! This particular fellow had sent Angie an e-mail that morning which stated, "We are on a very tight schedule. And because we have nine other places to sing that day, we may be either early or late. Therefore, make sure the audience is assembled in full up to 15 minutes before our scheduled start. Also, it has been noted in previous years that some of the facilities where we entertain allow people who are disengaged, sometimes even distracting. Please try to keep such people from attending. Please be aware also that the men in our Christmas Chorus are giving freely of their time and do so in the generous and festive spirit of the season. So we would greatly appreciate audience members showing appropriate appreciation for the choir that is bringing them this holiday gift. We suggest that staff members lead the patients in applause after each musical number. This will help encourage the choir members to be motivated to continue this outreach to your facility in the future."

Carolyn closed her eyes and shook her head. Under her breath, she whispered, "Lord, give me strength."

Angie didn't bother to hide her annoyance. "You see what I mean? Please, Carolyn, can I just write back and tell this yo-yo not to bother?"

"No, you'd better not do that," her boss cautioned. "Although he does have some nerve, doesn't he?"

"Nerve isn't the word that first came to my mind, Carolyn. I mean, really! For this guy, it's all about the comfort of his precious choir. The nursing home residents themselves? They exist merely to applaud him and his buddies. This fellow couldn't care less about the residents. No kidding, Carolyn, guys like this drive me nuts."

Carolyn looked over at Rita. "Angie certainly has a point. What do *you* think, Rita?"

Rita was slow to answer. She was, after all, awfully new at this and having her opinion asked for was nice but also pretty intimidating. She tried her best. "Well, this man obviously has no idea of what it takes to get residents down to the cafeteria. And a lot of them would undoubtedly be upset to go through all that just to hear a couple of songs and then be shuttled back to the rooms. So, in that sense, I agree with Angie that it doesn't seem worth it. However, I suppose there's always the matter of public relations that you have to worry about and we don't want to get you or Villa Vista on somebody's bad list. So it would be kinda hard to just tell this group to jump in a lake, right?"

Carolyn laughed. Rita had proved to be quite a find. Compassionate, a good worker, creative, wonderful with the residents, and bright. Carolyn was delighted (but not surprised) that Rita was growing into the new job so well. "Right," she answered. "We probably should avoid telling him *that*. And yes, there are always public relations to consider. But there's also the constant hope that some of these Christmas-only folks will see or hear or feel something when they're here that will make them want to come back and visit during other times of the year. Remember, that's how Vicki and Shirley got involved in doing ladies' nails."

"And Mrs. Tandey," Angie interjected. "She first came as part of a Christmas caroling group from her church. And from that one visit, we've now got the sing-along parties going strong." She chuckled and softly punched Rita in the shoulder. "Jump in a lake! That's a good one. And, of course, you're right, Carolyn. I'm done squawking…for a little while, at least."

Carolyn nodded. "Thanks. I know we would all love to have these December volunteers distributed throughout the year. It would be worlds better for the residents and an awful lot easier for us. But we've got to work with what we've got."

Carolyn rose to indicate the meeting was over. "Angie, what *will* you do to accommodate your nagging choir director?"

"Well, not what I'd like to do, Carolyn, so don't worry. No, I've already talked to Marsha Trinisi and asked if she could open the Christmas store early. I explained the situation to her and she's really gonna be a help. She said she would bring some girls from her church to sing a bunch of carols *after* the men's choir runs back to their bus. That way we're rousting the residents for a longer program and they won't feel cheated. What do you think?"

Carolyn beamed. "I think that's a marvelous idea. Very clever. The residents will like that a lot and it will be a great help to the staff. Thanks."

When Angie and Rita left the office, Carolyn returned to her desk for another forty-five minutes of work before her next scheduled appointment, this one with Lois Vendee to discuss tomorrow's family meetings. These "care plan" meetings were very important as they kept family members up to date on the condition and needs of their loved ones. At these meetings, representatives of the various branches of care were on hand: nursing, dietary, social services, activities and, when necessary, rehabilitation and the business office. Sometimes other staff members were present if they could shed light on some specific patient event. They met with family to make sure communication remained clear, full, and smooth – both ways. Carolyn tried to attend these meetings on occasion, especially when problems were anticipated or when major changes were imminent. Sometimes though, she came along to communicate special thanks to the resident's loved ones for their interest and cooperation. Since there were no problems on the horizon for the meetings tomorrow, the time Carolyn spent with Lois going over the agenda went pretty quickly.

The rest of Carolyn's morning was taken up with scheduling, a complex and ongoing task that involved not only her own staff, but off-site appointments that residents had with doctors and dentists. By 12:30 she was more than ready for a sandwich made out of the meatloaf Gloria had prepared as the main entrée for the residents' lunch. Before that, she wanted to take the revised schedule to the rehab unit in order to get Zachary to sign off on it.

But Zachary wasn't there, something Carolyn should have remembered. He was at a meeting with the architects who would be creating the exercise pool. She looked at her watch and realized he wouldn't be back for an hour or more. She thought of her sandwich again and decided to get to her lunch. On her way back to her office she stopped at the nurses station in the south wing. Greg Kwan, the physician's assistant was at the desk. Kendra London was filling the cups for midday meds, and Kate Stanwyck was unloading the lunch trays.

Carolyn asked no one in particular, "How are things going down here today? I know you're all awfully busy." They all knew this was an understatement and it drew a few chuckles. After all, this section had a new admission this morning, three residents to prep for doctor's appointments, and the aftermath of a manic episode with Mr. Orloff in which he had assaulted his roommate. Then, if that weren't enough, they had the responsibility of shuttling residents back and forth to the cafeteria for Christmas entertainments.

Kendra's smile helped reassure Carolyn that, though taxing, the responsibilities were being borne well. "Busy is right but they're okay. You heard about Mr. Orloff but he's in bed asleep now and we moved Mr. Campbell into 19. Mrs. Garcia is in the hospital still – recovering fine, we've heard – but they probably won't release her to come home until Thursday at the earliest. So a private room was all Mr. Campbell needed for a while. He was more perplexed than angry and so he took it pretty well. He wasn't hurt at all but it kinda shook the rest of us up."

"You fill out an incident report yet?" Carolyn asked.

Greg spoke without looking up. "That's what I'm finishing right now. I'll bring it in before I take off for lunch."

"Great. Thank you both. I've already heard you all handled

the whole thing very calmly and professionally. So, again, thanks and good job."

"Oh, Carolyn. One other thing." Kendra lowered her voice. "Mattie Gritzner has been in decline for some time now, as you know. But we had a tough time waking her up this morning and even with the diuretics, we are starting to lose the battle with fluid buildup."

"I've increased the dosage," Greg said with a sense of resignation. "But I have doubts it will do much at this stage. I'm going to swing by this evening. I have to look at that wound on Dr. Bonney's leg anyway – and if she hasn't improved, I'll send her over to the hospital."

Greg's despondency was apparent. Carolyn asked him, "And?"

"And...I don't think she'll ever come back here."

Carolyn sighed. This was never easy. She had never got used to the pain of losing people who had become dear to her. Thank God she hadn't. She nodded to Greg. "Thanks for telling me. I think I'll go down and see her. If you're right, Greg, it might be my last chance to say goodbye."

Carolyn couldn't remember approaching the Christmas Room with anything but an anticipation of warmth and good cheer. But not today.

Chapter 44
Goodbye and Hello

Mattie Gritzner surprised everyone by rallying and enjoying the best three days she had experienced in the past couple of months. But Greg Kwan was pretty certain that her improvement had little to do with anything he had prescribed. He firmly believed the change was due solely to the fact that Mattie's eldest son Durward had come to visit her from Chicago. The medicine of having Durward there, sitting and talking comfortably with Clark (from whom he had been estranged for years), was an elixir that he couldn't hope to match.

But Greg wasn't surprised either that this respite lasted only for those three days. And somewhere around two o'clock in the morning, after a long evening in which Mattie had sat up in bed for wonderful reminiscences with her family about Christmases past, the sweet lady died in her sleep.

Yoki Takahashi had checked on her just a half hour earlier and, at that time, her CPAP was operating smoothly and Mattie was breathing comparatively well. She had a fairly strong pulse, good color, and only a hint that she might be accumulating some more water around her heart. But when

Yoki came in later, she found Grace Trinisi sitting by Mattie's bedside. Grace had figured out how to unclip the cord that set off a buzzer and sent a signal to the nurses station whenever she was getting out of bed. Also, in what was quite a feat, Grace had managed to get to her friend's bedside without using her wheelchair or her old walker. Yoki found Grace crying softly as her hand smoothed out Mattie's hair. She looked up and said simply and softly, "Honey, Mattie died a little while ago. The poor thing, her body is already turning cold. I think you better call her boys."

***

Mattie Gritzner's funeral was a very small affair held in the chapel at the mortuary. Having spent almost all of her days in Chicago and outliving all of her contemporaries, there was no one to attend save the family, a couple of neighbors who had briefly known her, and some of the Villa Vista family. Joanna had suggested they keep the mortuary service as simple as possible and concentrate instead on a more meaningful memorial at Villa Vista. And that's what they did. Clark asked Tony Trinisi to lead things. After all, Mattie had become almost as attached to the Trinisi family as to her own in this last year. And he knew that Tony was a lay preacher or deacon or something at his church, so he'd know how to organize the service a lot better than he or Durward would.

Tony accepted the task and arranged a program with brief Scripture readings, a couple of old hymns that he knew were Mattie's favorites, and prayers. For his part, Tony didn't deliver a sermon. He only took a few minutes to explain the gospel and how Christmas, just a few days away now, was the promise of salvation that Easter eventually guaranteed. He told also of how Mattie had often spoken with confidence and joy about trusting Jesus as her Savior years earlier. The rest of the memorial service was given to remembrances and tributes by those who knew her best. Attending the ceremony were several Villa Vista residents and a dozen staff members including Carolyn, Zachary, Rita, Yoki, Ron, Greg, Angie, Zemi, and Ralph.

Tony had asked his mom if she wanted to say anything but she had said no. She would rather tell Mattie's family a few things in private later, maybe back in her room. That was fine. But others took Tony up on his offer. Brenda told some very sweet stories about her grandma. Joanna talked about her first encounters with Mattie and how her mother-in-law lovingly embraced her as the daughter she never had. Rita spoke of a late-night conversation between Grace and Mattie and herself, a conversation that had a life-changing effect on her.

When Rita finished and no one else rose to speak, Tony stood and made one last invitation. "When we finish here, Gloria has made coffee and tea and the girls have prepared some desserts so we can continue to share stories of Mattie's life. But before we have a final prayer, is there anyone else who would like to say anything?"

There was a moment of awkward silence with most of the eyes in the place decidedly avoiding Clark Gritzner. In Tony giving this last chance for someone to speak, everyone assumed he was doing it for Clark's benefit. And he was. But Clark sat quiet and unmoving, his gaze fixed on the floor in front of him.

Tony didn't drag it out. "Okay, then, let's take a moment…"

"Excuse me, Tony. I think I want to say something too…if it's okay." The delinquent speaker wasn't Clark, however. It was Durward.

Tony smiled. "Of course, Durward. Thank you." He motioned for the large man from Chicago, the "lost son" of Mattie Gritzner, to please come forward and take the floor.

Durward got up cautiously. He was a man with bad knees and it showed in his movement. Still, Durward was a tall, commanding presence, especially compared to the smaller and more fragile younger brother. Tony suspected that whatever else had separated the brothers in their past, Clark was almost certainly intimidated by Durward. But that alone could hardly justify the protracted and profound distance that had existed between them.

"I'm not in the habit of public speaking and I hadn't planned on doing so this morning. But, as Tony started to close things off, I realized there was at least one thing I needed to say to this gathering." For a person unused to public speaking, Durward was unusually effective. Diction, confidence, timing, eye contact. Tony smiled inwardly and thought, "This gentleman is much more than what he initially shows."

Durward continued. "That necessary thing is simply this…I want to express for the whole Gritzner family our deepest appreciation for the excellent care and tender mercies shown to our mother and," Durward nodded to Joanna and the girls, "to our mother-in-law and grandmother by the Villa Vista staff. I cannot name all of those who my mother mentioned by name in our phone conversations but you were all quite precious to her. She never had a complaint. She never voiced disappointment or worry. You made her feel safe and encouraged. And there's no doubt that you not only extended Mom's life, you enriched it."

"And, Tony, to you and Marsha, Ann, Margie, Albert and, most especially, to you, Grace, our family wants to express our undying respect and affection. Your contributions to my mother…*our* mother, were every bit as important as the part played by the facility staff. You showed love to Mattie. And it was the sweetest, most sincere, most uplifting love there is. We are tremendously grateful to all of you as well."

Durward paused for a moment. He looked down at his brother but Clark's gaze was still directed to the floor. It didn't matter. Durward's message wasn't for him alone. "You know, it is no exaggeration to say, the day our mother met Grace and made a new home in the Christmas Room was a day that would change not only *her* life for the better. It changed our whole *family* for the better."

A sob, not a loud or unwelcome one, burst from Reggie

Gritzner and her sister reached over and grabbed her hand. Joanna put her arm around her. And as Reggie quietly wept and Durward continued his remarks, Clark finally looked up. There were tears in his eyes too. And something else too, Tony thought. Gratitude? Maybe. Respect? Almost certainly.

Durward continued, "Through Mom's moving into the Christmas Room, she met the best friend she's had since her husband died almost 33 years ago. And she became part of a loving, loyal family – the kind I'm afraid she hadn't personally enjoyed for a long, long time. And in that family, and in the spirit of the Christmas Room, our mother's love for Christmas and its holy purposes were re-discovered. I am so, so grateful to God for that. And grateful to you, Grace, and your family, and to Villa Vista."

Durward was aware that Reggie wasn't the only one crying now and he decided it was time he lightened the mood if he could. It's what his mom would want him to do. So he chuckled aloud and took a deep breath. "But even those wonderful things were not the only presents to come forth from that Christmas Room. From what Mother told me over the phone, living in the Christmas Room guaranteed her a lot more friends and more pleasant experiences than if she was anywhere else. She told me that people were drawn there, that they liked to hang around. Therefore, she and Grace benefitted in many ways from the tree, the music, the lights, and the visitors. And, after being in the Christmas Room myself these last few days, I understand completely what Mom meant.

"And finally, I must mention what my mother considered the best blessings of all in coming to the Christmas Room. It opened up a new life for her daughter-in-law, Joanna, and it introduced her granddaughters to two handsome and honorable men. And finally, of special importance to me, it even brought her sons together again and that she lived to see it.

"So, again, thank you Villa Vista and thank you Trinisi family."

Tony started to come forward for the closing prayer but he sat back down as he saw Clark rise instead, take a faltering step toward his elder brother, and then wrap him in a strong and sincere embrace. Tony smiled upward and thought with a deep satisfaction, "That's certainly a better closing prayer than anything I could have come up with, Lord. Thanks."

Chapter 45
Another Lamb

Zachary O'Rourke opened his trunk so that Durward Gritzner could put in his suitcase. It was very early in the morning. It was dark and cold and windy. And though he would have loved to stay in bed another couple of hours, Zachary had gladly volunteered to drive Durward to the airport. Zachary had eaten a quick breakfast at the Gritzner home, Joanna having cooked "bacon butties" to go with fruit and Earl Grey tea. Brenda was there too, a little embarrassed to have her wet hair wrapped in a towel, but she wanted to greet Zachary and say goodbye to her uncle. Clark wasn't there for breakfast. He had begun going in early to work on a new project, part of his self-imposed sense of restitution. And that's why Zachary suggested that he take Durward to the plane.

The goodbyes were a little tearful but sweet. So too had been the parting between the brothers earlier. The Gritzner family was well aware of how much they owed to Durward's willingness to forgive his brother for grievous wrongs delivered at Durward through the years…and wrongs aimed at their mother and others in the single year past. But Durward deprecated and deflected the praise, stressing instead how grateful he was that the crisis had ended by repairing the long-broken bonds of brotherhood.

Driving through the windy darkness, Zachary had the feeling that Durward was relieved to be heading home. "Are you ready to be going back to Chicago?"

Durward sighed deeply. "Yes, I am, Zach. Very ready. There's a lot to do with Mom's property yet. And I miss my own work too." There was a moment or two when they listened together to the wind outside the car before Durward continued. "It's been an awful intense couple of weeks. Mom's condition and then her passing. And...well, everything else. It's been kind of stressful, I guess. So, even though it's been wonderful to be part of a family again, I guess I'm pretty steeped in my old bachelor ways."

"Yeah, I imagine so. But I'll tell you, Durward, you were a blessing and then some to that family. And," Zachary smiled broadly, "because I've got quite an investment in that family myself, I wanted to let you know how grateful I am personally."

Durward turned in the seat and looked at Zachary. "Thank you, Zach. I appreciate that. But you know the Scripture as well as I do, 'For to whom much is given, of him shall much be required.' And when it comes to mercy and forgiveness and new starts...Well, let me just say, I've been given a lot more than most. A *lot* more."

Durward turned back around and reached in his pocket. "Speaking of being given things, Grace gave me this the first day I came." Zachary looked down. Durward held in his hand a small plastic lamb. "It's from her nativity set. I had been sitting there in the afternoon next to Mom's bed and she was hard asleep and, I don't know, maybe my sadness and worry showed. Anyhow, Grace rolled over in her wheelchair and gave me this little sheep. I knew it had come from her nativity set – she had shown it to me earlier – and I started to protest but she put it in my hand and then closed my fingers over it. She said to me 'You hold onto this little guy. He will remind you of the meaning of Christmas, that Jesus came as the

Lamb of God Who would be the sacrifice to pay for our sins.'

"I started to explain to her that I knew that, that I was myself a Christian but she held up her hand to stop me. She said, 'I know. Your mother has told me all about you. I had a son who broke my heart once but God caught him too. I just wanted you to have the lamb to remind you of our Christmas Room and your mom and to give you comfort when she's gone.'

"I didn't have the heart to refuse it then. But I certainly don't want her nativity set to be without sheep. So, could you or one of the girls just slip it back in there? I don't suppose she'll notice it was ever gone."

Zachary took in the story and was touched both by Grace's act of kindness and Durward's sensitive nature. Yet he still couldn't help but respond to Durward's story with a hearty laugh. "I'm sorry, Durward, but I guess there's something you don't know about that little lamb."

"You think she *would* remember?" Durward asked. "I wouldn't hurt Grace or disappoint her for the world."

"What she will and will not remember at any given time is anybody's guess. No, that's not why I'm laughing, Durward. It's because I can guarantee you Grace is *not* going to miss that lamb."

Zachary's laugh had been infectious and Durward was smiling now himself. "Okay, I'll bite. How can you be so sure?"

"Because Tony Trinisi buys those plastic lambs by the bag. Grace gives them out to practically everybody who comes into the Christmas Room. She's given me four or five of them."

"Well, I'll be. That dear old girl."

Zachary completed his tale, explaining how Tony had replaced the first missing lamb, then another, then another, and then a fourth before he solved the mystery. "And rather than be frustrated at his mother's generosity, Tony was touched by it and decided to make sure she always has extras to hand out. He was telling me last summer he figures he's

235

bought more than 300 of those lambs so far."

Durward interrupted, "Where do they all go? What do people do with them?"

"Who knows? Some of the staff carry one in their pocket or purse. Others hang them on their own Christmas trees as ornaments. Lois told me she's used hers to make a whole little flock around her own nativity scene at home. Mine all sit on the windowsill of my bedroom. They are little pieces of the Christmas Room right there in my own pad."

The discussion went on from there, both men thoroughly enjoying the next thirty minutes while driving to the airport. Durward insisted on Zachary just dropping him off at the curb. After all, he wouldn't be able to see him to the gate anyway. The suitcase was retrieved and a firm handshake and mutual thank-yous were exchanged before Durward gave Zachary his card.

"Will you please give me a call every once in a while and let me know how things are going with Villa Vista and the friends I made there?"

"I'd be pleased to. And then, we will see you in June, right?"

Durward grinned. "Of course. How could I finally reunite with my brother's family and not be present when his oldest daughter is married off? I'll be there with bells on. Until then." Durward smiled and shut the car door. But as Durward walked to the airport entrance, Zachary saw him looking lovingly at something he held in his hand. One more of Grace Trinisi's little lambs had found a home.

Chapter 46
Christmas Eve: Daytime

There was a gentle snow drifting through the early morning darkness but the immediate scene was illuminated for David Youngville by the tower light above the parking lot. He appreciated very much the serene beauty of the snowfall on the west lawn. It was the perfect start to a Christmas Eve.

As was customary, David had come down to the cafeteria a little before 5:30 to find that Gloria had already brewed him a cup of decaffeinated vanilla tea. Gloria and Jess came in at 5 to start their breakfast prep. The rest of the kitchen staff would be there by 6 with the meal itself being served to residents beginning at 7:30. And that meant David had this time to himself. He had parked his chair in the corner, away from the noise going on in the kitchen and near the control button for the window shades. This was his best time to think, to pray, and to listen to music. This morning he had loaded onto his MP3 player a recording that Tony Trinisi had given him last week. It was a concert that had been recorded live at Boys Town, Nebraska, in the days Tony lived there. It featured both the famous Boys Town Choir and a terrific baritone who Tony had assured him had once been a big star in Hollywood and on Broadway, Gordon MacRae. David had never heard of him but the guy could sure sing. So could the boys in the choir.

The Christmas music was a bit more sophisticated than that which David was used to. What he was used to, of course, was the music Grace Trinisi played in the Christmas Room: Bing Crosby, Andy Williams, Nat King Cole, The Carpenters, Johnny Mathis, a country girls trio called Pure Heart. He loved them all. But Mr. MacRae and the Boys Town Choir were perfect for the reflective mood David was in on this snowy morning. For David had a big decision to make. Was he going to make the move to Harbor House or not?

David had long cherished hopes of one day being accepted into the Harbor House program. It was a dream first introduced to him by Zachary O'Rourke. In fact, Zachary had used it as motivation for David to better endure the pain and put in the work necessary to improve his condition. For not every disabled person qualified. And a year ago, even six months ago, David couldn't have made the grade. But Zachary's introduction of Harbor House as a real possibility had made a difference. David had worked harder. He had endured. He had tried to wait patiently but he had prayed hard too. He wanted to be accepted into the Harbor House program more than anything.

Part of the attraction was the sheer splendor of the place. Harbor House was a large, new complex surrounded on three sides by forest, the other overlooking Pelican Lake. David was also intrigued by the prospect of its state-of-the-art equipment, specialized arts and education programs, and the comfort of living with other young adults instead of being consigned to the ranks of the elderly and dying.

And then just last week, after the director of Harbor House had seen a TV news report of David's address to North High School, he had shown up at Villa Vista with a doctor and a physical therapist from their staff. They had put David through some pretty rigorous tests and then conducted a lengthy interview with him. David learned later they also had spent a long time talking with Zachary, Lois Vendee, and Greg Kwan. And, three days later, they had called. Harbor House would be pleased to accept David as their newest resident at his earliest convenience. Zachary's expertise and encouragement had borne sweet fruit. David's hard work had paid off. The dream had come true.

So why had David thus far refrained from saying yes?

That was the question David had been asking himself – and God – for several days. But it wasn't until this morning, this peaceful Christmas Eve morning, with the snow slowly obscuring the green of Villa Vista's west lawn, with the taste of his vanilla tea (sweetened with a teaspoon of Gloria's cinnamon honey) helping ease his anxiety, that the picture began to clear up for him.

David continued to watch the snowfall but his mind visualized other things too. He saw Clark Gritzner, a man who had been every bit as damaged (though in different ways) as himself. He had befriended Clark and had made a difference in his life. David had once believed his own life was over, that he was doomed to mere existence in a lonely shell, waiting through endless years to finally have the damnable struggle over with. But then Zachary had come into his life. And Carolyn. And Ralph. And Albert. And Patty. And all the others, including Clark Gritzner. They had all helped David see things differently, see himself differently as well. But, in particular, Clark had come on the stage and David found himself playing a role that showed him the opportunity for significance and worth – even in his condition. It was a liberating awakening of purpose. And it had come because someone had needed him.

And since then? David thought of his attendance at Thomas' wedding and becoming friends with Albert and the Gritzner girls. He reflected on the surprising success he'd experienced as a public speaker in these past few months. There was also his encouragement to Rita about attending college that he now rejoiced in. It had taken a lot but he had finally convinced her of the advantages that a degree would give for her future career plans, her earning power, her self-esteem. David had even coached her in the early mornings for a bunch of CLEP tests. When Rita danced into his room last Tuesday and announced she had earned 14 hours of college credit through those tests, David had been a prouder, more excited man than when he was given his own Master's degree. And he couldn't forget how valuable he had been for Patty Efron, his dear friend who had already made the transition to Harbor House and was doing outstandingly well there.

However, there was one other moment, a very dramatic one, that David knew was as critical to his decision about Harbor House as any. Indeed, he thought it probably the most important of all as it seemed to sum up the momentous changes that had occurred in his life this last year. That moment had come just yesterday afternoon. The lavish Villa Vista Christmas dinner had been completed and David had been invited by Tony and Marsha Trinisi to join the family and a few others down in the Christmas Room for some hot chocolate and Christmas carols. He had cheerfully accepted but he realized as soon as he wheeled himself into the room that great changes had been instituted.

Grace hadn't been given a roommate yet and, Lois had confided to him, Carolyn was determined to keep it that way for a while. Her idea was to make the Christmas Room a private one but with a difference. Carolyn had talked to Grace and Tony and received an enthusiastic response to her plan: namely, to make Number 14 in the south hall a more spacious and comfortable room. "Let's face it," she had explained at a recent staff meeting, "the number of visitors to the Christmas Room is creating a bit of a problem. Not that I want to close it down. Goodness, not that. It has been nothing short of terrific for the spirits of us all – residents, staff, and visitors alike. But it *can* get a bit crowded. And, poor Grace, she ends up having less living space than anyone else in the place.

"So, here's what we're going to do. I'm having Ralph

move the other bed out of there. He will put in a couple of chairs instead and leave the rest of the space for wheelchair residents to get in and out easier." Her announcement had been greeted with light applause but Carolyn ended with a quick warning. "Now, it's up to all of us to make sure that this doesn't get out of hand. We have to remember that it remains Grace Trinisi's home. Her care and comfort must remain priority number one. So, by all means, you can continue to drop in there for a moment or two of Christmas spirit to keep you going but we can't let it become a social hall. So, let's be sensitive and responsible and see if we can't make it work. Help the other residents understand that too, okay?"

Ralph Yarborough made the transformation in one day and the brand-new version of the Christmas Room made its debut on December 23.

And thus it was that David came to the remodeled Christmas Room for the party that had made such a difference to his consideration of Harbor House. The company gathered there consisted of Colin and Mary MacGregor from Sentimental Journeys, Dr. Bonney, Carolyn Kovacs and her daughters, Reggie Gritzner, and the whole Trinisi family. They drank their cocoa. They sang Christmas carols together. They listened as Colin read a poem called "The House of Christmas" by Chesterton. Being there in that group, that intergenerational company that had come to mean so much to him helped David see how his attitudes and priorities had shifted. And not just attitudes about himself and his faith but also about the inestimable worth of all human lives. Young or old. Fully abled or not. Healthy or ill. Content or anxiously battling need or discomfort. Socially connected or isolated and lonely.

Harbor House held out everything David Youngville had wanted a year ago. But a year had changed things so much. David now realized how much he was needed here at Villa Vista. He had friends here. He had graciously been grafted into a family here. And, most important of all, he had a ministry here. David was loved and appreciated here at Villa Vista. He had the best of care with Zachary and the others, care that would only get better with the resources of the new building project. And, he repeated to himself, he was needed.

David looked up to the clouds, discernible now with the first natural light of the morning. Yes, he would tell Zachary and Carolyn this morning and call Mr. Woodhouse after lunch. He would be staying at Villa Vista.

The kitchen door opened and Gloria entered the cafeteria. With her came the delicious aroma of cinnamon rolls. She carried one on a plate. "I thought I'd come warm up that tea for you and, while I was at it, get your opinion on these cinnamon rolls before I serve them up this morning." She had a grand smile and David couldn't help but think it was as pretty a sight as the snowfall outside.

"You promise not to tell Zachary. He keeps me on a pretty tight regimen where calories are concerned."

"I know. And I'm awfully careful about that. But it *is* Christmas Eve."

"Yes," David reached up to accept the treat. "It is Christmas Eve."

Chapter 47
Christmas Eve: Nighttime

It was a very merry and productive Christmas Eve at the Villa Vista Care Community. David's announcement that he was staying caused more joy than he could have imagined. Carolyn was thrilled and told him that, although she had been proud and pleased that he'd been accepted at Harbor House, she had despaired over losing the "chief morale officer" of Villa Vista. Zachary too was more than pleased and congratulated him on making a wise and generous decision. He reminded David too that the new plans for Villa Vista would ensure they would be able to provide the best equipment too. "And," David had said with a wink, "not even Harbor House is going to have the aqua therapy we will!"

The ripple effect of David's news delighted the rest of the staff too, adding to the already festive mood of the day. There were no organized volunteer programs today, but that was fine. Everyone seemed to welcome the calm. Even the weather had helped out by bringing just enough snow to make things pretty and Christmasy, but not enough to make driving difficult. A lot of family members were on hand throughout the day to visit their loved ones and, naturally.

Santa Claus came to call. In truth, it was three Santas who, after lunch, passed out cookies, brownies, and sugar-free fudge to the residents. Most of the residents recognized two of the faces behind the Santa beards: Albert Trinisi and Ralph Yarborough. But the third was a complete mystery. Only David Youngville and Ted Bonney recognized who was in the third Santa suit. And only they caught the blessed irony of the situation.

Clark Gritzner had come a long way.

***

By nightfall, everyone in the place was tired including Carolyn Kovacs who, although she had been around a few hours this morning, was now looking at starting a double shift tonight. Because they were working at minimum staff levels, there wouldn't be any time to coast during those hours either. But that was okay for Carolyn. Her Christmas stocking was full and she couldn't help but be grateful and joyful at the prospects for Villa Vista in the coming year. The foundation gift, the expansion, the increases in community support and involvement – all these were Christmas presents beyond her dreams. Yet she had been given a couple of extra blessings here on Christmas Eve. The wonderful news that David was staying was one. And the other was what she had witnessed just minutes ago in the Christmas Room.

Carolyn had walked in to check on Grace and there, amid the lights and color of the Christmas Room, Tony and Marsha Trinisi sat in pleasant conversation with Grace, who was seated in her green chair with a red throw over her shoulders. Beside her were Clark and Joanna Gritzner. Carolyn had joined that conversation for a few minutes before duties called her away. But she had been so touched and so grateful to God that He had given her today's winsome, uplifting pictures of Clark Gritzner to replace those created in their first awful meeting. Yes, it had been a marvelous Christmas.

A couple of hours later, Villa Vista was quiet. The Trinisis had gone to a Christmas Eve service at their church, accompanied by Ralph, Zachary, Yoki, and the whole Gritzner family. (Present also at that service at River's Edge Baptist Church was Lieutenant Ben Romero. Clark didn't notice him...but the lieutenant noticed *Clark*, giving the policeman's Christmas meditations a most interesting, but not unwelcome, twist.) In the other parts of the city, Rita Costello, Zemi Chukwu, Grant Katulka, and Angie Stewart were all celebrating the holiday with their families. Lois Vendee was enjoying a reunion with her younger brother, Fr. Armand Laurent, a missionary priest who served in a hospital in Côte d'Ivoire who was back in the States for just a short time.

In Chicago, Durward Gritzner celebrated a happy Christmas also. He had popped popcorn, watched Alastair Sim in *A Christmas Carol*, and read Calvin Miller's novel *Snow*, a lovely little story of Christmas, romance...and a divided family being made whole again. Durward was alone...and yet less alone than he'd been in years.

At Villa Vista, most were sleeping. Televisions were still on in a few rooms. Three residents were working a jigsaw puzzle on the oblong table in the foyer. A few more were in their wheelchairs parked around the nurses stations. David Youngville was in his room with headphones on. He was listening to an audio recording of Laura Hillenbrand's *Seabiscuit*, his Christmas present from Patty Efron. But most of the residents were asleep.

Not Grace, though. Yet whether Grace was even *present* at Villa Vista right now could be an open question. For she would have contended that she spent the rest of Christmas Eve with Mattie and Rosie, with her parents and her sisters and brothers, and, of course, with her beloved husband, Frank. Grace talked with them, rode horses through the snow, danced, played snap and charades, cooked the goose with Aunt Kit, knit scarves to give to the soldiers, bobbed for apples, and sang Christmas carols in the old log church down by the falls. Indeed, Grace celebrated a merry Christmas Eve with an exuberance and a lightness of heart unmatched by anyone in town.

However, there came a moment in the early morning hours when Grace descended to the material confines of the Christmas Room. She was awakened from her reverie by Derek Lewis holding her hand and asking if she was ready for bed. Yes, Grace said, she was. She told the young man, one of her new helpers, "I had a wonderful time with my son and his family tonight. And I talked to my other kids and their children on the phone too. It was such a nice Christmas Eve. But when they all left, I did some traveling."

"Traveling?" Derek asked.

Grace patted his hand. "You must humor an old woman. Maybe I was only dreaming." She gave him a smile. "But then again, maybe it was more than that. I don't know for sure. I'll be asking the Lord in person about these things pretty soon now." She sighed and set her wrap on the arm of her chair. "Anyhow, I feel as tired as if I have been traveling so I guess it's a good idea to get to bed."

"Okay, I'll get Gladys to come in and give you a hand."

Derek turned and started to go but Grace called him back. "One more thing, dear. You're new here, aren't you?"

Derek nodded. "Yes, ma'am, I am. I started here last week. I'm a student over at the junior college and I felt real lucky to land a job here."

Grace reached over toward her nativity set and grabbed one of the little lambs. "Let me tell you a little bit about that first Christmas, okay?"

A couple of hours later, Carolyn, Gladys Bergman and, from the north wing, Terry Price, were seated at the nurses station having their 2 A.M. "lunch" when Blanche McGill came back from the cafeteria with Derek alongside. There hadn't been enough staff available to mop the floors right after dinner, but it had to be done before breakfast. So Carolyn had volunteered them to take care of the job. Knowing the sacrifices she'd been making on behalf of her staff kept either of them from even thinking about complaining. But Derek did have something on his mind and Carolyn noticed it. "What's up, Derek? You look puzzled."

Blanche spoke up. "He's wondering about Grace Trinisi and the Christmas Room. He can't figure it out and he doesn't think he should hang on to the lamb Grace gave him."

Derek looked annoyed that Blanche had let that slip. "Mrs. Kovacs, I was going to tell you that on my own. You explained pretty strictly that we should never accept gifts from the residents and I tried to refuse it but the lady wouldn't have any of that. I didn't know what to do and so I figured I'd turn it in to you and…"

Blanche interrupted, "And I told him it was okay to keep it and I tried to explain why." She let out a little laugh. "I tried to tell him about Mrs. Trinisi and the Christmas Room while we were mopping but he's convinced I'm pulling his leg."

"How so?" Gladys asked. "What's she been telling you, Derek?"

Derek shrugged his shoulders and smiled. "Look, I understand I'm the new guy and I expect to be teased a little, you know, and be sent on a few snipe hunts and such. But still."

Blanche jumped in again. "But you don't believe in a nursing home room that's decorated for the Yuletide all year long? A room where Christmas carols are a regular feature in August? Where the lady's family brings Christmas cookies the 25th of every month? What in the world is hard to believe about any of that?"

The way the women were all smiling, some even suppressing laughter, convinced Derek all the more that they were having a joke at his expense. That is, until Carolyn Kovacs, his boss, asked him to have a seat. She smiled at him but took a serious tone. "Derek, first of all, Blanche is *not* teasing you. And *I'm* not teasing you either. We don't allow snipe hunts around here. We've got too many people to care for. Second of all, in the case of Mrs. Trinisi's little lamb, you can make an exception to our rules. I suggest you keep it. But if you continue to work the south wing, it won't be the last opportunity you'll get to have one! And finally Room 14 where Grace Trinisi resides is known around here, and even around the city, as the Christmas Room. All the things Blanche told you – and a whole lot more – are as true as they can be."

Derek had sat down. He was respectful but curious and still a bit incredulous. "So it's not a joke? It's for real?"

Carolyn gave him a very warm smile. "No, it's no joke. In fact, Derek, the Christmas Room is about as serious and as wonderful as it gets. It is a source of hope and joy that we all need for working in a place like this. I have no doubt you'll understand that for yourself soon enough."

Derek, looking at the faces of the women sitting there with him, realized this was a subject quite important and quite dear to them. He then felt the little lamb in his hand and remembered the remarks Mrs. Trinisi had made when she gave it to him. Maybe he was already feeling a bit of the magic. A nursing home that gloried in its year-round Christmas Room? Derek concluded he had come to a very interesting place to work.

***

Outside the snow began to fall again, slow and soft, blanketing the grounds with white. But there was color in the night too. Huddled in a burning bush beside Grace's birdfeeder were two pretty red cardinals looking into her window. The lighted cross and the twinkling bulbs on the Christmas tree were reflected in the cardinals' curious eyes. Grace saw them, smiled, and silently thanked them for stopping by. She wished them a merry Christmas and fell asleep.